MAGIS

SAM CHEEVER

ELECTRIC PROSE PUBLICATIONS

STAY IN TOUCH

I don't give away a lot of books. But I value my readers and, to show it, I'm gifting you a copy of a fun novella just for signing up for my newsletter!

SIGN UP HERE!

1

A light fog had settled into the zone. A cool mist that fell over my clothes and turned my chin-length brown bob stringy and limp. The miasma encapsulated the gently awful smell that always pervaded the street, invigorating it, turning it into something almost alive.

I grimaced as I shifted against the still-warm scratchiness of the roof. My boot stuck for a beat, clinging to the tar where a piece of the shingle had broken away.

Behind me, the soft glow of a lamp bathed the sharp slope of roof. Like a siren's melodious notes sifting through the fog of a storm-tossed sea, the light called to me.

I sighed, shifting again.

My stomach growled. I winced at the sound, despite the fact that it fell into the fog and was lost.

Nobody heard it but me. It was a stark reminder that it had been a long night, and I was ready for it to be over.

But it wasn't over yet.

Not until I found him.

Not until I confronted him.

A soft scuff had me straightening from my crouch, the sharp, wavy blade of my knife held at my side in a firm grip. The grip of the weapon was warm, as if I'd been holding it for a while. But it had been safe in its sheath against my thigh.

The shadows behind the mist swirled and gained density. I tensed, staring into the moving fog. "Who is it?"

My voice was soft enough to barely nudge the mist aside. But the creature that moved in an uneven shuffle in my direction heard me. He heard me just fine.

Perfectly round eyes glowed briefly in the light from my window. A small face, gray and leathery, grimaced as he took in my stance — the charcoal heft of my knife. "Sorry, Glynnie," the little gargoyle said. "I didn't try to sneak." Boyle ducked his head, his pointed ears shifting with guilt. A soft scraping sound preceded the sliding of his long tail across the roof, and his claws scritched softly as he sat.

"It's okay," I told the baby. I gave him a smile because he had a tender psyche and was generally unsure of himself. That was what happened when you were dumped with a stranger as an infant. "I should have been paying attention."

He shifted again, the scritch, scritch, scritch of his strong black claws a soft song in the night. "Is da man there?" he asked in a whisper so loud it couldn't help carrying across the street.

I hid a grin. "No." I turned back to the street below, watching the moonlit surface of the rough asphalt for signs of the creature who'd invaded my life and yanked what peace I'd managed to scrounge brutally away. "Not tonight."

My stomach growled again. A soft huff of amusement spilled between Boyle and me. I grinned, spreading my palm over my belly. "I'm hungry," I told him. "How about you?"

His round eyes, so dark in the night but a bright turquoise blue in the sun, sparkled with excitement. "Yeth!"

I grinned at the soft lisp. He'd almost grown out of the tendency with the arrival of his adult teeth. But every once in a while, one would slip through again. I loved the sound. It reminded me of the first years of his life. "Come on, then," I told him, moving toward the window. "I made stew."

The baby 'goyle gave a gentle huff of pleasure. He jumped through the window when I opened it, landing with a soft thump and then waddling across the room and flinging himself onto my bed.

Boyle loved my bed. He rolled happily, pulling

the covers over his small body with another huff of pleasure.

I climbed inside and turned, my gaze sliding across the street below for just one more minute. My heart pounded hard with expectation or worry. I was never sure which anymore.

He was out there. I knew he was. I just had to keep watch. Eventually, I'd catch him in the act of invading both my mental and defensive space.

It was only a matter of time. And then I'd ask him why he was there. Because his presence felt wrong. It felt dangerous. Like an omen of bad things to come.

H e stood in the shadows, his back pressed against the still-warm brick, and watched her. She was strong and attractive, with long, muscular limbs and thick brown hair that he guessed would have blonde highlights when the sun caught her out. Her lips were full, her eyes framed in thick arcs of golden brown. They were probing, intense. She stood on the roof of her three-story Victorian home every night, staring down at the street as if searching for something in particular.

Was she looking for him?

He shook off the question, knowing it couldn't be. He'd been careful. She had no idea he was there.

But she was lucky he was. Already he'd seen dangerous activity around her home. Deadly creatures that wouldn't hesitate to take her down. And it was his job to make sure that wouldn't happen.

He knew he should move on...expand his hunting area...but he couldn't bring himself to walk away. It wasn't just because of the woman. Though she was definitely part of it. Something about her intrigued him. Something called to his magic.

Still, there were others in the zone who needed protection.

Many others.

He should go.

Even as he had the thought, he knew he wouldn't leave. Not for a while. The feral energy he'd been chasing was thicker there than anyplace else he'd been. He didn't know if it came from her, or something in her sphere. Either way, she was important.

Either way, she was dangerous.

He lifted his head, inhaling the night on a long, deep breath. The sour reek of wet asphalt, flavored by the scents of a dozen cats, dogs, and heaven knew what other critters, filled the air. The normal stench was made worse by the soft rain falling around him like a shroud. And beneath all that, something else. The scent of some kind of energy he couldn't identify. It was what had initially drawn him to that spot. The smell of power. Along with the sheer numbers of animals converging on the street. Actually, most of them had converged on that one house.

Her house.

It had intrigued him.

Even now, with the rain falling in sheets from the iron-gray sky, the porch was draped in cats. The yard boiled with dogs that seemed for all the world as if they were keeping watch on the perimeter.

Dozens of raccoons chittered a warning from the massive trees surrounding the hundred-plus-year-old house. Squirrels gathered en masse to keep watch.

It was unnatural.

The zone had been mostly abandoned over the last few years, as magic contracted and sent its favor to other places. Places where money and connections created more opportunity for power.

It made a certain kind of sense that stray critters would leave the magic-dense areas beyond the zone. That wasn't what intrigued him. It wasn't what kept him there night after night, watching and waiting.

It was where they went. And how they behaved.

If he hadn't known that all the magic had been sucked from the zone a decade earlier, he would have suspected the woman was some kind of pied piper sorceress.

But that wasn't possible.

True magic couldn't survive in the zone. Sure, there were touches of the kind of energy humans created without realizing it. It was the power of instinct, of déjà vu. But no real magic lived there anymore.

If there was elemental magic, he'd have felt it when he arrived. It would eat at him, chewing on his flesh like an army of biting bugs. It would make his stomach twist and cause his pulse to pound in alarm.

He would know if she was magic.

He would know.

Still...

2

I dished up two bowls of stew as Boyle lumbered into the room, his slightly ape-like movements surprisingly light on the scarred wood floor. The kitchen was small, little more than a nook in the blueprint of the enormous house. The problem with Victoria, the home I had taken over after my grand-mother's death, was that its considerable square footage was broken into a myriad of rooms, each one small and oddly shaped. Going from one room to the next was like moving through a maze, with double French doors dividing the myriad spaces. Lead-glass windows, large and small, round and rectangular, offered plenty of light in the outer rooms, leaving a definite gloom to hang over the central spaces.

We spent most of our time in the main living room at the front of the house, the kitchen, and our bedrooms upstairs. Occasionally I worked in Grams' old office slash library on the second floor. The rest of the house was closed off, unchanged from when Grams was alive, and probably sporting dog-sized dust bunnies.

I was afraid to look.

I dropped a wooden spoon into the big iron pot and turned the fire off beneath it. Settling the bowls of stew on the table, I handed Boyle the oversized spoon he preferred. "It's hot," I warned.

Despite my warning, the little gargoyle scooped up a hearty bite, sniffing a tender chunk of meat before sticking out a long, pink tongue and slurping up some of the gravy pooled beneath it. "Yummy," he said in his high-pitched, raspy voice.

I grinned, pushing a thick slice of buttered bread in his direction. "Milk?"

"Yeth, pleathe."

I went to grab his sippy cup out of the fridge, an ancient affair whose golden color bespoke a much earlier time. Like my grandmother, I'd kept it alive through magic and herculean mechanical acrobatics. I had no specific magic of my own, but the big old house retained enough magic to keep things humming along for a couple of centuries. And I could enhance it to do just about anything I needed.

"Thank you," Boyle said, his cute pointed ears twitching. The cup was a favorite because he could easily grasp it with his claws, and there was no danger of dropping it or breaking it if he did have an accident.

I ruffled the soft tuft of orange hair between his ears. "You're welcome, sweet boy."

Sitting down across from him, I speared a tender carrot with my fork and watched him enthusiastically shovel stew past his thin, gray lips.

He clasped the sippy cup in his claws and drank deeply, his thick, leathery throat working as he swallowed. The little gargoyle slammed the cup to the table and made a sound of satisfaction.

I looked down to hide my smile. I knew I should scold him for his manners. But I just couldn't. He was too cute and he enjoyed the simple things in life so much, I couldn't find it within myself to turn his little face sad.

"What did you do tonight while I was working?" I asked, instead. I'd spent the better part of the night working in my garden, plucking leaves, shooing away rabbits and deer that had been drawn there by my presence, and picking vegetables that were on the edge of being too ripe. Other than checking on the little gargoyle several times and finding him safely ensconced on his perch on the roof, I hadn't seen him for a few hours.

Boyle shrugged, his eyes locked on his food. "Played in the basement."

I went very still, a bite of potato halfway to my mouth. "You what?"

He kept his gaze determinedly down, but I noticed he was no longer eating. Instead, he was shoving his stew around. His shoulders had rounded, and his ears were pinned back. "I was looking for treasure."

And I knew just the treasure he'd been looking for. Energy was like candy to a growing gargoyle, and it was all but impossible for him to ignore.

I set my fork into the bowl, my mind searching for just the right words. We'd had the conversation before—many times. *Stay out of the basement, Boyle. It's dangerous down there. You're going to get hurt if you don't listen.*

Every time he'd nod in agreement. He'd promise to avoid the space with the most earnest of expressions. Then he'd do it again.

I sighed. How could I make him understand?

It wasn't his fault, really. Gargoyles were creatures of magic. Magic called to them, whispering promises that I knew he found hard to ignore.

And he was just a baby. Only three years old. Gargoyles didn't reach adulthood until thirty, so he was barely past the newborn stage. He had no restraint...no impulse control. I was going to have to board up the door to the basement.

The lock I'd put in place hadn't even seemed to slow him down.

The baby had magical, lockpicking claws.

"Boyle..." I began.

His head snapped up, his round blue eyes filled with a plea. "I sorry, Glynnie."

I stared at that sweet face and all the irritation washed out of me. "I know you are, honey." I opened my mouth to explain yet again that the basement was too dangerous for a baby gargoyle.

Heck, it was too dangerous for me.

But my mouth snapped shut. I'd have to take care of it once and for all. "It's not your fault, Boyle. I understand you can't help yourself. But it can't happen again."

He tensed, tears shimmering in his eyes as his ears drooped with unhappiness. He pushed away from the table and dropped out of view. I heard his little clawed feet scratching across the floor and realized he was leaving the room. His tiny, bat-like wings fluttered behind him, testing the air.

"Boyle?"

"It otay, Glynnie. I go."

Horror swamped me. He meant he was *leaving*. He would climb onto the roof and try to fly away. And he would plummet to the ground because his wings weren't developed enough yet for him to fly. I hurried over and stepped in front of him, dropping to my knees to wrap him in a hug.

He let me pull him close, a soft sigh whispering past my ear. His breath smelled like cloves and sweet, freshly mown grass.

"I don't want you to go," I told the baby as he

sniffled softly. "I love you. I'm just trying to keep you safe."

He heaved another sigh, bigger than the last. "I sorry."

My arms tightened around him. "Don't be sorry. I'll fix it. Okay?"

He sniffled again and nodded.

"Now, go finish your dinner," I said, pulling back so I could meet his gaze. I gave him a smile. "I made peanut butter cookies for dessert."

Boyle's eyes widened in pleasure. "Can I have two?"

I tapped his tiny nose with a finger. "You can have two."

Watching him toddle back to his chair and hop onto it, my heart was heavy. When I'd found the little guy wandering around in the Victorian's yard, he'd barely been able to walk. He'd been skinny and his eyes had been red from crying.

I never found out where he'd come from. Or how he'd ended up at my house, but I'd taken him in that night. And I'd never looked back. I'd never even considered giving him up. Instead, I'd used every resource I had to figure out how to care for a baby gargoyle. It had been almost two years, and I'd never regretted caring for him. Not for a minute. But I was starting to realize I was going to need help soon. I had no idea how to teach a gargoyle what he needed to know.

Up to that point, love and basic care had been enough. But soon, he'd need to learn how to ride the wind. He'd need to figure out how to tap a lei line. He'd need to learn so many things.

And I wasn't equipped to teach him.

With a heavy sigh, I returned to my dinner. After I was done, I'd see what boards I could find in the garage.

I cringed at the thought. The garage was a nightmare of *stuff*. Some of it useful, some of it little more than clutter, but all of it dangerous.

It was the detritus of my grandmother's life. Culled from the house over the five years since I'd laid claim to Victoria. Much of it carried a deep reservoir of her considerable magic within its pores. It was stuff I'd never use. But it had been part of her. And I'd been unable to throw it away.

If there were any boards on the property, that was where they'd be.

I might as well get it done. The sooner the door was made impassable, the safer Boyle would be.

B oyle insisted on coming with me to the garage. It was a massive affair, big enough for at least three cars, and was detached because when the house had been built a couple of hundred years earlier, there'd been no such thing as garages.

I suspected it had once been a carriage house.

The little gargoyle clutched a cookie in each hand as he trundled along behind me, and I grimaced at the trail of crumbs he was leaving on the ground behind him. Then I winced as I realized the crumbs wouldn't be there for long.

Gargoyles scoff at the five-second rule. They roll on the floor laughing over it. There is no outside edge of time that removes the viability of any food that hits the ground. As far as Boyle was concerned, if it was edible when it was handed to him, nothing short of having someone pee on it would remove its viability after it hit the floor.

In fact, I sometimes suspected him of dropping food on purpose as a way of storing it for later. Once, I'd vacuumed up some cake crumbs he'd left along the stairs leading to the second floor. He'd thrown a fit, accusing me of eating them myself.

I'd had trouble calming him down after that one. And I'd vowed never to do it again.

I reached up and flipped the switch, illuminating the carriage house's only source of light, such as it was. A single bare bulb hung from the high ceiling, naked and covered with dust. It illuminated only the very center of the three-car garage, leaving most of it in shadow.

Good thing I'd brought a flashlight with me.

I stood there a moment, looking over the mess of broken furniture, boxes of clothing, and spellbooks. An enormous table along the outside wall was filled with cloudy glass beakers and stained with the residue of Grams' spell work.

Beneath the clutter, somewhere, was an old boat of a car. Grams had driven the classic Chevy she'd called old Belle all my life, as far back as I could remember. Belle was baby blue, chrome, and white, and sported actual fins along the back. She was a monster of a car that ran on magic rather than fuel. And she'd been indestructible.

I suddenly wondered if the old car would still run. But even as I had the thought, I realized it was unlikely she would run for me. Unlike Grandma Forester, I wasn't made of magic.

My grandmother had been a sorceress. Not just any sorceress, but one of the most powerful sorceresses in the known continents. She'd been spectacular, and her name had filled most in the magical universe with fear and respect.

There had been only one other who'd even come close to matching her skill. And I was pretty sure she'd once dated him. They'd never made anything of it, though. I suspected the competition had probably just been too much between them.

Grams had never admitted it, but I strongly suspected that my mother had been the result of that one encounter.

Grams had been the original women's libber. She'd believed she didn't need a man to be happy. And, as far as I could tell, she'd been right. At least where she was concerned. Except for bringing my mother into the world, there'd been no other evidence that Grams had even interacted with the male of the species.

My mother had followed in the same tradition, never marrying, and by the time my brother and I had been old enough to ask about our father, our mother was already gone. Grams had been frustratingly tight-lipped about our parents, saying only that we were loved.

That wouldn't have been nearly enough if we hadn't had Grams. But she'd showered us with enough love and protection to make up for the loss of two people we'd never known.

"Meow!"

I turned to find a small, black cat trotting into the garage from the pitch-dark night beyond. The cat wound around my ankles and then bumped up against Boyle, giving him a plaintive yowl.

Boyle looked at me. "Can I, Glynnie?"

I nodded. "Don't go far, though," I told him. "We don't know if the man's out there."

"Come on, kitty." Boyle grabbed a large bag of cat food from the cabinet near the door and headed outside with it, dragging the heavy bag along the floor as he went.

I turned back to the mess in front of me, eyeing the piles and stacks to determine where the boards would most likely be. I decided the back corner of the garage looked the most promising, and headed that way.

A dog barked outside and then another. I smiled. Boyle was like an old lady feeding pigeons in the park. He loved to feed the strays. And we'd accumulated quite a few of them along the way. So many, in fact that my kibble bill had tripled over the last few months. I sometimes felt as if I were feeding the entire planet of animals.

Deep down, I knew it wasn't Boyles' attentions that had brought the critters to Victoria. They'd been drawn to me. While I didn't have any inherent magic, I had the capacity to use and enhance the magic I encountered. And, I guessed that ability was a kind of magic of its own. Grams had once told me the source and core of my magic was settled in the animal world. I never really understood what that meant. But critters had always seemed drawn to me. Even when I'd been a baby. Grams had shown me photos of me in my bassinet in the yard, surrounded by a dozen bunnies, squirrels and deer as if they were protecting me.

It seemed only proper that I should feed them since it was my fault they were there.

"Woowoowoo, rowr."

I whipped around, my heart rate spiking in

surprise. I looked over at the enormous black dog and laughed with relief. "You startled me."

The big dog fixed me with intelligent brown eyes and whined softly in his throat.

I offered him my fingers and he moved closer, stretching his neck to carefully sniff the very tips.

The big dog had shown up in my yard several weeks earlier. At first, I'd thought he was a wolf. He was enormous, with long, long legs and a thick coat that formed a dense ruff over his shoulders. His tail was thick too, and beneath the midnight black of his fur, the undercoat was a soft, pale gray. His head was too wide for a wolf's. His muzzle too thick, with a silky fringe along his jawline. No. Not a wolf. Maybe some kind of hybrid.

Whatever he was, he seemed to be determined to introduce himself to me.

He'd been standoffish since arriving. Spending much of the day lying in the grass and staring at the house. When I'd gone outside to see him, he'd kept his distance, trotting away from me as I approached to keep a requisite ten feet between us at all times.

Trust was obviously an issue, and I had to wonder why. Had someone hurt him in the past?

I'd been trying to make friends with the big dog, all the while feeling as if he was trying to tell me something. Over the last few days, I'd managed to get close enough to touch.

He was wary. And he was magic. I felt the soft

sting of his energy dancing along my skin when I got within several feet of him.

But I had no idea why he was there.

I crouched down and offered him my hand again. "You're missing out on dinner," I told him, my voice low and soft. "Don't you..."

His head shot up and he spun, startling me into taking a step back. Then he gave a deep growl that brought the hairs on the back of my neck to attention.

And took off running for the door.

A beat later, Boyle's terrified scream tore the air beyond the light.

3

I took off after the dog, my heart banging against my ribs in pure terror. The night was pitch beyond even the dim light from the garage. In the distance, the silvery rectangles of the windows in the house did me little good. I stumbled over tufts of dense grass before remembering I had a flashlight in my hand.

My ears strained for some sign of what was happening as I fumbled with the power switch on the flash, not wanting to slow to mess with it.

Another cry, closer than the last, had me veering toward the house, where the glow from the kitchen window showed the abandoned bag of cat food, brown pebbles spilled in a trailing mound along the grass.

No animals pecked at it. In fact, nothing moved beyond the gracefully loping dog, whose fur had melded into the velvet tapestry of night, unseen except for when it caught an errant strand of weak light.

"Boyle!" I screamed, panic flooding me until I found it hard to breathe. My thumb finally found the power switch, and the flashlight snapped on.

Something leaped into the air in the dim glow. It plowed into me, crashing into my chest and sending me backward, to slam against the ground with an "umph!".

Arms like leather-covered steel wound around my neck, nearly choking me with their strength.

A soft sob rumbled against my chest.

My heart beating hard enough to make me dizzy, I sucked in a relieved breath and wrapped my arms around Boyle. "Are you okay?"

Growling filled the dense night beyond the house. Snarling and snapping.

I shoved to my feet, still holding the baby against me as I gripped the flash, intending to use it as a weapon.

I moved toward the sound. Instinct told me that the black wolf-dog was fighting a life or death battle, no doubt against whatever had terrified Boyle. I had to help him.

Without stopping to consider what I was doing, I sought the magic, finding a rich source of it nearby and siphoning it away to feed my own reserves. The magic was dark and spicy, unique, yet somehow comfortable to embrace.

And embrace it, I did. I yanked it close, wrapped the metaphysical blanket of my own energy around it and made it mine, assimilating it into my pores and expanding it until it danced against my skin, hungry and eager for release.

It was dangerous pulling magical energy from a source I didn't know. Terrifying. I had no idea what the magic I'd pulled would do.

Was it benevolent energy? Unlikely.

But it was powerful. And with a baby gargoyle shivering in fear against me, I forced my doubts away and...

I forced the magic into the flashlight, willing it to coalesce and build. The illumination flashed brighter, its light bathing the entire yard and painting the street beyond and even the buildings across from me in stark, white illumination.

What I saw made me step back, my breath trapped in lungs that had ceased to draw air.

Even in the light, it looked like a shadow, with indeterminate lines and frothy edges which filtered away as it moved.

The thing was vaguely man-shaped, with golden, glowing eyes and a huge mouth filled with massive yellow teeth. Its body drifted as it moved, occasionally disappearing, as if perched in the mouth of a vortex that would pull it back at the slightest provocation.

The thing swung something that looked like a scythe, its blade glossy with red blood. And the wolf-dog's fur was matted with the stuff over one shoulder, its gait hitching when it stepped onto its left front paw.

I watched the dog leap off the ground, faster than a normal dog by several times, and snap at the flowing robes of the apparition, ripping through them despite the fact that they didn't look substantial enough to grab.

The creature pulled back, most of its wraithlike form sucking into the protective vortex and then surged out again, the scythe making a neat arc on the air that sliced far too close the to dog's head.

A soft yelp of pain told me the blade had connected.

I growled in rage. Giving Boyle a quick squeeze, I looked down at him. "Hold on, baby."

He did, nearly breaking my ribs with his super-sized grip.

I barely noticed. I'd sent the magic into the flash-light again, my mind forming a far different picture from the first time I'd infused it.

The center of the silvery illumination thickened, coiled, and spread outward, spitting deadly energy like a drill bit that's been saturated with electricity.

I shoved magic into it and it grew, the coil spinning faster, and the energy becoming so rabid I had to tighten my grip on the metal canister to keep it under control.

"Get back!" I yelled at the dog and, amazingly, he listened. He stepped beyond the light and fell, his energy spent.

Worry thrummed through me. I almost abandoned the fight to check on him. But, if I did, he wouldn't be safe. Boyle wouldn't be safe.

Not until the apparition in front of me was gone.

The thing in the vortex refocused its eerie gaze on me. It stilled for a moment, and then lifted a long, bony hand, the skeletal fingers twitching upward in invitation.

I wanted to laugh. Did it think I was stupid?

"Yeah," I said out loud. "I'm going to take your hand and join you in your traveling nightmare." I shook my head. "I don't think so."

The thing dropped its hand, cocking the head I couldn't see beyond the constantly waving fringe of its hood. Only the glowing eyes and the sharp rows of yellowed teeth were visible. The fiend seemed to be waiting, watching with interest as I moved closer.

My foot stepped off the grass and onto the broken asphalt.

My magic wavered.

If I went any further, I'd be giving up any connection I had to the house—the source of my inherent energy.

That magic wasn't insignificant. I bit my lip, thinking. Should I risk it?

Boyle loosened his grip on me. "Glynnie?"

I hugged him close, kissed him on the fringe of hair between his ears, and looked into his little face. "I'm going to put you down. I want you to go over by the dog. Stay by him until I'm done. Do you understand?"

Boyle shook his head. "No, Glynnie. That's bad. Really bad." He slid a quick, terrified glance toward the vortex. "Don't go there."

I hugged him again. "I'll be fine," I told him, my voice sounding surprisingly calm. "The dog needs you, honey. He's hurt. Can you help him?"

The dog would keep the little gargoyle safe. He'd proven he would. And Boyle couldn't resist being needed.

An angry look puckered the adorable face for a beat. His bottom lip jutted, and he looked belligerent. "No. You need me more."

The thing in the street shifted slightly and, when I looked up, it had cut the distance between us by half.

All the little hairs on my arms stood at attention. "Boyle, I don't have time to argue."

He crossed his arms over his tiny chest.

"Boyle..." I began, and then it was too late.

The thing surged from its protective vortex and slammed into us. I hit the ground and rolled, covering Boyle with my body as the bony fingers dug into my sides, compressing my bones until they began to creak.

I screamed, the sound shrill with terror and pain. Beneath me, Boyle struggled to escape. I could feel his magic building and I panicked. If he did something to annoy the creature trying to pry me off him...

I looked frantically around for the flashlight, finding it nestled in the gutter two feet away from my outstretched fingers.

I'd never get to it in time. Not with an entity from Hell sitting on my back.

A snarl warned me the dog was back. It flew off the ground and landed on the creature riding my back.

The extra weight sank onto me and I collapsed. Just like that, I had a new worry. I was going to crush Boyle.

But the hound clamped its impressive jaws over the monster's neck and shook his head, flinging it away as if it weighed nothing.

I didn't hesitate. I jumped to my feet and grabbed Boyle, giving him a fear-infused shove. "Go into the house. Now!"

To my relief, he listened.

I waited only until I saw him disappear inside and then lunged for the flashlight.

The hound was a wild thing, lunging and

ripping and flinging, but it hadn't made much progress all the same.

And several glossy spots of blood painted its fur.

I lifted the flash and yelled, "Kill!"

The light spun into the coil of deadly magic again, but instead of a finger-thin coil, it had grown to the size of my wrist. And it was angry.

Fueled, no doubt, by my own rage.

I ran toward the monster, watching in horror as its scythe sliced downward, its trajectory ensuring a killing strike.

"No!" I screamed as the dog, presumably in a last-ditch effort to save itself, flew sideways and slammed into the big tree at the center of the yard, going limp as it hit the grass.

I didn't hesitate.

My hand coming up, I gave a feral scream, the sound warbling on the edge of a growl, and lunged at the wraithlike monster.

4

The sizzling coil of energy speared the thing high on one shoulder. I'd been aiming for the heart...if it even had one...but the monster was the epitome of constant movement, the flowing and shimmering robes confusing the eye and making it hard to pinpoint its exact location.

The coil met little resistance as I pulled it back, and I wondered if there was anything beneath the robes other than foul black energy.

It had certainly felt substantial when it was crushing me into the ground.

I withdrew and rolled back on my heels for a beat, trying to discern a pattern in its movements.

The creature flew at me again. I ducked, swinging the coil above my head as I spun away.

The searing white energy sheared off a piece of the robe, and it hit the ground with a meaty plop.

The creature's head flew up and an inhuman sound permeated the night.

Thank the goddess. It could be hurt.

Good to know.

It spun again with superhuman speed and flew at me, claws outstretched and the golden gaze glowing with renewed ferocity. I stumbled backward, no time to rise to my feet, and lifted the energy blade again, slicing it sideways.

The blade caught the thing across the chest, digging deep.

Blood, thick and dark, flowed from the wound. A feral scream filled the night. But rather than retreat, the thing lashed out, hitting me like a runaway train and throwing me across the yard. I landed hard, my head slamming into the patchy grass a beat later than my body and wrenching my neck.

Pain sliced through me. My gaze wavered and darkened around the edges. I was dimly aware of movement around me—claws skittering over the broken concrete sidewalk and fur rustling softly against my skin.

I tried to move my arms. My legs. And push myself off the ground with my hands. Nothing worked.

Then the thing was on me again. It slammed down hard, crushing me against the ground and driving a large rock into my hip.

I cried out, my vision still wonky and my brain

like mush. My hand hit the thing in the chest, just above the still bleeding gash I'd created, and I shoved. But it had been all I could do to lift my arms. I had no strength.

And the magic I'd sifted from my surroundings was being siphoned off. I knew it as I looked into the brightly flaring gold eyes.

The monster was pulling my energy away. Consuming it just as I...

I swallowed hard, my brain shoving the thought away. In a last, desperate effort, I tugged the knife I kept on my thigh free and plunged it into the fiend's side, my bloody hand sliding down the hilt with the force of my strike and the blade slicing my palm.

The creature screamed, washing my face in putrid, sulfurous air.

I wanted to twist the knife, to tear the blade through its flesh. But I was so weak. So tired. I'd just lay there and...

My eyes started to close. The world swirled beneath my lids, unreal and indistinct. I felt myself fading.

My life bleeding away like the energy I no longer had.

It was okay, I thought, as my limbs grew heavy. A soothing warmth slid through me. Peace descended.

It was okay...

I'd just rest a while.

From deep within my brain a terrifying reminder fought free of my lethargy. *Boyle!*

I started, my eyes snapping open. I had to protect the baby. It was my job...

But the realization wasn't strength. I couldn't draw on it to live. I sent out my siphoning energy and found minimal magic in the air. I pulled in what I could and reached further...to the house. My siphon hit the wall of the big Victorian and flailed. The house was densely warded against outside magic. My energy signature was too weak to compel the ward. I felt Victoria's energy throbbing behind the barrier, a bright promise of life and strength. But I couldn't get to it.

I was going to fail. Tears leaked from my eyes. Anger flared but had nowhere to go. I looked up into the fiend's too-bright eyes and felt nothing. I was done.

A long, dark shape flew against the monster, slammed it sideways. The attack interrupted the thing's feeding pattern and sliced off the energy drain.

Good, I thought. *That's good.*

A shadow fell over me. A deep voice filled the silence. But I couldn't understand the words. Fog filled my brain, thick with static sounds. I reached up and touched hard, warm flesh. "Thank..." I managed. But that was all I had.

I closed my eyes and let the darkness take me down.

Warmth.

I tried to pry my eyes open, but they wouldn't cooperate.

Crackling sounds.

A fire.

I focused on my body and realized I was lying on something soft.

It smelled slightly musty but with a twinge of Grams' lilac body wash scent.

My couch.

I focused on pulling breath into my lungs, filling them with slightly smoky air. The cushions beneath me shifted, and something small and warm wrapped itself around me.

"Glynnie?"

Shock brought my eyes open. "Boyle." My arms felt like lead when I lifted them to wrap around him. "Thank the goddess, you're okay."

The baby snuggled against me, his little head tucked beneath my chin.

That soft tuft of orange hair tickled my nose, and I wrinkled it to keep from sneezing. "I was so worried," I told him.

"I okays," he said, sighing.

We lay there a long moment, the heat of the fire bathing us and warming the cold from my bones.

Then a floorboard creaked.

Alarm pierced the calm that was embalming me. I jerked upright, startling Boyle. My grip on the baby tightened. My gaze cleared under an adrenaline rush, and I saw him standing across the room. "Who are you? How did you get inside my house?"

The man stood half in shadow, half bathed by firelight. His lean jaw was shadowed with the stubble of the previous day's beard and his full lips pressed together as he looked at me. The cheekbone I could see was sharp and high, the nose straight, with a nostril that flared wide at the tone in my voice.

I watched a thick, dark-blond brow arch and his jaw tighten. "The 'goyle let me in."

Goddess's galoshes! "He wouldn't do that," I said. Though I sounded unsure, even to me.

The man held my stare, seemingly unwilling to argue the point.

I glanced down at Boyle, finding the answer in his guilty gaze. "What did you do?"

The baby deflated, folding into himself. "He not bad, Glynnie. He saved you."

The tiny voice was filled with tears and made me feel like an ogre. "You don't know that, Boyle. He could be mean."

Boyle shook his head, unusually determined. "He not bad."

I glanced up to find the stranger's lips curved into a wry smile.

I narrowed my eyes at him. "You're the man who's been watching me."

Since it wasn't a question, he didn't bother confirming it.

But he didn't deny it either.

"Why?"

He crossed his arms over a wide chest, the muscles in his biceps bunching impressively. "I have my reasons."

All the air left my lungs. It *was* him! I'd known it as soon as I clapped eyes on him. "You need to go."

He stared at me for a long moment. Panic flared as I considered that he might not leave.

But then he inclined his head. "It was nice to meet you...Glynn."

I blinked, shocked at the sound of my name on his lips.

Mutely, I watched him stalk toward the door, admiring the view despite my fear. As he pulled the front door open I swung my legs around, dropping my feet to the floor. "Wait!"

He turned, humor sparking in his hazel eyes.

"I..." confusion swept every thought from my head. I didn't even know why I'd stopped him.

Those expressive brows lifted again, and he

finally smiled. "You're welcome, Glynn." He lifted a hand to Boyle. And then he stepped outside.

Son of a bunion! My heart was pounding. Stars danced before my gaze. He'd been in my home. And I'd been... The panic deepened. He could have hurt the baby. He could have killed me.

But he hadn't.

I frowned. What was he up to? I shoved to my feet. "Watch him through the window," I told Boyle. "Let me know when he's gone."

Boyle bounded across the room, launching himself into the recliner in front of the biggest window and leaning on its back to watch through the glass. "What you doin'?" he asked in an uncertain tone.

"We're going to talk to Mitch."

Boyle quivered with delight, forgetting for a beat to watch the man.

The baby loved our resident seer. Mitch gave him ginger cookies and juice.

"Watch him, sweet boy," I reminded. I tested my balance and discovered I was still a bit wobbly. But it dissipated quickly. "I'm just going upstairs for a minute. Don't open the door," I told him, a thin thread of censure in my voice.

"Yeth, Glynnie."

He'd disappeared into the shadows across the street. But I still felt him there, like a fracture in the natural energy of the street—a rough spot.

Boyle and I went out the back of the house, picking our way across the wild and wooly back yard to a copse of enormous evergreens at the back corner of the property.

Correction. I picked my way across. Boyle bounded and bounced and skipped across the grass, just happy to be involved in another adventure.

Watching him, I sighed. He made me feel old at thirty-two.

We came out the other side of the trees and started across the ranch house's hard-scrabble yard. I glanced toward the dimly-lit window at the end of the house that was farthest from Victoria, my hackles rising as I did. There was a shape behind the sheer curtains. A head with hair that drifted around it like a sun flare. Narrow shoulders below the unkempt head shifted slightly as I glanced her way, and my unease doubled.

She didn't like it when I crossed her yard.

She never had.

The trees behind me shifted in a soft swing of movement and a long, dark shape trotted out.

Panic eased at the sight of him. "Are you okay, big guy?" To my shock, the big dog trotted right up to me and pressed his muscular bulk against my leg.

Remembering the glossy stains on his coat during the fight with the vortex monster, I ran my hand over his fur, searching for the damage so I could assess it. I found nothing. No wounds. Not even the dried residue of blood.

I dug my fingers into the thick scruff between his shoulders. "I knew you were magic." I frowned. "What are you?"

His response was to snuffle against my leg, thick tail sweeping the air behind him.

Boyle bounded back to me on a soft squeal of delight. "Puppy!"

I tried to grab him before he launched himself at the enormous dog, but he managed to evade. He hit the dog's broad chest hard and wrapped himself around the creature's neck.

My hand shot out to grab the dog's muzzle before it could bite.

But all it did was swipe an enormous black tongue over Boyle's face, making him giggle.

The figure in the window across the yard twitched again. I grabbed Boyle's hand. "Come on, sweet boy. We need to keep moving. Della's not happy we're in her yard."

His face turned to the ranch house and his little face folded into a frown. "She mean," he stated unnecessarily.

Understatement of the millennia, I thought.

I started off again, watching as Boyle bounded along beside the dog, who it appeared was coming with us. The baby was chattering as if he'd found a long-lost friend.

The sound made me smile.

5

He stood in the street, staring at the big old house from the shadows. He wasn't wrong. An enormous power pulsed from within it. He *had* been wrong about the woman. She wasn't the source of the power. At least, not all of it.

The energy he'd sniffed within the walls was unlike anything he'd ever tasted. It was both offensive and defensive. Alien but familiar. He hadn't decided if it was centered within the bones of the house, or if something else fed it.

His research of the area told him there was a lei line beneath the home. He suspected that was what he was sensing. But he'd sniffed out lei lines before. And this one was different. A convergence maybe? A collection of energy at the crossroads of two or more lines?

He stared at the house, seeing the multi-hued

lines of power rising in ripples from its walls and roof. The house might be sentient. He'd bumped against a couple of those in the past. They were rare and generally were believed to be fed by lei line magic.

But this house...this old, slightly worn Victorian home was different somehow.

That difference worried him. The people of the Body would be much too interested in it if they knew.

A shock of realization hit him. He'd wondered why they'd sent him to that goddess-forsaken little corpse of a town.

They'd wanted him to find the house and maybe the girl.

He thought of the report he'd been painstakingly writing. He'd been walking a thin line between reporting enough to keep his boss interested, but not telling him a sufficient amount to bring the man to Render.

It was a tightrope he was becoming used to. A dangerous game. But one he increasingly felt compelled to play.

Mitch didn't have a last name as far as I knew. At least, if he did, he was as reluctant to share it as he was to reveal anything else about himself.

I didn't even know what he was, exactly. We called him a seer because he knew things nobody else knew. Things he shouldn't have known. Things he couldn't have known.

I felt the sting of his magic as I stepped through the curtained door of his shack. It left a sour taste on the back of my tongue. And smelled like pickles.

A man sat cross-legged on a pile of rugs in front of a well-worn leather recliner. His form was encompassed in a purple housecoat that had once had rick-rack along the edges. Beneath the housecoat, a pair of threadbare cotton pants gathered around pale, hairy ankles. His feet were bare. His fiery red hair was neatly combed, parted on one side, and looked only slightly greasy as usual.

"Hello, Glynn," the seer said as Boyle and I stepped through the door. Boyle ran over and hopped around in front of Mitch, his ears twitching and the little shock of hair between them bouncing manically with his movements. "Hi, Mitch!"

Mitch smiled, turning his bright brown gaze on the excited baby. "Cookies and juice are on the table over there, buddy."

With a happy squeal, Boyle bounced toward the

table in the "kitchen" which consisted of a short counter with a microwave, a small refrigerator, and two cabinets that apparently held everything Mitch needed in the way of food and utensils.

I had no idea how he did it. I'd managed to fill every cabinet in Victoria's kitchen and still needed to put stuff into baskets.

I sat down on the floor in front of our host, crossing my legs as he had, and waited. I didn't need to tell Mitch what was going on. He would already know. I didn't need to ask him what I wanted to ask. He'd already know that too.

He knew everything that happened on the entire street. And I had no doubt he knew more than that.

Boyle pulled the chair from the small table, the legs scraping noisily across the curled and stained slab of linoleum Mitch had thrown over the dirt to delineate the kitchen. He jumped up and claimed his first cookie, stuffing it happily into his mouth.

"He's a shadow in my mind," Mitch said.

The words made my heart thump. I frowned. "What does that mean?" Maybe Mitch was speaking in code.

He shrugged, digging in one ear as he thought about my question. "I've been watching him since he arrived. But there's nothing. Only a black smudge that sits across from Victoria."

"Is he magic?"

Despite the greater world's assumption that all the

magic had been pulled into the cities, the residents of Render knew better. In our small, forgotten place in the universe, we all held our magic close, hiding it from the few non-magic humans who still resided in the dusty, broken town. And from those who would try to bend it to their will beyond the small town.

Mitch nodded without hesitation. "There's no question. But it's a different magic than any I've encountered. Either he's really good at masking it, or..."

I waited for the "or" to be fleshed out a bit. Unfortunately, Mitch didn't seem so inclined. Finally, I asked, "Or?"

Mitch shook his head. "I'm still working on that."

Frustration filled me. "Is he dangerous?"

"My instincts tell me, no. But he's not of Render. So that makes him inherently dangerous, yes?"

I nodded. Leaning closer, I lowered my voice. "Boyle let him into Victoria tonight."

"Yes."

"He trusts him."

That made Mitch frown. Gargoyles were natural protectors. And, though it was true that Boyle wouldn't come into his magic for a decade or more, the roots of the magic he'd someday exhibit were already in place. His instincts were generally spot-on. Though, because he was so young, I had to believe they were susceptible to outside influence.

As if reading my thoughts, Mitch said, "The boy isn't infallible. He could be swayed by a sweet treat or a smile."

I knew he was right. Yet...

"I met him. I sensed magic, but it didn't feel hostile."

Mitch nodded. "I'm inclined to agree, Glynn. Though if you're looking for surety and promises. I can't give them where this man is concerned."

I sighed. "Okay. You'll let me know if...when that changes?"

"Of course."

Mitch glanced at the door. "Why didn't your friend come inside with you?"

For a beat, I was confused by his question. "My friend..." Then it hit me. "The dog?"

Mitch folded large, freckled hands together. "The dog."

"I don't know. Maybe he wasn't sure you allowed dogs."

Mitch chuckled, lifting his hands to indicate the fifteen foot square shed he lived in. It had once been a gardening shed for the abandoned mansion on the property. I'd asked him once why he'd chosen not to live in the big house. Nobody would have known or cared. The house had been abandoned when the magical family who'd lived there left Render. But Mitch had just shaken his head, giving me an enigmatic smile. "This is my place," he'd said. "It will always be mine."

I hadn't known what he'd meant, but I trusted he knew what he was talking about.

"What do you know about that thing that attacked us tonight," I asked him.

"Wraith," Mitch said, grimacing. "Nasty creature."

"Any idea what it wanted?"

"No."

I blinked, my gaze widening. "No?"

The seer fidgeted uncomfortably. He fixed me with an angry gaze. "What do you want me to say, Glynn? I don't know everything!"

A small hand touched my shoulder, and I looked at Boyle. He still had a cookie in his hand, but he was watching Mitch, clearly as surprised as I was that the seer was yelling at me. I couldn't remember a time when Mitch had been short or angry.

"Mitch?"

His face was tense, his shoulders rigid. He finally scrubbed a hand over his eyes and sighed. "I'm sorry. I'm just frustrated."

Boyle slid into my lap, his warm little hands wrapping around my wrists as he chewed the last of the cookie, his cheeks bulging.

Crumbs filtered down to my legs, dotting my jeans.

"Why are you frustrated," I asked, feeling worry

scrape up my spine. I'd never seen Mitch discombobulated. Never.

"Something's happening, Glynn. Something's coming. And for the first time in my life, I can't see it."

A chill swept over me. I didn't know what to say to that. Anything I asked would only frustrate him more.

"It okay, Mitch," Boyle said, spitting crumbs as he said the man's name.

Mitch nodded, smiling indulgently. "It will be, Boyle. Don't worry."

"Will it?" I asked softly.

Mitch lifted his bright gaze to mine, his jaw tight.

The fear in his eyes was all the answer I needed.

"Glynn, Glynn, Glynn, Glynn!" a happy, excited voice sang out through the night. I was smiling even before I turned to find the petite, blonde woman running toward us across the broken sidewalk.

I caught her as she flung herself at me. "Hey, girlfriend." I hugged her, laughing at her exuberance.

In the distance, the big dog gave a deep-throated bark of alarm.

My assailant rolled back on the heels of her pink sneakers. "Whoa! Why do you have a wolf?"

I laughed. "He's not a wolf." Then I frowned, not sure at all that he wasn't. "I don't think."

"Sissy!" Boyle squealed, running toward us with the dog protectively at his side. "I miss you!" He didn't even slow before he threw himself at my best friend, and despite the fact that he was a third her size and weight, she caught him easily, laughing with delight. "I miss you too, munchkin!" She sprinkled his small face with kisses as Boyle cringed and giggled. "Ach!" he said, mimicking Sissy's usual response when he did that. "Witch kisses."

In response, she kissed him right on the nose. "Witch kisses are the best, munchkin."

Sissy let him slide to the ground and offered the wolf-dog her fingers to sniff. He didn't hesitate to extend his nose, sneezing heartily as he got a whiff.

Sissy rolled her eyes. "Pepper. I just made myself a bacon, lettuce, and pepper sandwich."

"Ugh!" I said, knowing it would earn me a belt on the arm from her tiny fist. Her eating habits were a constant source of amusement for me. Though, I'd noticed lately that she was infecting Boyle with them. Gargoyles are nothing if not gastronomically adventurous, making my best friend the perfect role model for him where food was concerned.

"How was your trip?" I asked as she fell in beside me. As usual, I felt like a giant next to Sissy. She was five feet two inches tall and, though shapely, probably weighed about as much as my left leg. By contrast, I was tall for a woman at five feet ten and big-boned. Or, at least, that's what I told myself each and every time I broke down and let myself have dessert with Boyle.

"Exhausting," Sissie admitted. "I had to hold my cloaking spell for eight full hours today."

"Eight hours? How is that even possible?"

She sighed. "Two brownies, almost an entire cherry pie, and a large bag of chips made it possible."

I envied my friend, who burned a massive number of calories when she did magic and needed to replenish them in whatever way possible. Just standing next to her while she ate that stuff made my butt an inch wider. I would have hated Sissy for the ability to eat whatever she wanted if I didn't love her so much. "I don't know why you risk it," I scolded gently. "If anybody realized..."

She touched my arm with a soft hand, the nails of which were painted a cotton candy pink. "Nobody knew I was a witch," she told me, smiling. "And, I risk it because somebody needs to, and I'm the only one who can."

Sissy came from a wealthy and powerful family who lived in New Indianapolis. Her mother was on track to be the next Mayor of the city, and her father was a Statesman for the Magical Body, similar to a Senator in the human government. The Body was the governing force for Indy and the surrounding area, even usurping the Mayor's power in many areas. Though it was generally thought that their power ended at the city limits. Those who knew the Body more intimately, like Sissy's parents, understood they would extend their power until they came up against resistance.

Even then, they'd been known to use unreasonable force to overwhelm any but the staunchest opposition.

The Valkyr family was high-magic, but their positions made them the perfect advocates for Render. And Sissy's assurances that the town was magic-free was all that kept the Marshals from descending on us and dragging us all into the city.

Sissy pretended she was low magic to distance herself from her family. According to Sis, her parents hated that she lived in Render. But she insisted she couldn't stand living in a city with, "All. That. Magic," as she put it with much drama. Though I found it hard to believe her parents didn't know she was a witch, I never underestimated their ambitions. Or their full awareness of what would happen to those ambitions if it became widely known their beautiful daughter was a witch who preferred living in the countryside to taking her place with her family in Magical Indy.

6

Sissy blew bubbles at Boyle and he poked them with a claw, giggling hysterically as they continued to rain down on his head. A particularly large one floated to his pert little nose and hung there, glistening in a rainbow of refractive light.

"Pretty!" the little gargoyle breathed, his eyes crossing with delight.

"Okay, you," I told him. "Time for bed."

"Aw, Glynnie," he whined.

I shook my head. "Nope, no arguments now. It's an hour past your bedtime. The sun will be up soon."

He harrumphed, but couldn't hold back a jaw-cracking yawn. "Can I sleep with you?" he asked softly. And I realized he was still spooked from the night's events. Though I would normally insist he climbed the stairs to his attic bedroom, provided with a gargoyle's love of heights in mind, I gave in because, to tell the goddess's honest truth, I was a little spooked myself. "Okay. But just this once."

His grin was wide as he flung himself at my legs, giving me a bone-creaking hug. Then he climbed agilely onto Sissy's lap and gave her a kiss on the cheek. "Night, Sis."

She hugged him, kissing him on the nose. "Night, sweet Boyle. I'll see you tomorrow?"

He nodded happily and scurried up the stairs to the second level.

Sissy and I sat in silence for a minute, enjoying the quiet and our steaming cups of coffee. She sighed. "It's so nice here."

There was a familiar tang of longing in her voice —one which she only got after she'd spent time with her family. Sissy didn't like living a false life in Indianapolis. She didn't, in fact, much like the big, busy city itself. But most of all, she didn't like the cool, shallow affection that was all she got from her parents. I knew she'd always longed for a sister. Or even a brother. Even the nickname she'd insisted on since she'd been a moody pre-teen spoke to that desire. Sissy wasn't her real name. She wouldn't tell me what that was. But I suspected it was something refined and stuffy. Like Persephone or Charlemagne.

Unfortunately for Sissy's sibling aspirations, having one child had been the extent of the Valkyr's parental capabilities. An argument could be made that even having one child had stretched them beyond those capabilities.

I reached over and squeezed her hand. "It's late. Why don't you stay over?"

She considered it long enough that I gave her a nudge. "There's plenty of room on the bed for three. As long as you don't mind Boyle's snoring, or having his cold little feet kicking you all night long."

She laughed. "As tempting as that sounds..."

"Come on," I nudged her with my foot under the table. "We can make popcorn and watch old vampire flicks." I waggled my brows and the sad look finally left her eyes.

Sissy was a sucker for cheesy horror movies.

"Okay, you talked me into it. But I'm sleeping on the couch. I love that little munchkin like a rabbit loves carrots, but I'm not up to being pummeled by those icy little feet all night. That little sucker packs some power."

"Tell me about it." I climbed to my feet, biting back a groan from my treatment at the hands of the wraith. But Sissy noticed.

"Let me heal those bruises," she offered.

I shook my head. "I'll be fine by morning. You don't need to waste your energy."

The magic of the house would heal me. If Sissy did it, she'd pay a higher price. Recently, Sissy had begun to suffer debilitating headaches whenever she used too much of her magic.

I suspected the issue was an emotional one, the result of over twenty years trying to pretend she was "normal" and denying her gifts. But Sissy's hackles rose whenever I suggested something along those lines. So, I'd stopped suggesting it and had just tried to minimize her magic use whenever possible.

Sissy shrugged. "I'll go pick out a movie?"

"Good. I'll pop the corn."

We'd just settled in a few minutes later, Grams' hand-knitted throw over our legs and a truly cheesy werewolf movie flickering into life on the television mounted over the fireplace, when the first rumble shook the house.

Sissy and I shared a look.

We waited for a beat and, when nothing else happened, I shrugged. "Probably just Victoria settling. She's old and creaky."

Sissy stuffed popcorn into her mouth and sighed happily.

The movie was twenty minutes gone when the second rumble hit, and something in the kitchen crashed to the ground.

I jumped up, heading into the kitchen to find the coffee cups I'd washed out and set to dry on a towel on the counter shattered into splinters on the floor.

Goddess's galoshes! I thought with irritation. Those cups had sentimental value. They'd belonged to Grams.

"Earthquakes?" Sissy asked, still munching popcorn.

We were used to the occasional earthquake in the countryside around the magical city. The general consensus was that it was caused by an abundance of magic being used in a relatively compact area. Mostly the quakes were just annoying and we ignored them.

I didn't think Victoria was succumbing to earthquakes. But I wasn't sure, so I nodded. Hiding my expression from my friend, I picked my way gingerly around the mess and plucked a broom and dustpan from the corner where I'd tucked them. Electricity came at a premium in Render and worse, with strings. People monitored its use, using it to keep track of Renderites and, when necessary, to control us. The result was that, like most of us in the small town, I used as little of it as I could. Sissy held the pan for me while I swept the broken glass into it, and then dumped it into the trash.

Another rumble hit the house, strong enough to shake a glass jar filled with teabags toward the edge of the counter. I caught it just before it went over the edge. "Okay, that's it!" I yelled to the air.

The reverberations cut off, mid-growl and the house fell to silence.

Sissy eyed me with surprise. "You control earthquakes, now?"

I sighed. "It's not earthquakes."

Her smile slipped off her face. "What is it, then?"

I chewed the inside of my lip. No way was I going to tell her. If I did, she'd want to help. And I couldn't let her do it. It wasn't her responsibility. "It's nothing. But I need to take care of it. Maybe we could take a raincheck on the sleepover?"

Confusion morphed to hurt and then to anger in her gray eyes. "Glynn, I'm going to help you with whatever this is, so you might as well stop trying to get rid of me. Now tell me what we're dealing with, so I can prepare."

"Siss..."

"Uh!"

"But..."

"Eh!"

"I don't want..."

"Inh!"

I gave up. "Okay. But I don't think you can actually prepare for this. I would appreciate the backup, though. Just in case..."

Sissy's expression, always clear enough to see straight through, showed her concern.

I didn't really blame her. I'd passed through concern weeks ago and was currently teetering on the sharp edge of terrorized.

It would be a relief to finally share some of that terror with a friend.

The door opened with a soft whoosh, sucked back on its hinges on a gust of grave-scented air from the ward. Magical energy sifted over me, a stinging wash of icy air that left me feeling like I needed a shower.

The stairwell was pitch dark, the magic of the portal having made electric lighting a luxury we couldn't afford. Every time the magic flared in the portal, it blew out the fixtures we'd installed in the ceiling above the stairs and the main room.

Standing at my back, Sissy gave a soft gasp of alarm and her hands found my shoulders, squeezing hard enough to leave bruises. "Glynn?"

I shook my head. "I need to move fast. You can stay up here if you want." I started down the steps, stopping on the third one and turning to look back at her. She hadn't moved. "Keep an eye on Boyle for me," I said, trying to keep the fear-infused wobble out of my voice.

A moment later, I heard a soft exclamation and the steps vibrated under Sissy's weight as she hurried after me. "I said I'd help."

I'd have felt better if she hadn't sounded so terrified. And if her usually pink cheeks weren't an unhealthy chalk-white hue.

Sissy reached over and grabbed my hand, squeezing it tightly enough to make my finger bones creak. I appreciated the anchor. Even if I was pretty sure it was to make *her* feel better.

We descended the last few steps, moving past the unfinished drywall of the stairwell. As I stepped down onto the dirt floor, the basement opened up around me in all its horrible glory.

Sissy yanked my hand, her feet refusing to leave the last step. "Um, Glynn..."

I gave her hand a squeeze and forced myself to pull free. "Stay right here."

She nodded, her gaze locked on the nightmare across the space.

I didn't blame her. The fiery tunnel that led from the ragged hole in the rocky wall was definitely an attention-getter.

I stepped forward, my hand reluctantly releasing the wood railing. My fingers had probably dented the soft wood from the pressure of my grip. I sucked air at the feeling of magical energy rolling through the basement.

Behind me, Sissy drew a long, ragged breath, her eyes bright.

"Are you okay?" I asked.

Her gaze shot to me and widened, her mouth opening but no words finding their way past her lips. She nodded, clutching the same railing I had been abusing.

The fire that roiled inside the tunnel spun with

unusual vigor, the force of its energy telling me something bad was coming.

"Goddess's galoshes!" I muttered. I'd known the energy was building, but I'd had no idea it had gotten so bad.

"What is that thing?" Sissy whispered in a hoarse voice.

I forced my fingers to release the railing. "Portal." She'd known my job was to protect Victoria from discovery. A magical house would be a rare and coveted find for the power-hungry Body. But I'd never told her about the portal in the basement. The fewer people who knew the better. Sissy was my best friend. She'd proven her loyalty to me many times over the years. I trusted her. I just didn't want her having to carry around knowledge she might be forced to lie about later. "It's not too late to leave," I half-joked.

She ignored me. "Where does it go?" the question was breathless. When I glanced her way, I saw that her chest was heaving.

"Sis, are you sure..."

"I'm fine," she said, her voice sounding more normal. "It's just...amazing."

"Yeah," I said. "That's a word for it." I could think of many others. But maybe that was because I'd seen the worst the thing could spit out. And it was bad.

I thought of the wraith in the yard and couldn't help wondering...

The house rumbled again, dust from the ceiling sifting down on my head. High above me, I heard the ominous sound of something crashing to the floor. Dread filled me as I wondered what fresh heartache I'd find when I went back upstairs.

"It leads someplace we don't want to go," I answered vaguely. The truth was, I wasn't sure where the portal led. Grams had told me the house rested atop a lei line, and that the energy from the line bubbled up and infused the old house with magic. I only felt a small fraction of that energy because my power isn't of the earth, my energy is centered in the animal world. Human animals included. But even I gained a soft bump of power from the thing in the basement. And I knew how seductive it could be.

"What are you going to do?" Sissy asked, her voice sounding closer.

I turned to find her standing just behind me, her gaze locked on the fiery portal. "You should get back," I said, frowning.

She didn't acknowledge my warning. Her gaze stayed riveted on the roiling magic.

"Sis?" I waved a hand in front of her face.

She blinked and grinned. "No wonder you don't like to come down here. That's seriously cool and vastly terrifying."

"Yeah." I frowned toward the stairs. I knew my friend. I wasn't going to be able to talk her into staying back. So I'd just have to finish what I'd come down there to do and get us both back upstairs. "Don't get any closer, okay?"

"What are you gonna do?"

Grabbing the special clay pot Grams had designed for the purposes of siphoning energy from the portal, I quickly spread large-grain salt and iron pellets over the bottom. The pot was about a foot wide on the bottom and top, widening to eighteen inches in the center. It was infused with nullifying magic so that any of the energy that entered the pot was immediately voided. The sulfurous residue left behind by the process of nullification fell into the mix at the bottom, dissolving the salt and iron and turning them to sludge. When I was done, I'd empty the sludgy mess into another specially warded pot and carry it outside to work into the soil at the back of the property.

It sounded toxic, but the pot's magic turned it into something that fed the earth instead of poisoning it. In the area where I buried the sludge, enormous trees reached toward the sky. Some of them only a couple of years old.

It was a tedious process, made even less palatable by the burn I always got when siphoning the energy. The pot had to be held on its side, opening toward the portal, and I had to get as close to the fiery heat as I could stand to go.

I'd get what amounted to a bad sunburn from the process. Painful, but not disfiguring in the long run. The process was like releasing pressure in a pressure cooker. Making a volatile magical force safe and harmless.

For a while.

It was something Grams had gotten used to during her time in Victoria. And it was something I was learning to manage, though I had a tendency to put it off until it got way too volatile.

Like it currently was.

Sissy watched me prep the siphoning pot, her face intent and her gaze speculative. She didn't ask any more questions, and I assumed she was saving them for when we went upstairs.

The house rumbled again, the floor beneath our feet rising upward in a rippling movement that threw us to the ground. I just barely managed to hold onto the pot, protecting it with my arms as I fell.

My elbow slammed painfully against the hard ground and pain radiated down my arm, turning my fingers numb.

Sissy cried out and my head whipped around as she fell, her body limp and her eyes closed. One arm was outstretched toward the portal, the fingers twitching slightly.

The portal spit fire into the room, its tentacles barely missing me as I dove to the side.

Aggression!

I remembered Grams' voice droning over and

over. *You need to siphon the energy while it's still passive. If it turns aggressive, you'll be in danger.*

I'd waited too long.

Fire burst from the portal again, its tendrils forming into the shape of a hand, the fingers curved like claws. It raked the air where I'd been, but I'd rolled away as soon as I saw it coming.

It knew what I was planning to do, and it was trying to stop me.

I jumped to my feet, the pot wrapped protectively in one arm.

With a soft sound, Sissy's body slid closer to the portal.

Her eyes were still closed, her chest rising and falling in shallow breaths. But somehow she'd moved. She slid closer again, and a phantom burn appeared on her wrist, taking the form of the fiery fingers that had searched for me.

I ran for her and was hit by a sizzling wall of energy, flinging me back to slam against the table holding the siphoning objects.

Agony speared through me. Something cracked inside my body, slashing fresh misery through my ribs.

The table fractured under my weight, and salt and pellets slid to the floor. The secondary siphoning pot crashed downward and broke into two equal pieces.

"Sissy! Wake up!" I screamed, praying she'd hear me.

But she didn't respond. She just lay there as the energy tugged her several inches closer. The burn around her wrist turned darker, and blisters formed from the fiery clutch of the magic.

I shoved painfully to my feet again and started running, snatching up the pot and throwing myself to the ground before the wall of energy could catch me again.

I skidded across the floor, snatching at Sissy's small form as she shot toward the fire.

But she flew out of my grip, sailing quickly toward the burning maw of the portal, her small body limp and helpless. And I couldn't do anything to stop it.

7

Footsteps pounded down the steps. They sounded thunderous in the closed, heavy air of the underground space.

I didn't have time to wonder who it was. I'd managed to wrap a hand around Sissy's ankle and had turned myself into a physical anchor, trying to keep her from being pulled into the portal. I tried pulling her away from it, but the power tugging her forward was too much for me.

It was as if I weighed nothing. She continued to be drawn forward, inches at a time.

A large hand reached out and grasped my arm.

I screamed in frustration as the hand wrenched Sissy out of my grip. "No!" I lashed out, reaching for a swirling wave of residual energy and yanking it deep inside.

It hit me with the force of a punch and the sweet-

ness of a favored treat. The energy slammed through
my system and exploded, infusing me with pleasure.
Without thinking, I gathered it into a bludgeon and
threw out my hands, sending it toward the man
who'd taken Sissy from me.

He flew backward, crashing against the stair rail
with a grunt, and slid slowly toward the floor.

I blinked in surprise.

It was him. The guy across the street.

And he had Sissy clutched against his chest,
cushioning her from the impact of my magical
tantrum. "Get her out of here," I growled, my voice
three octaves deeper than usual because of the
power I'd pulled into my body.

He shook his head and carefully laid her on the
floor. "You need help."

"I'm fine," I growled. "Go!"

The irritating man shook off my order and found
the pot. "We don't have much time. Siphon, fast!"

I didn't stop to wonder how he knew what I was
about because he was right. We *didn't* have much
time. The walls of the basement had started to flex,
bowing outward as rock dust filtered down on us.
Above our heads, things were crashing against the
floor as the entire structure was tested against a
massive wave of foreign energy.

I grabbed the pot and braced it against my
belly, bending my legs as a super-heated wave of
energy flared outward from the portal, searing me

in fiery agony. "*Porta nomine protectoris virtutem cedere hinc,*" I shouted as the energy beat against me.

Fire lashed out, sizzling the air an inch from my face. The flame formed into a fiery fist but my innate protections, fed by Victoria's energy and my role as the portal protector, kept it from touching me again.

The air became superheated.

The rock walls were lost behind a wavering wall of energy and heat so powerful the surface of the rock began to melt, dripping downward in glistening streams.

Sweat poured off me. The stench of burning hair filled the partially protective bubble around me. And a grave-scented wind burst from the portal and shoved at me, forcing me backward. I leaned into the powerful gusts, knowing I was playing a dangerous game as I did. If the portal entity withdrew the windy barrier, the loss of resistance would send me hurtling into the gateway.

Hard arms suddenly encircled me from behind, a powerful body braced against mine.

Gratitude filled me as I realized the man had figured out what I'd just realized and was making sure it didn't happen.

I watched the skin on the muscular arms bubble under the deadly heat, the hairs curling as if on fire.

He tensed against me, no doubt in excruciating pain, but he never wavered. He held on as the energy finally gave up its resistance and pulled the fiery fist back into the portal.

"*Porta nomine protectoris virtutem cedere hinc,*" I screamed again, my voice devoured by the driving wind.

For a moment, I worried the command was lost. But then the energy began to coil at the center of the portal, oozing slowly outward, thicker at the source and growing thinner in increments. Like a telescoping lens oozing reluctantly toward the pot braced at my center.

It continued to fight the command in the protector's directive. But, ultimately, the laws of magic wouldn't allow it to resist. The first wave of energy slammed into the pot. It hit so hard it lifted me off my feet, driving into me like a firehose, relentless and steady.

I clung to the pot with everything I had, feeling the man at my back through the tension of his unyielding musculature.

He was strong. And he was stubborn. And he might have been the only thing that kept me from slamming into the rock wall at our backs as the energy hammered and hammered and beat me senseless with its impossible force.

Then suddenly it was gone. The fire snapped away with a final angry hiss. The edges of the deadly portal retracted, folding inward until nothing was left but a rough-hewn reformed rock wall.

We crashed to the ground in a pile of heaving chests and painful limbs.

The wind died. The heat fell away, returning the space to its usually clammy temps. And the basement fell eerily silent.

The man beneath me pushed me gently aside and rose to his feet, grabbing me under the arms and pulling me toward the stairs.

I almost laughed, understanding the sentiment. He no doubt worried the portal might fire up again at any moment and resume its assault. "It's okay. It's closed now," I told him.

I climbed slowly to my feet, the pot still clutched against my chest. The magical energy inside the pot swirled in a rainbow of colors, sparking as it hit the edge of the magic containing it. The pot was very warm, on the edge of uncomfortable, but the spell infusing the clay kept it from becoming too hot to handle.

My gaze fell to Sissy as the man bent over her, and my relief at having the siphoning behind me fractured as I looked at her too-still body. "Is she okay?"

He scooped her up. "She's still breathing," he said unhelpfully. "Beyond that, I can't say." He started up the steps and I followed. I took the siphon with me, unwilling to let it out of my sight.

He laid Sissy on the couch and placed a finger at her throat.

I headed for the kitchen, setting the pot in the sink so it wouldn't topple to the floor if the house, goddess forbid, decided to give a final shake after its magical tantrum.

I opened the cabinet near the back door and pulled out the first aid kit Grams had left me.

Soft footfalls hit the floor behind me. I turned in his direction with the scratched and rusted metal box that held the first aid items clutched in my shaking hands. "Who are you?"

I hadn't meant to ask him that. Had no idea why I'd done it. But it was something I needed to know, so I didn't regret the question.

He shrugged. "That's not important."

"Yes," I said, frowning. "It really is."

We locked gazes for a moment. He finally lowered his, giving me the win. "My name is Wilder Hawkins. But most people call me Hawk."

I stared at him a moment, seeing the truth in his eyes, and then nodded. "Glynn Forester. People call me Glynn."

He smiled. "I'm glad you told me. I'd have never guessed."

Reluctantly, my lips curved upward. Then I remembered Sissy. "I need to..." I motioned toward the door that he was blocking with his big body.

He nodded. "Her pulse is strong. She doesn't seem to be having any trouble breathing. Except for the burns on her wrist, I don't see anything wrong with her."

I nodded. "Thanks." The word felt inadequate and, at the same time like it was too much. I mean, he *had* broken into Victoria and forced himself into my business. I wanted to know how he'd gotten past the wards. I wanted to know why he'd interfered. I wanted to know...so many things.

But I had to tend to Sissy.

I moved past him and hurried to the couch. Boyle was sitting on the couch next to her, his little form tucked into the curve of her body. One, long-fingered hand rested on her arm above the burns. He looked up as I approached, his bright gaze flicking to Hawk and back to me, dismissing him. "Sissy sick."

"I know, honey. I'm going to make her better." I shooed him off the couch but he didn't go far. He jumped to the padded back and squatted there, watching me as I opened the metal box.

"You give Sissy the nasty medicine?"

He looked so appalled I almost laughed. "No, sweet boy."

His face softened in relief. He looked up at Hawk, speaking to him as if he'd always been around. "That purple med-cine tastes like butt."

I heard the smile in Hawk's voice. "Butt, huh? I've never tasted butt."

Boyle giggled happily.

I pulled a jar of ointment out of the box and unscrewed the top, dipping my fingers into the foul-smelling concoction. I carefully rubbed it over my friend's hand and arm, grimacing at the red and swollen skin. The burns went from her fingertips all the way up to her elbow. Guilt ate at me, turning my amusement at Boyle and Hawk's banter on its head.

Sissy wouldn't be hurt if it weren't for me.

A warm hand dropped onto my shoulder. "It's not your fault," Hawk said as if reading my mind.

I shrugged him off. "You don't know that."

He fell silent, but I looked up to find Boyle eyeing me with an unhappy look. He didn't like it when I was rude to people. That was my doing since I'd been trying to teach him by example that he should respect other people and be kind unless they tried to hurt him.

More guilt chewed on my insides. I shoved the jar back into the metal box and pulled out a tiny bottle, removing the lid and holding it under Sissy's nose. The jar contained smelling salts, with a bang. A special herb that could pull people from magical oblivion.

For a moment, nothing happened. I was starting to panic when she finally coughed, her hand pushing the jar away. Then she winced. "Ow." Sissy's eyes opened, her gaze unfocused for a beat and then narrowing in on me. "Glynn?"

I tucked the salts away and closed the kit. "How

are you feeling?" I asked my friend.

"Like a dog's backside," she murmured, trying to shove herself to a seated position and wincing again. "My arm's killing me. What happened?" She looked down at the swollen skin and frowned. "It looks burned."

"You got too close to the portal," Hawk said.

Sissy jumped and gave a surprised yelp.

Despite myself, I felt my lips curve into a smile.

"What in the..." She widened her eyes at the big man standing next to me. I understood her shock. I never allowed strangers into Victoria.

Especially not big muscular ones with piercing hazel eyes.

"Sis, this is Hawk."

The surprise left her face, and a sly smile replaced it. "Yes, he is."

I cleared my throat and she turned to me, horror filling her expression. "Did I say that out loud?"

I nodded.

She covered her face. Laughing nervously, she started to offer him her hand and then realized it was the burned one and switched. "Sissy Valkyr."

I tensed, but Sissy didn't seem to notice.

They performed an awkward left-handed handshake.

Then Hawk said, "Valkyr? As in Statesman Valkyr?"

All the color left my friend's face. She didn't

generally share her last name for obvious reasons. At that point, she couldn't exactly deny the connection. Since she'd turned the color of paper at the question. "I shouldn't have told you that," she said instead.

He nodded. "No, you probably shouldn't have."

Shocked silence filled the room.

Hawk looked from one to the other of us and seemed to realize how that had sounded. He lifted his hands as if in surrender. "I'm not a reporter and I don't work for a rival politician. Believe me, I couldn't care less. You don't have to worry about me spreading gossip."

I wasn't sure if his denial made me feel better or not. From the tense look on Sissy's face, I didn't think she was sure about it either.

Hawk turned to me. "I need to know about that portal."

"No," I said, plucking the kit off the couch and standing. "You don't."

I started toward the kitchen and he grabbed my arm, stopping me. I glared down at his hand and then back up to his face.

He got the message, releasing me. "Look, that came out wrong. I'm not trying to stick my nose into your business."

"For a man who isn't trying to stick his nose into my business, your nose seems to get into my business an awful lot." I didn't wait for his response.

Heading into the kitchen, I stowed the kit back in its spot in the cabinet. When I turned back around, he was leaning against the doorframe, watching me with his hands shoved into the pockets of his jeans.

"Glynn..."

I shook my head. "You want me to tell you my private business. I don't even know you. For example, I don't know why you showed up in Render and why you've been watching my house. I don't know why you keep injecting yourself into my life. And I don't know how you keep getting into my house." My voice rose at the end because that was the part that bothered me the most. Victoria was my safe haven. It was how I protected Boyle and me. And the man standing in front of me, sexy face looking stern and judgmental, had breached it twice.

"That last part is simple," he told me. "The boy let me in again."

That stopped me in my tracks. I was going to have to have a stern discussion with Boyle. "He shouldn't have. He knows better. What did you do to him?"

Hawk blinked at that, anger bringing fresh color to his face. "I don't hurt children."

I shrugged. "I don't really know if that's true, do I? I don't know you. And when I ask you a question, you rarely answer with the truth."

"I don't lie."

"Maybe not. But you're pretty good at evasion, aren't you?"

He stared at me for a long moment, his body resembling the side of a mountain for its rigidness. Then he pushed off the doorframe and inclined his chin. "Have a good day, Glynn."

And he left.

8

"Don't you think you were pretty harsh?" Sissy asked.

I turned around to find her standing in the doorway, arms holding her stomach as if she still felt ill. I hurried over and wrapped an arm around her waist, guiding her to a chair. "Sit. You shouldn't be on your feet."

She let me ease her into a chair, which told me more than I wanted to know about her condition. Worry spiraled through me.

But then she lifted an angry gaze, her mouth tightening. "He helped us," Glynn. "He might have saved our lives. Why were you so mean to him?"

I rubbed my arms, suddenly cold. "You don't understand."

"No. I don't. Which is why I'm asking."

"Would you like tea?"

She opened her mouth, her brows lowering as if she were going to yell at me, and then sighed, nodding. "That would be great. And if you have any cookies, I wouldn't object to a couple of those either."

I quickly obliged, realizing she was probably burning through tons of calories healing the burns from the magical attack. An attack she should have never been close enough to experience.

I was a terrible friend.

I placed half a dozen of my home-baked peanut butter cookies on a plate and put it in front of her before starting the tea.

She ate quietly for a minute, leaving me to my thoughts. Which was both good and bad. I couldn't answer her question, because I wasn't even sure myself why Wilder Hawkins scared me so much. He'd scared me from the beginning when I'd started seeing his shadow lurking across the street. He was an unknown quantity in a place where the unknown could be deadly.

But it was more than that. There was something about him that felt like a threat. And the fact that everyone around me seemed to immediately like him made the threat feel even more dire.

I set a steaming cup of tea in front of Sissy and turned to the fridge. "I have leftover stew?"

She nodded, sipping the tea and closing her eyes with pleasure. "Oh, that's so good." When she opened her eyes again, they looked less hostile. "Thanks."

The pitter-patter of tiny clawed feet told me Boyle had joined us. "Me too, peeese," he said, jumping onto a chair and grabbing one of Sissy's cookies.

"Hey!" she scolded, a grin on her face.

"Good," the baby declared as crumbs sifted to the table.

"No more cookies," I scolded half-heartedly. "Stew first." I'd given up on convincing Boyle to eat a true breakfast long ago. He didn't seem to care for breakfast foods, and I'd finally decided it was better to get food into his growing belly than to force him to eat things he didn't like. So, he generally ate leftovers for breakfast.

Apparently, that was what I'd be eating for breakfast too.

"So," Sissy said as I turned the flame down on the stove, stirring the stew. "Why don't you like him?"

I turned to find both of them staring at me, matching looks of curiosity on both of their faces. "Don't gang up on me, or anything," I groused.

Sissy shrugged. "We just want to know."

"Yeah, we's just wanna knows."

I smiled at the baby, then narrowed my gaze on the cookie in his hand, which seemed to have mysteriously gotten larger than the last time I'd glanced his way. I turned a glare on my friend.

Sis gave me a totally non-repentant grin. She pressed her finger against the last of the crumbs on the plate and stuck the crumb-coated finger into her mouth.

I was outnumbered and disrespected in my own home.

"You still haven't answered my question," Sis said. "If you're not careful, we'll think you're *evading* the answer."

I stiffened, taking the barb right between my shoulder blades. Then forced a neutral expression and spooned stew into three bowls.

"I'm not evading, I just honestly don't know the answer," I finally told her. "Something about him bothers me."

"I'll bet," Sis said, waggling her brows suggestively.

Boyle tried to waggle his tiny orange brows, but his whole face moved instead. Sissy and I both laughed at the sight. Boyle cackled. He loved being a clown.

"Stop it, you're corrupting the baby," I told my friend, relieved to be sharing a grin.

"Why don't you go over there," she suggested.

I sat down and picked up my spoon. "Over where?"

"To his place."

"I don't even know if he has a place," I responded.

She nodded enthusiastically. "The old fire station across the street."

I just stared at her for a long moment. "How would you know that?"

She took a big bite, smiling as she chewed. The rat was deliberately making me wait for my answer. I raised my brows, spoon poised in the air.

She finally swallowed. "Mother asked me about the new resident when I was home. I had no idea who she was talking about, of course. But now I realize it had to have been Hawk. She said someone had bought the old fire station. And since you thought someone over there was stalking you, and it appears that it was him..." She let the thought trail away, too obvious to finish.

The realization that Magical Indy kept such a close watch on who bought and sold what real estate in Render iced my spine. "Why wouldn't he just tell me that, then?" I wondered aloud.

Sis blew a raspberry. "You mean, like drop by with a plate of brownies and say, 'Hey, my name's Hawk, and I'm a mysterious stranger who randomly helps people when they need it. Oh, and, by the way, I'm really hot too.'"

She burst into laughter and Boyle joined in, though he couldn't have any idea what he was laughing at.

I shook my head. "Har de har har, Sis."

"But I'm serious. Why don't you go over there and take him some cookies or something? Hit reset. Maybe he didn't mean to scare you with the stalking. And maybe you shouldn't have been so mad at him for piercing the Victoria sanctum." She said the last with air quotations around sanctum.

I rejected the idea immediately, quickly directing the conversation away from Hawk and onto less volatile issues. Unfortunately, my mind kept returning to the suggestion. And it finally started to gain a certain sneaky appeal.

I decided I'd like to visit his lair. See how he lived and try to suss out if he was hiding something that would make life more dangerous. Maybe a little reconnaissance mission was just the thing for putting me back into my happy place.

By the time Sissy left, she was looking much better. Food, Boyle's antics, and healing time had made a huge difference. As always, I was amazed at her healing powers. And a little bit jealous. Because of my ability to pull magic from the air and amplify it, I tended to heal faster than non-magics, especially inside Victoria. But my healing power was nothing like Sissy's, who'd basically healed third-degree burns from her fingers to her shoulder in a matter of hours.

I wished eating cookies and stew would give me superpowers.

Sighing, I glanced at the sky beyond the glass and took in the spectacular sunset on the horizon. Vibrant streaks of pink, purple, and cornflower blue melded together to create a natural painting that was far more stunning than anything an artist could create.

Boyle had finally slept for a few hours and then disappeared to the roof, taking his usual perch at the highest peak, where he would safely "guard" the house until I called him in for dinner.

Yawning widely, I pulled a bag of dog food from the cabinet and headed out the front door. I was greeted by a chorus of meows, yips, and chittering as I stepped foot onto the porch.

I stood at the top of the wooden steps and looked around, searching for the small, feral faces tucked within the branches of the trees, the protective prickles of the bushes and, for the more secure of the bunch, draped over the grass and along the porch railings.

"Meow!"

A cold nose touched my arm. I glanced toward the small black cat with the startling blue eyes. "Hi, kitty." I ran my hand over the little creature's back, giving him a scratch in that spot in front of his tail that made him arch and purr.

He'd walked along the narrow railing as if it were six inches wide, instead of the inch, inch and a half max that it was. "Hungry?"

My question created a chorus of responses and caused an enormous shadow to disengage from the glooms under the large oak and trot in my direction.

The black dog.

A family of raccoons scampered higher on the tree, and several cats scuttled away as he came close. I quickly scooped the cat up to protect him, but that proved to be an unnecessary precaution. As the dog made short work of the four shallow steps, the cat's purring rumbled through its small body. He seemed unconcerned by the giant dog, even stretching to touch noses with the beast.

The dog was surprisingly gentle with the little thing, allowing the feline to rub its head on his wide muzzle and giving it a polite sniff in response.

"Good boy," I murmured, scratching him under the chin.

His reaction was to fix me with an insulted look as if I'd been rude for assuming he'd misbehave.

All right, then.

"What's your name?" I asked the dog. "If you're going to hang around, I need to call you something."

A shrill scream rent the air. My head jerked up and, before I could react, the dog was already running. He ran into the night, moving like a shadow but with the speed of a wolf.

I took off after him. "Boyle!"

I turned as I ran, my gaze sliding upward.

"I know, Glynnie. I stay here."

"Don't come down from the roof," I instructed. He'd be safe up there. It was warded to repel dark intent. And if trouble came his way, he could duck inside in the blink of an eye, where the deeper warding would protect him.

Shoving aside the sliver of worry over Boyle, I ran toward the screaming that had only increased since that first, blood-curdling shriek.

It was coming from Della's house next door.

Goddess's galoshes! Of all the places...

Glass shattered loudly up ahead and my gaze snapped in that direction. A tattered curtain was pulled into the house and yanked downward, ripped partially from the rod.

The dog hadn't waited for someone to open a door for him. He'd just barreled right inside.

He reminded me of someone else I'd recently met, I thought. Then shoved the thought aside because it was too distracting.

The screaming stopped abruptly, sliced off in a way that made me fear the reason why.

Halting just outside the large broken window at the front of the house, I listened for some clue of what was going on inside, hearing nothing but a wheezing sound that I didn't like.

Soft footfalls approached from the street. I turned, seeing the familiar bulk of my new neighbor loping toward me with a feline kind of grace.

I hid my hands behind my back and reached for the magic in the air, feeling it bite at my fingertips with an acidic eagerness, the feel of it oily and black against my flesh.

I grimaced, fighting the urge to fling it away. Della was in trouble, and the only way I could help was to siphon the energy I'd need against whatever was attacking her.

"What's going on?" Hawk asked as he slowed to a stop a couple of feet away.

I shook my head. "I just got here."

He moved up close to the broken window and lifted his head, his nostrils flaring and his big form growing tense. "Demonic magic," he declared.

I frowned. "How do you know that?" I gave him a wary smile. "Did you smell it or something?"

He skimmed me a look. "Or something." He grabbed the sill and leaped through the window, offering me his hand.

I appreciated that he wasn't going all Alpha male on me, telling me to stay there while he took care of it himself.

"There's a dog in there," I whispered as I ignored his hand and jumped through the window on my own. My sneakers crunched down on broken glass and I stilled, the sound like gunfire in the sodden silence. "He's on our side."

A surge of pain seared the hand I'd braced on the sill, but I didn't react, not wanting to give him the satisfaction of knowing that I'd put my hand down on a sliver of glass.

He nodded. "Big black one?"

"You know him?"

"I've seen him hanging around your house."

Another evasive answer.

"I'm hoping he's the reason the screaming stopped," I said, frowning at the thought. The alternative reason was unthinkable. Della hadn't been a good neighbor. She hadn't even been an okay one. But I didn't wish her harm.

Though, I wasn't sure I could say the same about her when it came to me.

9

Unfamiliar magic saturated the air. It throbbed against my skin like a living entity, a much livelier energy than the kind I was used to.

Or should I say, lifelier, because at its core it was life for the home's inhabitant, an odd kind of life, but a life all the same.

The pulsing beat of the magic had a rhythm I quickly noticed. A lazy beat whose pattern was uneven, hesitant. Even as I had the realization, it slowed further, sliding over my awareness like sludge.

"Something's wrong with Della," I told Hawk.

He didn't ask any questions. He moved quickly forward, his lithe grace carrying him unerringly through the overstuffed home and down a hallway that no doubt contained my neighbor's bedroom.

He stopped before we reached an open doorway,

hitting the wall with his back and sliding slowly forward until he could peer around the frame into the darkened room.

One hand clasped the wood of the door frame and one was stretched toward me, a silent request that I stay back and remain silent.

I tugged some of the foreign magic into my core, tasting it and finding it bitter and weak. Della was in bad shape. I wasn't sure if she could be killed, given that she was already a spirit, but if there was a state beyond death where a fairy spirit could go, Della had both feet and one hand over the threshold to that place.

I didn't siphon magic from the air for fear that I'd pull energy the spirit needed. Instead, I engaged my other magic and began enhancing the sliver of energy I'd drawn, giving it density and heft. Adding power.

I had no experience with fairy magic. Had never tried to enhance it before. But I would do what I could to help Della recover. And I'd trust Hawk to deal with whatever had harmed her in the first place.

It was a solid plan. One I could live with. So why had all the hair on my arms risen to attention at the sound of a pain-filled moan? And why did the icy breeze wafting over us, which was filled with the stench of death and decay, make me want to run screaming from the room?

A low growl emerged from down the hall. My head whipped around and I saw eyes, glowing a red the color of fire, slitting the darkness like twin blades.

I pressed back against a hard, warm body. "Hawk..."

I felt him shift to see where the sound was coming from, felt his muscular form turn rigid against my touch, and jumped when one of his hands found my wrist, tugging me slowly backward. "Into the room," he whispered, the command so low and throbbing with menace I barely understood the words.

I didn't argue. I wasn't stupid.

I let him pull me behind him and hesitated, my fingers finding the back of his shirt. The cotton was hot and slightly damp, and the flesh beneath it was like rock. "I can help," I wheezed out, not sure at all if I could.

He didn't respond, only pressing me toward the open door. "Lock yourself inside."

I hesitated for another beat, remembering my earlier designation of duties. It had made sense. Suiting each of our strengths to a tee.

So why then was I reluctant to leave him there all alone?

A spittle-drenched snarl rent the air and I jumped, falling back against the wall as Hawk shot forward and disappeared into the darkness.

A terrible snarling, followed by the sound of bodies slamming into furniture and walls, had me taking a step forward. But a soft plea stopped me before I could do something really stupid.

"Glynn?"

Della's voice was a sigh upon the air. If weakness was given voice, that breathy call would be it.

I turned toward the darkened room, seeing a soft glow across the room. "Yes. It's me, Della. Are you okay?" I moved into the room, setting aside the battle in the other part of the house as my eyes filtered out the shadows and focused on the pale glow of the woman draped across the floor.

She was lying beneath a window, the sky beyond showing the silvery orb of a nearly full moon. The moonlight filtered through the waving branches of an ancient walnut tree and made the woman on the floor appear to be moving.

But she wasn't, I realized as I dropped to my knees beside her. She couldn't possibly be. There wasn't enough left of her to move.

My fae neighbor had always been diminutive. Under five feet tall and weighing no more than ninety pounds. She had a wispy halo of soft white hair that tended to fly around her head on an unnatural breeze. I suspected the white was her natural color because she wasn't old by a fairy's standards. The skin of her face was flawless, and her body was lithe and strong. The spirit's silvery gaze was ringed with a thin band of icy blue. From what little she'd told me about herself, she'd died in her early forties, and in the way of her people, her body should have been given over to the rich soil of her fae homeland so she could be reborn. Except that, for some reason she hadn't wanted to return to fairy. So she hadn't completed the rebirthing process her kind generally underwent.

Instead, she'd become a fairy spirit. A prisoner of her home, where fairy soil kept her spirit alive and thriving, and fairy wood and stone gave her form corporeal properties.

But something had happened to her that had robbed her of that corporeal form and yanked her healthy color away. And the wispy aspect of her tiny form told me she was in danger of fading completely away.

Della's colorless lips moved and sounds emerged. But they weren't words. More like emotions given auditory form.

She was quickly running out of time.

Beyond the door, something crashed, the impact so massive the pictures on the walls trembled. Growling sounds were interspersed with the wet sound of ripping flesh. I shuddered, forcing myself to concentrate on the task at hand.

I reached out and took Della's ghostly hand, nearly dropping it again. The flesh was worse than cold. There was a rubbery and clammy feel to it, like death, which made me wish I'd never pressed my skin against hers. But I gritted my teeth. "I'm going to try to enhance your magic, I told her."

Her fingers tightened against mine and the cold seared my skin, a painful jolt that had me reaching deep for the will to hold on.

Della's lips moved again but, though I leaned close, I couldn't understand the words.

I closed my eyes and reached for the ribbon of fairy magic I'd pulled into my core, wrapping magic around it where it sat, inert and unresponsive.

The power I tried to infuse it with fell away as if the two parts were opposing magnetic poles and inherently repellent to each other. I tried again and again to reinforce the energy...to make it stronger... but nothing worked.

Della's lips moved, her grip tightened on mine, surprisingly strong and shapely fingernails digging into my flesh. I leaned close. "What is it? What are you trying to tell me?"

Her insubstantial form wavered, blipping like a hologram that was losing its ability to transmit. The grip on my arm increased, belying the wispy quality of her form.

Her lips moved, her silvery gaze locked on mine.

I strained to hear.

Her body shuddered, her nails slicing through my flesh.

I winced, losing the battle not to pull away. But

somehow she held on. And her gaze slipped past me, to the door.

Fear became a living thing on her translucent face. Her lips moved again...drawing on energy she could scarcely afford to spend. And I finally heard what she was trying to tell me.

Run!

10

The snarl was mere inches from my ear. Hot spittle hit my cheek and, before I could dive away from it, fangs sank deep into my throat.

Agony speared through me, hot and bitter, like a sour taste on my tongue.

The horrible thing wrapped me in a spidery grasp and sucked, the sound terrible in the sudden silence of the house.

Vampyre? I asked myself, immediately dismissing the idea as something deep inside me tore and magic began to rip from me in a wash of white-hot agony.

The thing was drawing my enhancing energy, making itself stronger even as it drained me of my life-giving blood.

I screamed, tugging on the magic in the air and yanking it blindly to me. Purple energy glowed around my hand and I reached up, smacking the monster in the chest and spearing the power into him in a wild, untamed rush.

It hit him hard, ripping him away and flinging him across the room to smash against the wall.

Della lifted an insubstantial hand and squeezed it into a fist. In response to her command, the floor buckled in a violent groundswell and the soil beneath the floor surged upward like a wave, covering the horrible creature and pulling it beneath a rich, black wave.

I placed my hand over the ragged tear in my throat. It came away covered in my blood. Hot blood streamed down my throat, saturating my tee and weakening me with the force of its loss.

Dizziness swamped me as the blood flowed, but I gritted my teeth against it. The thing that had attacked me wasn't gone. It would be back and stronger than before, thanks to the energy it had stolen from me.

I forced myself to my feet, staggering toward Della. "What is that thing?" I asked her. "How do I stop it?"

She shook her head. "Go. Leave me."

As tempting as leaving was... "I'm not leaving you with that thing."

"You can't..." She stopped, narrow chest heaving as if she was finding it hard to breathe. "You can't help."

Across the room, the soil rolled and I knew the monster was digging its way upward again.

I clasped her icy hand. "Tell me how to help you."

She licked her dry lips. "You can't."

"I'm not leaving. Please, Della."

Her eyelids fluttered closed and I thought I'd lost her. "Della!" I shook her slightly, her weight insubstantial as air in my hands.

"The soil," she rasped out. "There's magic in the soil."

The earth geysered upward and the fanged monster it had imprisoned flew out of it in a spray of black dirt.

The thing hovered a foot above the earth, chalk-white flesh stretched over its skeletal head. Its fangs were brown and curved, the canines an inch long apiece with a deadly-looking row of triangular teeth between them. A bright red stream of blood...my blood...trailed down its chin. The monster had glossy black eyes and dull black claws at the ends of its skeletal fingers. There was no flesh on its form, only dead-looking skin stretched over bones.

As I stared at the creature, its colorless lips curved slowly upward. "You have a tasty soul," the thing rasped, its voice coming from several places at once.

Despite my resolve to fight, I found myself taking a step backward as the voice scoured over my senses like sandpaper. My knees wobbled and I nearly hit the ground.

"You need to leave," I said, despair rising at the breathy, uncertain sound of my voice.

It laughed, the maniacal sound layered on the air as if there were several of the monsters in the room instead of one.

I took another step back, icy fingers sliding up my spine from the sound.

"I will leave," it said. "As soon as I've eaten my fill."

"Goddess's galoshes," I breathed out, my heart pounding painfully against my ribs. I needed backup.

The thought made me wonder where Hawk and the dog had gone. Fear razored through me at the realization that they'd been too quiet for too long.

Had the thing across the room already dispatched them?

The floor shifted beneath my feet. I jumped back as it rolled upward, spilling Della into the earth. The boards rolled and undulated toward the creature across the room, shooting toward the ceiling as the monster leaped into the air.

I heard him slam against the scarred wood as I dropped to my knees, plunging my hands into the earth. It was cool against my feverish skin, a rich, loamy scent wafting from its moist surface.

Across the room, the wooden floor shuddered, a

board splintering as a clawed hand broke through the barrier.

I forced my gaze downward, my attention locking on my goal. Energy rose from the soil, its imprint ancient and its touch like silk against my skin. It was unlike any magic I'd ever handled. Still, when I tugged at its strands, the magic seemed eager to come to me. I pulled it deep into my core, wrapping my enhancing magic around it and feeling it grow and swell against the edges of my core. I let it build, feeding it energy until it fairly burst from my skin. I stared in wonder at the violet glow rising above my skin and reveled in the feeling of power swelling my every cell.

The wooden barrier exploded outward and the thing flew at me, fangs wetly gleaming and claws outstretched.

I braced for it, not wanting to expend Della's magic on the monster when I needed every bit of it to make her whole again.

Fortunately, I didn't need to use the pulsing energy that saturated me.

An enormous black form flew through the door, hitting the monster with the force of a runaway train. The attack carried the monster and the giant black dog across the room and through the window, their entangled forms disappearing into the night beyond the shattered glass.

I didn't waste any time taking advantage of the

respite. I dropped to my knees, placing a hand over Della's heart and one on her forehead. I tried to push the energy into her, but it resisted, clinging to my skin.

Panic flared as the sounds of growling rose beyond the window. Something slammed up against the outside of the house. My panic grew.

What if the magic wouldn't take?

I tried again to ease Della's fae magic into her flesh, despair filling me as it resisted again.

I was too late. She was already gone.

My hands slid off her cold form, falling against the cool soil.

I'd failed.

The dirt rose around my hands, wrapping them in a silky embrace and drawing the enhanced magic from me.

I watched in wonder as the violet-colored energy formed a network of what looked like veins in the soil. A network that spread and branched a dozen times like the veins beneath a person's skin. And then they began to flow toward Della's lifeless form, sliding over her skin and sinking inside. Carrying the magic into her as they went.

A moment passed as I stared at her, transfixed by the process I'd just initiated. She lay perfectly still, her form hardly more than a glistening wisp of color on the air.

I blinked, frowning.

At some point, without my noticing, the fairy spirit had become more substantial. Her wispy form gained solidity and her gray cheeks turned a healthy pink again.

Suddenly, her thin chest rose and she gasped in a healthy breath. Her eyes opened. And her head turned slowly to me. It wasn't until her once again pink lips turned upward in a weary smile that I finally breathed.

"Thank you," Della said.

I clasped the hand she offered me. It was still cool, but that was probably normal. Her skin no longer felt like dead flesh. "You're welcome." I panted. "You scared me for a minute."

She just shook her head, her smile fading away. "Is it gone?"

"I…"

Footsteps pounded down the hall and I tensed.

I shoved to my feet and turned toward the door, yanking energy from the air. The power slammed into me, nearly taking me down again, and boiled eagerly at my fingertips as I faced the door.

Hawk stumbled inside. He was too pale and had blood dripping down the side of his face.

His gaze slid around the room. When he spoke, his voice was a soft growl. "Where is it?"

I let the energy fall away, breathing a sigh of relief. I wasn't sure if the relief was because I didn't have to fight the nasty thing again. Or if I was glad to see that Hawk was alive.

Probably both.

"The dog carried it outside." I looked toward the window, only just then realizing the night beyond had gone quiet. "I hope he's all right."

Hawk sagged against the door, one hand rubbing blood from his face and onto his jeans. "Well, that was fun."

The tension shattered in the room and I laughed. I couldn't help myself. "Yeah. Tons of fun."

A soft whining sounded outside the window. The dog's head appeared within the empty window frame. Its gaze brightened when it saw us.

I hurried over, "Are you all right?" I asked the big canine, my hands reaching through to test his fur. There were glossy patches of blood, but he didn't seem to be damaged in any substantial way. "Good boy," I told him, resting my forehead against his and earning a long, wet lick on the cheek for my concern.

"I need to name you, don't I," I asked him.

He whined softly.

"It's Nicht," Hawk's deep voice said behind me.

I turned in surprise, finding him standing only a foot away. I hadn't even heard him move. "You must be part cat," I told him, my hand covering my suddenly pounding heart.

He shook his head, his expression filled with horror. "Please, don't insult me. Cats are bossy."

I lifted an accusatory brow and he shook his head, though a grin trembled on his lips.

Then his words sank in. "Wait. What did you say about his name?"

He nodded toward the big canine, reaching out to scratch it beneath the chin. "His name is Nicht."

I felt my eyes go wide. "You know him?"

Hawk held my gaze, a thread of worry sliding through his. "You could say that."

"What else could I say?" I asked, narrowing my gaze on him.

He sighed. "You could say that he was my dog. Or, to be more specific. He's *my* hellhound."

11

I sat on the roof between my bedroom window and the tallest peak, staring at the horizon as the sun began to rise in a spectacular play of color.

Tiny nails scritched along the shingles as Boyle came down from his favorite perch on the peak to snuggle up next to me.

I wrapped an arm around his tiny body and sighed. Watching dawn come was a favorite activity for us. We'd been doing it since he came to me as an infant. Even then, he'd laugh and point toward the flares of distant color and grab his adorable little toes with excitement.

His joy in the sight had become slightly more reserved as he'd grown, but it was no less real.

"You tired, Glynnie."

It wasn't a question. He could feel when I was tired. As he could sense when I was in danger. I counted my blessings, again, that he'd listened to me and hadn't followed me to Della's house. Though I'd found him clinging to the roof on that side of the house, his tail wrapped around the chimney so he could lean out into the night and make a quick leap if he thought I needed him.

It was the hardest thing about having a baby gargoyle. Gargoyles are innately protective, especially of those they love. Boyle was far too young to protect me in any but the most basic sense. He would have just put himself in danger.

But he'd have been a delicate meal for the soul swallower Hawk and I had encountered at Della's.

I shuddered, and his head lifted from my shoulder. "Bad man?"

Nodding, I kissed his warm forehead. "Very bad."

"Puppy and Hawk hepped you stop him?"

I rested my chin on his head so he couldn't see my frown. Hawk's revelation had been a shock. For several reasons. The most important of which was the fact that he hadn't told me about the dog — hellhound — sooner. I gulped at the realization that Boyle had been very rambunctious around Nicht. The big hound could have hurt the baby. And that made me crazy with anger.

So why hadn't Hawk told me? It was the question I'd been chewing on before Boyle joined me. And I still hadn't come up with an answer that didn't feel like betrayal.

And snooping.

"Yes." I looked down at Boyle. "The puppy's name is Nicht."

Boyle's orange brows lifted in surprise. "Glynnie name him?"

"No," I said, forcing my expression to remain neutral. "Hawk did. He's Hawk's dog." I pulled Boyle into my lap, wrapping my arms protectively around him. "He's a hellhound," I told the baby. "Hellhounds are dangerous. So I want you to stay away from him."

"Aw, Glynnie!" he objected.

"No arguing. I want you to promise."

Boyle's bottom lip stuck out, and he frowned up at me.

After a minute, I strummed a finger over it, making it vibrate. He giggled and I smiled. I tapped his adorable little nose. "Just until I know for sure who he is and what he wants. Okay?"

Boyle gave me a long-suffering sigh and nodded. "Otay, Glynnie."

"Good. Are you hungry?"

He jumped up, bouncing energetically on his toes. "Yeth, yeth, yeth!"

I followed him to my bedroom window and waited while he climbed inside. He was bouncing happily on my bed as I slid a leg through and hesitated.

Headlights cut across the front yard, bathing the

big tree in yellow light and causing a family of raccoons to scurry higher, chittering angrily at the intrusion.

I frowned down at the unfamiliar car, watching as the passenger-side door opened and a long, slender form unfolded itself, a handsome face turning upward, unerringly finding me where I sat sideways on the sill.

He lifted a hand but I only frowned, not bothering to return the wave.

The man leaned back inside the car and his voice trickled upward as he pulled a suitcase from the back seat. He thanked the driver and waited while the car pulled back out of the drive, wasting no time hightailing it back down the street.

"Goddess's galoshes," I grumbled unhappily. "What is *he* doing here?"

A rtur Forester, a.k.a. my older brother, stood on Victoria's front porch and glowered at the door, which refused to open for him.

If I'd been a bit more mature, I would have helped him out. And, I would...eventually. But in the meantime, I stood in front of the large picture window with the lights off so he couldn't see me, and grinned like a high school teen watching a mean girl get rejected by the star quarterback.

It was just too sweet to cut short.

"Glynnie, open the demon-possessed door."

My grin widened. "It's open," I called out, a mean chuckle escaping before I could stop it.

There was a growl. It might have been Nicht, but I doubted it.

"Who dat?" Boyle asked, his cheeks full of the chips I'd given him to keep him from barging onto the porch and letting my unwelcome visitor inside. "That, sweet boy, is your Uncle Art."

His eyes got big and he crunched loudly on a particularly large chip. "Dat Uncca Artur?"

I frowned down at the little gargoyle. "You remember him?" My brother's absence from Boyle's life was actually one of the reasons I was ticked at him. My brother had neglected a lot of things in his thirty-six years. Boyle was one of them. And Victoria was another. The old house was currently letting her feelings on that neglect be known.

And she had my full support.

"This demon-spawn house won't let me in and you know it. Now, either open this door, or I'm going to do something neither one of you is gonna like."

Art tugged a fire stick from his pocket and flicked it on. He held it toward a tatty rocker whose dried and cracked weave would no doubt grab hold of the flame and create an easy bonfire.

My pulse didn't even rise. Instead, I reached out and touched the wall. "You gonna let him get away with that?"

The wall warmed beneath my fingers and I stepped closer to the glass, eager to view the results of my brother's ill-conceived threat.

It didn't take long.

Boyle tucked up in front of me, crunching loudly. He pressed his little face to the glass, leaving a greasy handprint where he spread his palm over the window.

To my utter delight, the porch bucked violently underneath Art's pristine loafers and he flew backward, arms akimbo, to land in an ungainly heap on the grass. The suitcase he'd brought with him rolled end over end, a beat later, and landed atop his head with a meaty thump.

Shoving the hard-sided bag off his face, Art lay there a moment, groaning loudly.

At which point, a large black dog trotted out of the shadows and lifted its leg, letting loose an enthusiastic stream of urine that extinguished the fire stick lying next to Art in the grass.

I burst out laughing as Artur jumped to his feet, screeching with rage. "Is everything in this place demon-possessed?"

I opened the door, stepping out onto the porch and glowering down at him.

"Not everything," I told him, a laugh burbling in

my throat. "But Nicht definitely is. Thanks, buddy," I called after the disappearing hound.

A soft "woof" carried back to me.

A warm weight hit my leg and I looked down, finding Boyle pressed against my thigh, his expression leery. I reached down and placed a reassuring hand on his head.

"What are you doing here?" I asked my brother.

He brushed at a dark spot on his slacks, grimacing. "I don't need a reason to come here, Glynnie. Or, are you forgetting that I own this place?"

The door slammed shut behind me in a clear message. "Victoria isn't owned by anyone," I told him.

He shook his head. "Tell that to the lawyers who drew up Grams' inheritance papers."

I crossed my arms over my chest. It was a sore point with me, and of course he knew that. I was pretty sure I'd never understand why Grams had given Victoria to Art. He'd never shown a second's worth of interest in the place. And his siphoning magic, weak compared to mine, wasn't enough to keep the portal in check for an hour, let alone the decades required. "The house doesn't want you here."

He shrugged. "Victoria will listen to you."

It was true, but that didn't mean Victoria wouldn't resent me for interfering. My brother wasn't worth that resentment. "You can come in if she allows it."

Rage filled his expression, turning his normally golden brown complexion a deep red.

The shadows shifted and Hawk appeared, Nicht trotting at his side. He glanced at Art. "Is there a problem, Glynn?"

"No problem. My brother has come for a visit."

Hawk's expression was set into a neutral mask. I had no way of knowing what he was thinking. But his gaze, when it turned my way, was filled with a question.

I barely kept from shrugging. How did I tell him my older brother and I had made a lifetime of quarreling with each other? That, I was pretty sure neither of us would ever give in and allow our relationship to warm? Or, that I couldn't even justify my hurt feelings with any specific examples that made sense.

Finally, he smiled. "I look forward to getting to know him," Hawk said.

And to my shock, he and the hound climbed the steps onto the porch. Grabbing up Boyle and depositing him on his shoulders amid rapid-fire giggling, Hawk walked inside.

Artur looked at me, his brows lifting in what had to be a chorus of questions. Coward that I was, I turned on my heel and followed them in.

12

I don't know which was more surprising to me. One, that Victoria let Artur into the house. Or, two, that she seemed to have embraced both Hawk and his hellhound as part of the family.

I watched my neighbor talking to Artur, the two of them seeming thick as thieves, while Boyle and Nicht played rambunctiously in the living room behind me.

Beyond thanking me for the beer I'd given him, and skimming a glance my way every few minutes as if checking to make sure I was still there, Hawk paid no attention to me. Every bit of his formidable consideration was locked on my brother, who'd responded to that attention with the quick and easy charm he was known for. A charm that had served him well as assistant to a powerful Magistrate of the Magical Body.

Art's charm had never worked on me. I knew him too well, and I saw beyond the charisma to the cynical politician beneath.

A happy squeal caught my attention. My eyes went wide as Nicht trotted past, a shrieking baby gargoyle on his back. Boyle's tiny hand clutched the thick ruff between the dog's shoulders and his skinny legs kicked Nicht's sleek sides.

"Oh!" I exclaimed, diving for Boyle. But Nicht chose that moment to rise up on his hind legs, pawing the air like a horse. He turned his big head and fixed a kind, brown gaze on me as Boyle melted down with hilarity, almost sliding off the hound's sleek back as he laughed.

The white cowboy hat Artur had brought him fell over Boyle's eyes, and the tiny clawed hand that was clutching his new six-shooter waved wildly above his head.

"He seems to like the stuff I brought him," Artur said a beat later.

I glanced up, surprised. I hadn't heard him approach.

"He does. Thanks for bringing him something. It wasn't necessary."

Artur's brow furrowed. "But it was necessary, wasn't it? It's actually long overdue." He slid a look over the romping duo—circling the couch as if it were the sun and they were planets—and grinned. "I'd forgotten how cute he is."

I chewed on my lip to keep from snapping at Art. Part of me...the part deep, deep down, beneath the automatic anger...knew that he was trying. And that should count for something.

When I was pretty sure I wouldn't snarl, I finally said. "What I meant was, the toys are nice. But he'd be just as happy with your time. Your affection."

The furrows in Art's brow deepened. "You're right." He sighed. "I've been a cad, Glynn. I know it. But I let the excitement of being there...at the Body... overcome my good sense. It was exhilarating and..." His handsome face lit with excitement. "It made me feel as if I was doing something significant with my time." He shook his head, the glow in his expression receding. "I romanticized it all, I'm afraid."

"You're talking like you don't work there anymore," I said, panic beginning to rise. If Art had left his big, important job in Magical Indy, would he want to come back to Render and live there? In Victoria?

The old-fashioned, domed ceiling light above our heads flickered with agitation, as if Victoria had come to the same terrifying conclusion. I knew that wasn't possible. The house wasn't a sentient being. Not really. But a century of magic saturated its bones and painted its skirts, and all that power had created a type of magical AI.

Yes, I thought, pleased. Victoria was like an artificial intelligence. I'd struggled since taking over my portal duties to decide how to categorize the old house. That description fit as well as anything.

My lips curved in a smile.

"What's so funny?" Art asked, his own smile tight, humor not reflected in his eyes. I'd learned early in our formative years that Artur Forester took himself way too seriously. If he thought someone was laughing at him, he never took it well.

I shook my head. "I was just thinking about something," I said dismissively. I cocked my head, narrowing my gaze. "You haven't told me why you're really here, Art."

He sighed. "I guess telling you that I missed you won't be enough?"

I bit back an answering laugh. Barely. "Not unless you're dying..." I joked. And then felt panic slicing through my chest. "You're not...dying...are you?"

Art didn't withhold his laughter. "Not even close." He looked around the room, his gaze falling to the crackling fire behind me. The fireplace always contained a fire in Victoria. The thick walls held off what heat the exterior threw at it during the day, and that was considerably less than in the old days.

It might be late summer, but Render and the surrounding countryside had dropped a dozen degrees when all the magic users had left. We generally experienced mid-seventies to low-eighties during the day in the summer, and the temperature dropped into the forties and fifties when the sun went down.

People in the countryside called it the great cooling. Or lumped it into the transfer of magic into the city and called it the great exodus. Either way, some of the residents in Render hated the cool weather. Or maybe they just hated what it represented. Personally, I loved it. Humidity and heat were not my favorite things. Though fall and winter could be a little brutal in Render.

"...what I want to do," Artur said, poking absently at the logs to encourage the flames to flare.

I realized I'd been daydreaming and refocused on him. "About what?" I asked.

He gave me an irritated look. "You weren't listening, were you?"

I held his gaze, refusing to admit he was right.

After a beat, he sighed. "I'm starting to rethink my job at the Magical Body. I used to think everything we did there was good for the community."

"And you don't think that anymore?" I asked, surprised.

"I wouldn't go that far. But lately, some things have happened that I'm not comfortable with."

"Like what?"

"You know I can't tell you that, sis."

I blinked at the term. He hadn't called me sis since I was fourteen years old and he was preparing to leave. To move to the city and become an intern at the Body.

"I was hoping I could stay here for a while."

And there they were. The words I'd been dreading. All the color left my face and my head was shaking before I even realized it. "It won't work," I told him, frowning at the thought.

"Why not?" His face flushed with irritation.

"I'm the portal keeper, Art. Your being here will only confuse things."

"I want nothing to do with that portal," he said, his brown eyes, so like mine, sparking with anger.

"You say that. You might even mean it..." the words trailed away, mostly because I knew that what I was about to tell him would make him really mad. Despite the fact that they were the truth. Or maybe because of it.

"Have I ever shown any interest?" he asked as if that proved his case.

All it really did was annoy me. His indifference only made the idea of his moving in on my territory even worse. "No. But you won't be able to help yourself," I said, snapping my lips together before I opened that particular can of slithering snakes.

"You believe I'll be irresistibly drawn to the portal?" he asked me. He barked out an angry laugh. "I assure you, that won't happen, Glynn."

I cast around for words that wouldn't cause an explosion and finally realized there weren't any. So

I'd have to settle for trying to present my argument in a gentle, non-judgmental way instead. "Art, you had a dream. You followed it and it made you really happy. I totally get that."

He nodded. "But?"

"But, you're used to taking charge. Your personality demands it. If you come back to Victoria now..." I let the words sink in, praying he caught my meaning, so I didn't have to come right out and tell him he was a control freak.

He shook his head. "What? If I come back, what?"

I twisted my fingers together, annoyance flaring. He was going to force me to say the words. I struggled for patience.

"Glynn, just say it, you're making me crazy!"

I looked him in the eye and said, "If you come back, you'll try to control everything. Boyle and I have a life here. We have schedules and routines. We have rules. We like our life the way it is. But you'll try to change it all. You can't help yourself."

His lips pressed together. His gaze flashed. I was pretty sure I could hear his teeth grinding together.

A warm weight pressed against me. I looked down as Boyle twined his fingers with mine. His little face looked worried. He leaned against my thigh.

Art saw it too. And to my surprise, he reigned in his rage. He stared at the fire a moment, seemingly trying to regain calm. Then he expelled air in a burst and looked up, his gaze sliding past me. "You can stand down, guardian. I'm not going to hurt her."

I turned in shock to see Hawk standing just behind me. It shocked me that I hadn't seen him move. His handsome face was tight, and his gaze was narrowed on my brother. His big hands were fisted, the muscles in his forearms bulging and taut. He didn't say a word. He didn't need to.

"I understand," Art told me, forcing his lips into a smile. He suddenly looked tired. "I know I can be a little..." He shook his head, laughing. "A lot, actually. You're right. My need to control things served me well at the Body. But I realize it won't work here. You've built a life and you deserve to live it. All I'm asking for is a few days. Just a little mini-vacation. Time for me to figure out where I'm going with my life."

It sounded very reasonable. It would probably be irrational of me to deny him. Still...

"You have my word that I won't interfere." His gaze slid to Hawk's. "And, if I do," he went on, "You can always sic your guardians on me." He grinned at Boyle and nodded toward Nicht, who'd stayed glued to the baby's side. "All of them."

I decided I could live with that. "Three days?" I offered. He looked relieved.

"That's perfect. Thanks, sis."

Relief swelled inside me. "Good. I need to feed

Boyle. I could hear his stomach rumbling from across the room."

Art inclined his head. "I'll just get out of your way. My old room?"

I nodded. "Sure. But you'll join us for dinner." I said, realizing too late that my tone had been bossy. "Okay?"

That time, his smile was genuine, and it totally lit his brown eyes. "I'd like that."

13

S oft snoring woke me from a deep, dream-filled sleep. I started upward, confused at the sound.

The covers next to me were mounded, something moving beneath them. Fortunately, I recognized the soft, whistling snores and smiled. I tugged the blanket off Boyle, who was curled in a tight little ball with his long, skinny arms covering his head.

He twitched in his sleep as if he was having an active dream.

Maybe a nightmare, since he'd come down from his attic bedroom and climbed into bed with me.

I covered him again and reached for the glass of water I kept on the nightstand, finding it empty.

Goddess's galoshes, I muttered. I'd never manage to go back to sleep without taking a sip of water. Once my mind decided I was thirsty, it wouldn't stop obsessing until I gave it what it wanted.

It was the curse of a bossy mind.

With a sigh, I climbed out of bed, heading downstairs with the glass to refill it from the pitcher of cold, filtered water I kept in the fridge.

I never made it to the kitchen. As I descended the final three steps, my gaze slid to the open door in the hallway—the basement door. The heavy lock was still attached, but someone had found a way to open it without a key.

"What's going on?" I murmured, my mind roiling. But my thoughts quickly moved to the real issue as a wisp of all-too-familiar magic burned over my skin like flame.

The portal! I realized, panic slicing through me. I didn't even realize I'd set the glass down. I could have dropped it for all I knew. I was suddenly descending the unlit wooden steps, wondering how whoever was down there had managed them without falling. I was as familiar with them as I was my own face, and I still clutched the railing tightly to keep from tumbling down the stairs if I missed a step.

A soft light infused the space once I'd stepped out of the stairwell. An illumination spell. The magic cast a subdued yellow light around the basement, not bright enough to really see anything, but enough to move through it without a flashlight.

The light wasn't bright enough for me to see into the darkened corners of the stone-walled room. But it was plenty bright for me to recognize the familiar form of my brother standing in front of the portal wall.

Artur's dark hair stuck up in tufts over his head as if tousled from sleep. He was wearing a pair of cotton sleep pants and a tee-shirt that glowed white in the meager light. His wide feet were bare, the bottoms shadowed with dirt from the floor.

"Art?" I kept my voice soft because he wasn't moving. He simply stood staring at the wall, one hand resting against the stone where the portal would be if it had been open. The fingers on his hand were splayed, the palm resting against the flat, irregularly shaped stones. They would be warm to the touch.

They were always warm.

But the rock would only heat to the melting and burning point if the portal was open.

Art hadn't opened the portal. I wasn't sure he could. He'd never done it before as far as I knew, and I didn't think his magic was strong enough for him to try.

Unless he'd found a way to augment his power since he'd left Render.

"Artur? What are you doing down here?"

Not a twitch. His hand stayed flat against the wall. His face remained pointed toward it.

He didn't appear to have heard me.

I took another step. Then another. Until I was

close enough to reach out and touch his shoulder. I reached toward him, fingers extended, with the intention of doing exactly that. But he finally moved, so I dropped my hand.

"Why are you down here?" I asked him again.

Art turned around and I gasped. His eyes were open but they were set and blank. His movements were stiff, and he didn't seem to see me as he moved past me toward the stairs.

I watched him climb the steep stairs in robotic movements, not even looking down at his feet or touching the railing as he climbed.

I followed, keeping several feet of distance between us.

Below us, the illumination spell blinked off, casting the basement once more into darkness.

I followed Art to his room and watched him disappear inside. I heard the covers on his bed rustle and the springs creak as he climbed inside. A moment later, I heard him sigh as he did when he was settling into sleep. I closed the door and went back downstairs, relocking the basement door to hopefully keep Boyle from wandering down there.

Then I went back to my room. Boyle had thrown off the covers and was twitching like somebody was poking him with a finger, but his lips were turned up in a smile and he was laughing softly. I grinned at the silly baby and tugged the covers over him again, knowing it was probably a lost cause. He was too active of a sleeper to keep them on.

Still, the room was cold.

I shivered, stretching out next to Boyle. But I couldn't sleep. My thoughts swirled around the possibilities of what I'd seen.

Had my brother been sleep-walking? I'd never known him to do it. And, if so, why had he come down the stairs? And how had he gotten past the extra lock I'd put on the door?

I should have boarded it up. I'd meant to, after finding out that Boyle was playing downstairs. But things had happened and I'd...

I sighed. I was boarding that door up first thing when Boyle woke. I didn't want to wake him with the pounding. And, if I was honest with myself, I didn't want to leave him alone in Victoria with Art while I went to get the stuff I'd need.

A stab of pain sliced through me at the thought. I didn't trust my own brother. How pathetic was that?

I resettled myself, seeking the perfect position that would allow me to sleep. Shivering, I pulled the covers up under my chin. Burrowing into the soft mattress, I trembled until the warmth of the covers chased away the chill of the room, and tried to wipe my mind of worry.

I didn't think I'd be able to manage it. In fact, I spent another hour lying there trying to push my whirling thoughts away. But I somehow fell asleep.

And dreamed of terrible things.

My jaw cracked on a yawn that nearly broke my face. I flipped the eggs I was frying and took another sip of my coffee. I'd eschewed my usual cup of tea and broken out the coffee pot, hoping the caffeine would help me wake up.

Behind me, sitting at the table, Boyle bounced energetically in his seat, his busy fingers slashing crayons across paper to create pictures he'd have to decipher for me later.

Whatever the baby gargoyle was going to become when he grew up, I sincerely doubted he'd be an artist. Though, what did I know about such things? For me, art was a painting of fruit or vibrantly colored flowers, with maybe a bee or two buzzing around them.

"It smells good in here," Artur said from the doorway.

I slid a look his way. "There's coffee on the stove."

I'd long ago given up on the luxury of fast coffee when Victoria had fried my fancy coffee brewer for the fifth time. There was way too much magical energy flooding the house for most electronic gadgets to work.

The television worked if I only used it every few

days. But, I was lucky the lamps and heating unit somehow managed to keep plodding on. Though I had to replace the lamps every few months, so I didn't have very many of them.

Grams had left me a decent stash of gold and silver coins to keep Victoria running. I bartered with the people in Render and the surrounding areas for most of what I needed. A man came through town with a horse-drawn wagon selling household items and non-perishables once a month. And I sold home-canned vegetables and fruits twice a year to add to the coffers. But without sustainable work in the area around Render, I'd had to be frugal with my funds.

If I really needed something I didn't have, there were several small towns like Render within an hour's walk that sometimes had what I needed.

I'd found the French drip pot buried in a cabinet a couple of years earlier and had figured out how to use it by trial and error. It took forever to make a cup of coffee. But the output was delicious.

Art eyed the hourglass-shaped metal pot. "Fancy."

I shook my head. "Practical. The electric brewing machines kept dying. Victoria's too hot for them to handle."

My brother and I shared a grin.

He rubbed a hand over Boyle's orange tuft and

the baby looked up, giving him a shy smile. "What are you drawing, Boyle?"

Boyle gave him a long-suffering look. "Bananas."

I enjoyed the look of consternation on Art's face as he cocked his head one way and then the other to try to pull the form of a banana from the slashes of purple, brown, and green covering the center of the sheet. "Ah," he finally said. "A Picasso banana. I get it." He nodded, grinning at Boyle, and the baby looked pleased.

Hunh, I thought. Lying worked. Why hadn't I thought of that?

"You want eggs?" I asked Art. He sipped his coffee, his expression lightening in surprise. "Mm, this is good." A beat later, he seemed to realize for the first time that I was waiting on him to respond and nodded. "I'd love some if you have enough to spare."

His comment was intended to be polite. It wasn't his fault I took it as an assault on my ability to provide. I frowned at him.

He shifted uncomfortably. "I mean because you weren't expecting a third mouth."

I lifted a brow.

He sighed. "I'd love breakfast. Thank you."

He said it so primly that I couldn't stay ticked. I laughed, shaking my head. "The eggs come from my friend Sissy's chickens. We always have lots of them."

He nodded, taking another sip from his coffee.

I set the plate of eggs in front of him and settled a basket of warm, freshly baked bread in the center of the table. "Eat while everything's warm."

Boyle took that as an order and reached for the napkin covering the bread. He tugged it off and started to grab a piece.

I cleared my throat.

He stopped and gave me a startled look, then smiled, offering the basket to Art. "Would you, um, likes bread?"

Art was chewing but he smiled, plucking a slice from the basket. "Thanks, buddy. Such nice manners."

Boyle's gray skin flushed with pleasure. "Tank tou."

I placed a plate of butter on the table and a small bowl of jelly next to it. "You should spoon up some of that jelly before Boyle gets into it," I warned.

Art didn't argue, he placed a large glob on his bread. "Is he as messy as you were when you were little?" My brother's teasing smile made a warm spot in my belly.

I laughed. "Worse. I don't know how he does it, but he paints the whole table, the chair he's sitting on, and a circle of floor beneath the chair in jelly every time."

Art watched in wonder as Boyle used the jelly spoon to paint everything on his plate, including the eggs, with grape jelly. Watching him watch the baby, I thought about the discussion my brother and I needed to have.

I couldn't talk about the basement episode with him in front of Boyle. But the kid was the duke of dillydallying, and it would be a while before he finished playing with and then eating his food. Then it would take me just as long to clean him up.

I sighed, realizing I'd have to settle for small talk.

I was terrible at small talk.

Fortunately, Art saved me from having to make the opening salvo.

"So, what's the plan for today?"

I blinked at him, irritation flaring. Surely he didn't expect me to entertain him?

He must have read my expression. "I mean, is there something I can help with?"

Okay, that was better. And it gave me a segue into the subject he and I needed to discuss. "Actually, there is. I've been meaning to batten down the door to the basement, and I keep getting distracted." I watched him closely for a reaction but didn't see any. He stabbed a last bite of egg and nodded. "I can definitely help with that. How do you want to do it?"

I glanced at Boyle, my brows lifting so Art would get my meaning when I said, "I need to remove access to the room completely. But every couple of months I need to be able to go down there myself. You know...to do what needs to be done."

He let his eyes go wide as he slid a look toward the oblivious baby. Boyle was painting the edges of his plate with jelly, using the back of the spoon as his paintbrush. "Oh. Oh no!"

"Right." I was relieved he got my message without my having to tell him that Boyle had been going down there. "*Nobody* should be down there unless absolutely necessary." Again, I watched him carefully. He didn't react to my statement except to nod in agreement. "Does this have to be pretty?"

"No. I was thinking of just nailing some boards over it."

"That works. Do you have the stuff, or do I need to go into town?"

Talk of the project consumed the next several minutes, until Boyle seemed to grow bored with playing in the jelly. "Can I go ou'side, Glynnie?"

"You can, if you stay on the roof. I'll take you across the street to see Nicht in a little bit. Uncle Art and I have one thing to do first."

He gave his long-suffering sigh that proclaimed me a too strict, overprotective parent, and then agreed. "Otay, Glynnie."

Twenty minutes later, after I'd scoured grape jelly from his tiny hands, nose, ears, neck, and feet... don't ask...Boyle scampered away with a shouted goodbye and I dropped, already exhausted, into my chair.

"He's adorable, sis," Art said.

His tone was sincere and it made me smile. "He is, isn't he?"

To my delight, Artur had begun cleaning the table, chair, and floor as I'd scoured the baby, so we were able to head out to the garage much faster than I'd thought we would. As we exited the house, I looked up to Victoria's highest peak, where Boyle clung invisibly in the darkness. "We'll be right back, sweet boy," I called softly. "You stay up there until we get back, okay?"

"Otay," said a soft voice from above. "I watch for Hawk."

The night was soft against my skin. The sweet scent of the roses planted along one side of the house wafted over me, warmed by the previous day, and I sighed, reveling in the moment.

"It's so quiet out here," Art said.

I realized he was right. I rarely gave it much thought anymore. The only sounds that broke the silence were the constant drone of crickets and the occasional croak of a bullfrog down by the pond. "It is." I turned to him. "Did you have any trouble sleeping? I know you're used to traffic noise and people shrieking outside your windows at all hours."

He chuckled. "That's an accurate statement."

I knew because I'd gone to stay with Sissy's parents once for a few days. Sissy'd had to be there for a family wedding, and she'd begged me to come along so she wouldn't be bored out of her mind. The experience had been fascinating. The Valkyr's lived in an enormous home...a mansion really...in the new part of town. During the magic wars that had initiated the pulling of magic into a single regional location that could be controlled and monitored, the entire northern quadrant of the city had been pretty much leveled. When the rebuilding began, the new construction had taken on a completely new footprint. One that was heavy on large, expensive homes for the newly formed managing body and low on "regular people" or the simple, homey restaurants and retail they preferred.

Like Sissy, I'd felt like a fish out of water in that part of the world. And by the time we'd left, I'd been vastly relieved to be getting back to Render.

Artur didn't live in that exclusive neighborhood. But he lived as close to it as he could manage on his modest salary. And I suspected his aspiration was to one day own a mansion the equal of Sissy's family home.

"What are you going to do while you're here?" I asked my brother as I opened the door to the garage.

He shrugged. "To be honest, I'll probably sleep a lot. I'd like to spend some time with Boyle and you," he gave me a shy smile that was surprisingly endearing. "And help around the house if you'd like. I just needed some time away from it all."

I flipped the switch and the watery fall of light illuminated the center of the big space. Turning on the flashlight I'd brought, I played it around the edges until I spotted the boards I wanted to use. I pointed them out, following Art toward the back of the big building with the flash. "Is there something going on at the Body that's worrying you?" I asked him.

He examined the boards, selecting two that would work perfectly and tucking them under his arm. "Nails and a hammer?" he asked.

"This way." I picked my way carefully through the clutter to the tool bench Grams had built against the sidewall.

"Nothing specific," Art responded. "Just the usual jockeying for position and power."

I glanced his way in time to catch a frown. "I can't believe I'm saying this, but I'm getting tired of it all."

Something about the way he said it made me wonder if someone hadn't hurt Art personally. He'd always loved the jockeying and power-grabbing in the past. I grasped a metal toolbox and we headed for the door. "Well, there's certainly none of that in Render."

We shared a grin. But, as we stepped back out into the night, his expression turned serious. "You love it here, don't you?"

"Of course..." I began, finding his question odd. I'd always loved Render. Though, if someone had asked me why, I'd be hard-pressed to explain it. The beautiful, quaint little town of my childhood no longer existed. What had once been a place of old-fashioned beauty, lifelong friendships, family, and comforting tradition overlaid by useful and safe magic, had become a place of deprivation, decay, and loneliness with an under-layer of fear that affected every thought and action.

But the small group of people who'd clung to the town watched out for each other. We all used our individual energies to create a protected whole. And despite it all, we'd managed to carve out our own little haven in the midst of all the ugliness that stained Render's history.

"Glynn?"

I realized Art was waiting for me to finish my thought. "Sorry, I was woolgathering."

"You're happy?"

His question felt oddly specific. As if he thought I might have reason not to be. Like he'd been worried about me.

"I am."

A weight seemed to leave his shoulders and I was glad. Something was going on with my brother. Something had interfered with his perfect life... intruded on his plans in a big enough way to bring him back to his childhood home, despite the ugli-ness he no doubt saw on its broken and untraveled streets.

Still, whatever it was, I decided I was glad he'd

come. And maybe, if he'd be willing to share it with me, I could find a way to help.

We rounded the front of Victoria and something drew my gaze skyward. I flinched back with a cry as a huge, dark creature swooped down on us, enormous bat-like wings pounding the air almost soundlessly above us. I gave a sharp cry and grabbed Art with one hand, shoving him toward the house. "Run!"

Yanking magic from the air, I focused my siphon on the creature hovering eight feet above my head.

The demon's eyes were a throbbing ruby glow in the night, its fangs painted in their terrifying illumination as if bathed in blood.

The thing jerked as I yanked magic from its core and, lifting its veiny black wings, it plunged from the sky with a blood-chilling shriek.

Diving right at me.

14

The demon's scream was immediately followed by a second call. I dove to the side and rolled, feeling the creature's too-sharp talons ripping the air inches from my hip. I shoved to my feet and threw out a hand, hitting the demon center mass as it changed direction and headed for me again.

Cool night air wafted over me as something flew past overhead. To my horror, I realized it was Boyle, his tiny wings working overtime to keep him in the air.

He gave a shriek that was too small to be scary but managed to terrify me anyway. "Boyle, no!"

The baby shot toward the demon, somehow staying outside the range of its claws and raking his claws over its chest.

Still stunned from the wash of my power, the demon made a grab for him and missed. Unfortunately, that was the last piece of luck the baby was going to get. The creature shifted in the air and swung its wing, smashing it into Boyle and sending him flying on a breathy cry of pain.

"No!" I screamed, blinded by my tears and barely able to move as my heart pounded against my ribs. I was dizzy with horror, immobile with pain. "Boyle!"

Enraged, I threw both hands into the air and let everything I had fly, sending a boiling wash of uncontrolled energy into the beast.

It hit the demon like a wall of fire, sending the creature flying toward Victoria on a scream of pain. He smashed into the house and a wall of answering magic shot away from Victoria, its power feeding the flames trying to engulf the creature.

The demon was immune to its own magic. Fire was its element. I'd only hoped to overwhelm it into fleeing. But Victoria's magic was a foreign thing, as deadly to the demon as its magic would be to me.

The demon blasted away from the house, shooting toward me like a bullet, and hit me head-on before I could dive away.

The impact knocked me off my feet, sent me flying toward the street, and we hit the broken asphalt so hard we skidded several feet before we came up against the curb on the other side.

Bones cracked in my back and fire ate at the hand I was using to keep his deadly fangs away from my neck.

A scream ripped through my throat, leaving it feeling bloody and torn but doing nothing to save me from the demon's determined attack.

The monster screamed too, the red glow of its eyes fading to black. Victoria's magic ate at its wings, creating black lace from their leathery surface as it nibbled holes in the ugly, slick surface.

Something warm slipped down my cheeks—either tears or blood. I couldn't tell which.

I was going to die, but my greatest fear was for Boyle.

I had to help him.

I tried to lift off the ground, but the demon's weight pressed against my hand and my arm gave way.

Sizzling hot saliva bathed my throat. I screamed again, the sound broken and weak. I could do nothing as I felt the knifelike fangs touch my skin. Felt them sink into flesh.

The air above me shifted in shades of charcoal and black, and the demon's weight was suddenly gone, his claws lifting me several inches off the street before ripping free of my clothes.

I slammed back down into the street, my head hitting the curb hard enough to make stars burst before my eyes.

I gritted my teeth and fought oblivion. I couldn't pass out.

I had to find Boyle.

I shoved at the street with hands and arms that felt like rubber. My cheeks were bathed in frustrated tears. "Boyle!" I croaked, my throat raw and torn.

I shoved one more time, managing to gain a couple of inches before my arms gave way again. "Boyle!" I shrieked, finally gaining some strength behind the single word, which throbbed with terror.

Someone bent over me. Hot, calloused hands skimmed along my throat, felt the back of my head and came away sticky with blood. "He's okay, Glynn," a deep voice reassured. "He's safe. Your brother's got him."

"Thank the Goddess," I said, my lips moving but the words caught in the ravaged tissue of my throat. *Thank the Goddess*, I murmured again in my mind. *He's safe.*

I grabbed hold of the heated hand sliding over my arm, holding on to it like a lifeline. "Thank you..." I whispered brokenly. And then I let the shadows in my mind drag me under.

Lights flickered over my face, bathing me in heat. I lay there for a moment, listening to the gentle dance of the fire and smelling the familiar tang of smoke on the air.

My eyes were closed and I had no desire to open them any time soon. My body ached all over. Some irrational part of my mind told me the real pain would stay away as long as I didn't open my eyes.

But I made it a personal rule not to let the irrational rule my life. So I forced them open.

The room was dark except for the flickering firelight. There was no sound beyond the crackling of the fire.

That silence made my pulse quicken. *Boyle*? He was never quiet. Had Hawk lied? I tried to stand, but my legs got tangled in the gentle prison of Grams' throw. "Boyle?" I called out, my voice husky. Forcing my legs over the side of the couch, I tried to tug the knitted blanket from around my ankles. "Boyle! Where are you?"

Footsteps, light and quick, hurried toward me from the kitchen. Sissy quickly cut the distance between us, her pretty face tight with concern. "He's fine, Glynn. Don't get yourself upset."

I fell back against the couch, sucking air into lungs that had seized with panic. Sissy wouldn't lie to me. Boyle had to be okay. "Where is he? Why is it so quiet?"

"He's...napping in his room," she told me, sitting down on the couch. "He cried for an hour when Hawk carried you inside. Nothing anybody said would comfort him. I..." Her gaze slid guiltily away. "I'm sorry."

Panic flared again. "What? Is he sick?"

"No." Sissy shook her head, tucking a glossy

strand of long blonde hair behind her ear. "I hope you don't mind. I gave him a suggestion."

Irritation flared. Sissy had no right putting the baby under a spell without asking me first. "You spelled my child?" I hated the tone of my voice even as the words came out. But I couldn't stop them. I'd been so worried. And her admission seemed like verification that I'd had a right to be.

"I'm sorry," she repeated. "He was making himself sick with worry. He wrapped himself around you and hissed at anybody who tried to pull him away."

I blinked. Boyle had hissed at them? A gargoyle only hissed as a prelude to violence. *Not my sweet baby boy...*

"It was just a light spell. There won't be any after-effects. It just encouraged him to sleep. And he was so exhausted he fell right under."

She reached out and tucked the blanket under my thigh, looking miserable.

She'd been right to do it. I knew it. But I wasn't feeling reasonable at the moment. "He was terrified, Sis. That demon could have killed him."

Her gaze found mine. "It could have killed both of you." She frowned. "Where do you suppose it came from?"

I shook my head, rubbing shaking hands over my face. "First the soul swallower and now this. What's happening in Render?"

"Don't forget the wraith," my best friend reminded me.

I groaned. "How could I forget that?"

"You saw Mitch, right?"

I nodded, reaching for her hand. I squeezed it and some of the tension left her expression. "Thank you. For helping Boyle."

She nodded, looking relieved.

"Yes. I saw Mitch. But he didn't say anything about this," I told her.

"What did he say?"

I expelled air. "Not much. I mostly went to ask him about Hawk."

Her eyes went wide. "And?"

"Mitch knew only that Hawk is magical. But he doesn't know what he is. He couldn't even tell me if he was good or evil."

Silence pulsed between us for a long beat. I knew what Sis was thinking. I was thinking it too. But I didn't want to say the words.

So she did. "The timing is suspect, Glynn."

I tensed as if struck. I had no idea why. It wasn't like Hawk and I were romantically involved. But Boyle really seemed to like him. And he'd saved us more than once. "I know." I swallowed hard, the words tasting vile against my tongue.

She patted my arm.

"Where's Art," I asked, seeking the comfort a change of topic would give.

"He and Hawk are trying to figure out where that demon came from."

Before I could stop myself, my gaze slid to the basement door, which still hadn't been boarded up. *Goddess's galoshes!*

Sis didn't miss my skimming gaze. "You think it came through the portal?"

It wasn't possible, was it? "No."

"How can you be sure?"

"I'd know if it had been opened. I'd feel if something came through."

"But you've been telling me that something's changed. It's been erratic. And the energy has been building."

She was right. And that had me worried. There was one way something could have used the portal, possibly without my knowing. It was something Grams had told me about once, a long time ago. But it was too horrible to consider. "Yes." I let a moment's doubt flood me and then sliced it off. If the creatures we'd been facing were getting through the portal under my watch, I was responsible for Boyle almost getting killed. And for Della...

I shook my head again, mostly because I wasn't ready to face that possibility. "I'd know, Sis."

She didn't look convinced, but she let it drop. "Do you want something to eat? Or some chamomile?"

I didn't want anything. Except to see Boyle with

my own two eyes. "I'm going to go check on the baby."

Sis nodded. "I'll make some tea. For when you come back down."

I didn't argue, though I knew I wouldn't drink it. The last thing I wanted was to be soothed. I was going to check on Boyle, and then I was going to follow the monster's trail. I was going to find out where it had come through. Somebody was responsible for the attacks. I knew it in the center of my core.

But, even as I climbed the steps toward the third floor and Boyle. I said a silent prayer that somebody wasn't me.

I sat on the edge of Boyle's bed, staring down at him. His little chest rose and fell in sleep, his thick, dark-orange lashes fanning out across his cheeks. He looked even more adorable in sleep.

One hand rested on the bed, fingers slightly curved and twitching in what was probably a harmless dream. I was fairly certain that wasn't just wishful thinking on my part. The baby often dreamed of flying with the bats in a night-darkened sky or playing with the critters who always surrounded Victoria. He didn't seem upset and his breathing was soft. My hand crept out before I could stop it and I slipped my fingers through his. The tiny digits tightened around mine, warm and baby-soft.

He sighed in his sleep and I smiled.

Tears burned my eyes. If anything ever happened to Boyle...

I sniffed, scraping hot tears from my cheeks with the back of my hand, anger making the action quick and overly aggressive.

Nothing was going to happen to Boyle. I'd keep him safe if I had to keep him inside Victoria until we figured out what was creating the magical chaos in Render. I thought of Mitch's dire proclamation, *"Something's happening, Glynn. Something's coming. And for the first time in my life, I can't see it."*

I shuddered.

I couldn't see it either. But I needed to. I needed to figure out what was going on before anybody else got hurt. And I had a feeling I needed to do it fast. Because whatever was happening, it seemed to be happening at an accelerated rate.

And it had already threatened everybody I loved.

15

I was getting ready to go looking for Artur when the door to the kitchen opened and he stepped inside, his expression grim.

Sissy and I glanced his way, and she frowned. "You didn't find anything?"

He shook his head. "No. But there's something in the air..." He broke off, looking worried.

I thought of Mitch's words again and shook off the sliver of fear slicing through me. "What kind of something? Where? Does Hawk know what we need to do?"

Art threw me a strange look. I didn't blame him. We barely knew Hawk. I had no idea why I'd assume he'd know more than we did, especially about something dark that seemed to be stalking Render.

But my brother didn't call me on it. He just shook his head. "We walked the entire street with Nicht.

The dog was agitated, his eyes glowing red..." Art grimaced. "That's disturbing on so many levels."

I nodded. "Nicht is a hellhound."

Sissy sucked air, her face paling. "Say it ain't so!"

I chuckled. "I'm afraid I can't do that."

Art shoved his hands into his pockets and leaned a hip against the cabinets. He didn't look surprised about Nicht's species. Hawk must have told him.

"But aren't hellhounds evil?" Sissy asked.

I shrugged. "Apparently not. Unless he's putting on one heck of an act. He's saved us more than once," I reminded her.

"And he lets Boyle ride him like a horse," Art said, shaking his head.

"Still," Sis said, looking worried.

"He's fine," Artur said. "I might not have Glynn's powers of siphoning magical energy, but I have a sense about these things. I can feel malevolent energy and that...hound...doesn't have any."

"What about Hawk?" Sis asked my brother, skimming a quick, guilty glance my way.

Art frowned. "I can't get a full read on him. My gut tells me he's okay. But there's definitely something dark there."

My brother was echoing my own feelings about Hawk. His behavior since we'd met him had been helpful and kind. I had no reason to doubt that was what he was. Except for an uncomfortable tightness in my chest whenever he was around. My head didn't trust him, despite what my heart was telling me.

"What were you feeling out there?" I asked, shoving aside concern that I was changing the subject again. I really needed to get a bead on Hawk soon. There were currently too many unknowns in our lives. And I didn't like unknowns.

"There was a spike of something really dark around Della's house," he told me, his gaze finding mine. "Hawk thought it was just residue from the soul swallower attack."

Sissy grimaced. "I can't believe what's happening in our little piece of Heaven."

Art and I laughed. Render was a lot of things. But it was a real stretch to call it any kind of Heaven.

Sissy's brows lifted. "What? I love our little community."

I did too. But I supposed I had a more realistic... or maybe cynical view of it. "Did you check on Della?" I asked Art. "Maybe that thing came back. Or it wasn't alone."

He nodded. "Yeah. She's still really weak. We barely got anything out of her. But she was alone and, from the sting of magic as we stepped into her home, she's warded the heck out of the place."

"That's good," I said, relaxing. "Did you see Mitch?"

Art's gaze darkened. "He wasn't in his shed."

Silence plunged between us. Sissy and I exchanged alarmed looks.

"That's not right," Sissy said. "He's always in that shed."

"I suppose he does need to leave once in a while," I said, "To get groceries and stuff." Even as I said the words, they sounded unsure.

"No," Sissy said. "He gets everything delivered. Mitch hasn't left his place since the Body sent that Representative down to snoop around the big house."

That was what we all called the mansion on whose property Mitch lived. About a year previous, someone had apparently reported that a magic-user was living in the old mansion. Whoever it was had evidently seen Mitch moving around in there one night, his flashlight skimming the furnishings that had been left behind in the family's frenzy to leave.

The rep had questioned everyone on the street, looking for Mitch and asking if we knew about him using any magic. Those of us who had magic had learned to keep it hidden. To help with that, Sissy had provided us with a small tattoo that masked our special energies when they were engaged through a particular word. We each had our own words, like private passwords, to keep from being detected.

Mitch had refused the tat, claiming it would interfere with his power. He'd retreated to his shed after that and hadn't left it that anybody was aware.

"We need to check on him," I told Sissy.

She nodded, climbing to her feet.

Art held up a hand. "Wait a minute, you two. Hawk and I have already checked on him. He's not there."

"What if something happened to him?" I demanded.

"Then you two don't need to go marching down there and endanger yourselves."

We glared at each other for a long moment. Artur had used the "I'm a big strong man and you're a weak, stupid woman" thing on me all my life. It had never worked out well for him, but that didn't keep him from pulling it out of his arsenal whenever he felt it was needed.

I used to punch him in the gut when he tried it. But that had gotten me into too much trouble with Grams. So I'd learned to settle for beating him down with my words.

Not nearly as satisfying, of course. But as I'd gotten older and smarter, I'd learned it could be just as effective. I narrowed my eyes on my bossy brother. "I'm going to check on my friend. Can you be trusted to stay here and protect Boyle?"

Art bristled, just as he'd always done when I'd basically accused him of being a coward for not charging into adventure with me. "If you're going to see Mitch, I'm going with you."

I looked at Sissy and she sighed. "I'll protect the little bug. But if you need help..."

"I'll give you a call," I said, knowing Boyle would be perfectly safe in my friend's capable hands. "If we're not back in an hour..."

"I'll go get Hawk," she told me.

I nodded and gave her a quick hug. Then I slid Art a look. "Let's go, big brother. Try to keep up."

The area around the shed was silent. Only the annoyed squeak of a passing bat disturbed the quiet. I crept closer, all my senses on alert. Despite my jibe, Artur had more than kept up as we'd navigated the shadows along the street on our way to Mitch's place. For all his faults as a brother, Art knew how to move almost silently through the dark.

Somewhere along the way, we picked up Nicht. The big dog trotted up and pressed against my side, big tongue lolling comically out the side of his mouth.

I grinned at him, digging my fingers into the thick scruff over his shoulders and giving him a quick scratch to thank him for joining the party. As we came within several feet of the shed, Nicht speared off into the darkness, disappearing as if he'd never been there. I assumed he was doing a perimeter search of the area and felt some of the tension leaving my shoulders at the thought.

There was nothing visibly wrong about the space. But I remembered Art's worried voice saying, "...there's something...". He was right. There was... something. A tension in the air. An unsettled feeling to the area. It made my hackles rise and made me want to turn around and run.

I slid silently up to the door and reached out, feeling the knob with a fingertip. Electricity chewed on the skin of my finger and snapped a thin band of light into the night. I turned to Art, lowering my voice to a whisper. "It's warded."

"That's good, right?" Artur asked. He'd spent enough time at the Body to understand about magical security methods. "If the ward's intact, he probably left of his own volition."

I wished I could agree. But there were ways of killing someone and disposing of them without breaking a perimeter ward. As a portal protector, I knew that all too well. Unsanctioned portals weren't exactly common, but they did exist. The portal in Victoria's basement wasn't sanctioned by the Body, which was why I'd worked so hard to keep it secret.

Art touched my arm. "You're thinking portal, aren't you?"

He'd always been able to read my expressions. "Yeah. That would explain the tension in the air." And the slight stench of sulfur I was smelling. But I didn't mention that because it would set my brother off. Unsanctioned portals were one thing. But portals that led to the dark dimension were too dangerous not to report.

At least, if you were a rule-obsessed, starched collar, stick up the backside, paper pusher like my brother. His stint at the Body had sucked any rebel tendencies he'd had right out of him. And he hadn't had much of that to start with.

I held my hand over the knob and felt for the energy pulsing through the ward. It came to me with only the smallest resistance and slid through my palm. The energy burned as it slipped beneath my skin, making itself known before allowing me to weave my own energy through it and claim it for my own.

The ward on Mitch's home snicked off when I touched the knob again, recognizing the familiar energy of the spell. I glanced at Art. "Wait out here. Let me get a look at what's going on before you come inside."

Moonlight slipped over his face in thin streams, obscuring his features. But not enough to hide the belligerent expression. "Not happening, sis."

"Mitch doesn't know you. If he's inside, he might attack." What I didn't mention was that Art didn't have the magic to deal with whatever might be inside.

See, I could be diplomatic if I had to.

"You'll be right here if I need help. And Nicht's around here somewhere. It'll be fine. I just want to siphon some of the energy inside and read it. It'll take five minutes. Ten tops."

He reluctantly allowed me to precede him into the shed. But he refused to leave the doorway. I could feel his judgmental glare biting the skin between my shoulder blades.

Goddess save me from a bossy sibling.

I slipped into the tiny home and stared at the empty chair in the center of the space. It was weird to see the chair empty. Mitch spent ninety percent of his time there, even sleeping in the chair most nights. Its position allowed him to see whatever came through his door, and he'd infused the age-scarred leather with his seer magic so that it was nearly plug and play. He plugged his narrow back-side into the chair, and visions just rose up around him.

Anyway, that was how he'd described it to me. The chair wouldn't work for anyone else, he'd assured me. But then, he hadn't accounted for a Magis.

I could make the chair plug and play for me too. And I fully intended to do it. As soon as I finished my search of the shed.

Pulling out the flashlight I'd brought along with me, I painted the small space with light. I focused it in the corners and along the ceiling before moving deeper into the room and skimming it over every inch of the chair.

I found what I'd dreaded on one overstuffed arm of the chair, following the trail of dried blood down one side with the light.

I knew without having it tested that I was looking at Mitch's blood.

And there was a lot of it.

I hung my head, feeling worry turn to a certainty that made my stomach churn.

Mitch hadn't left his little home under his own steam. He'd been attacked. And if he was still alive, he was badly hurt.

I turned toward the door as soft footsteps approached. Art bent over the chair, frowning at the blood my flash illuminated. "That's not good," he said.

I sighed, straightening. "No. Not good at all."

I finished examining the rest of the place, which consisted only of the tiny kitchen and a five-foot square space with a camping toilet and a sink with running water that Mitch captured in a roof cistern and fed through a simple plumbing system leading to the kitchen and bath.

I didn't find anything in either place, which worried me. If Mitch had been hurt and had washed up at either sink, I could convince myself that he'd left of his own accord. But there was nary a single drop of blood in either sink. No bloody towels left behind—no med supplies in the trash.

Mitch had been taken.

"Anything?" Art asked.

I shook my head. "You need to wait outside for this next part." I fixed him with a look that I hoped he could interpret properly. I didn't want to put him into the position of seeing me access Mitch's magic and then having to lie to the Body.

His gaze sharpened. "What are you going to do, Glynn?"

I just stared at him.

"Glynn?"

"Two words, Art. Plausible deniability. I'll be out in a minute." Or ten.

He stared back at me for another minute. Long enough that I was afraid he was going to fight me on it. But then inclined his head. "I'm leaving the door cracked. If you need help..."

"I'll call you," I promised, knowing I wouldn't. No matter what happened, I couldn't allow Art to see what I was about to do. Not only was my magic status illegal outside of magical Indy, but I was going to insert myself into another magic user's energy and siphon it off for my own use. That was considered by many in the magic world to be the ultimate violation unless it was done in self-defense. Akin to energy rape.

It was bad enough that Art might feel he had no choice but to report it.

I waited until he'd stepped through the door and then pulled the door closed behind him, infusing it quickly with the ward magic I'd siphoned.

"Hey!" Art yelled from outside.

I ignored him and headed for the chair, my heart thudding against my ribs.

Art began pounding on the door as I settled my flashlight onto the floor and turned to lower myself into the chair.

My heart was pounding so hard I was having trouble breathing. Panic swelled inside my chest, tightening my lungs and churning acid in my belly.

I was about to do something I'd never wanted to do. I'd always believed being a Seer would be horrible. I'd never wanted to know the future because if there was something bad there, I wouldn't be able to avoid it. I'd only worry about it until it happened.

Mitch could sometimes change the future from his visions. But that was well beyond my ability to do. Even siphoning his magic wouldn't give me that power.

So, whatever I was about to see, I wouldn't be able to stop it.

No matter how horrible it was.

16

As soon as I touched the worn leather, the warm sting of Mitch's magic slid into me, tightening my skin and sending a rolling tremor sliding beneath it.

The sensation was so uncomfortable it was all I could do to stay in that chair. My flesh crawled beneath the magical onslaught, and my fingers tightened against the soft leather of the overstuffed arms.

The magic swelled and took me.

I gasped, my eyes flying open as the air around me shifted, changing form against my skin. I didn't have any idea what I'd expected to see. But it wasn't what I was looking at.

The place was beautiful. Vivid and bright, with a golden sun high overhead. The grass beneath my feet was thick, my feet sinking deeply into its cool embrace. I wriggled my toes with pleasure, realizing that I was barefoot.

A soft breeze wafted past, its touch a gentle caress against my bare skin.

Bare?

Panic sliced pleasure from me as I looked down and saw...

Goddess's galoshes!

"Whew!" I wasn't naked. Not totally anyway. I was wearing a summery dress, made of a light fabric that felt silky against my skin and was so lightweight it was almost see-through.

But I wasn't naked, thank the goddess.

A bright splotch of color flashed in my peripheral vision. My gaze snapped up and I smiled. A butterfly fluttered past, heading for a bush that was thick with large chartreuse and purple flowers. I realized the bush was the source of the delightfully sweet scent that perfumed the air.

I was so engrossed in my surroundings, it took me a moment to realize that I wasn't in *my* world.

The place where I stood wasn't Render. It wasn't even Magical Indy, though I knew Indy had some of the best gardens of any of the country's magical cities.

But they had nothing like that butterfly, whose wingspan had to be something like twelve inches and whose body looked to be five inches long.

It was the size of a bird.

My gaze slid upward. Indy's gardens, though beautiful beyond compare, didn't have trees whose branches were formed into arrowhead shapes, and whose leaves were a vibrant shade of scarlet, perched atop perfectly straight trunks covered in black bark. The trunks were wide enough to drive a car through. And they rose next to each other in nearly perfect formation, like a giant, verdant army from another planet.

The ground shook and something snapped out, snatching the butterfly from the air above the flowery bush.

I blinked and my head whipped around.

The creature had to be thirty feet tall, with a lizard's head and impossibly long claws on too-long arms.

The monster had a humanoid frame, but that was the end of any resemblance to humans. A long, disgusting tongue slithered out from between reptilian lips and tasted the air. I shuddered with disgust.

Without warning, the thing dropped to all fours and started toward me.

I panicked, trying to run, but my feet wouldn't move. I stood there, my heart pounding hard enough to make me dizzy, and watched it lumber right at me.

The creature's stench hit me several feet before it did. It smelled like rotten fish and feces, and its eyes glowed with a terrible amber light. Each time a heavy paw hit the ground, the branches on the bush beside me rustled, mirroring the quaking of the ground beneath my feet.

I fought desperately to move, but my feet were stuck fast, the thick grass wrapped around them like steel bands.

With a small, terror-filled sound, I crouched low, covering my head with my arms, and said a prayer that the thing might somehow miss me.

The stench deepened, coating the air like paint, thick and viscous, and its touch on my skin was clammy. I shuddered as it flowed over me, feeling each rumble of the creature's footsteps in my bones.

And then it was gone.

The air was cold and I shivered. I slowly uncovered my head and blinked, blinded by darkness.

"What the...?"

I was in Render again. I stood, staring around at the familiar sight of my street. And it was nighttime. Had I somehow left the chair, sloughed off the visions and returned to reality?

I tried to move but my feet, clad in my familiar sneakers once again, were glued to the broken asphalt.

I looked at Victoria, terrified of what I might find. If I saw a vision of the house burning, or worse, of Boyle being harmed, it would be real and I wouldn't be able to stop it.

I suddenly wanted out of that chair, away from the visions. I couldn't shake the feeling that, if I didn't know about the bad thing, somehow I could stop it.

It wasn't a logical feeling. But feelings were rarely logical.

Victoria rose into the darkness. Unchanged. Golden light bathed the space behind the windows of my room and higher, in Boyle's attic bedroom. The tension that had turned my muscles to rock eased.

I took a deep, relieved breath.

A husky, pain-filled cry broke the night.

I swung my vision to find the cause, seeing Hawk and Nicht in battle with something...something...a long tongue snapped out and caught Nicht across the muzzle. He jerked away with a painful yelp.

Hawk swung a long blade and the monster reared back, emitting an ear-shattering squeal that sliced along my nerves. His strike severed the lizard thing's disgusting tongue, the meaty flesh hitting the ground with an acidic sizzle.

A soft warmth slipped over my leg. I jumped, crying out in shock. I looked down to see the small black cat rubbing against my legs. It looked right at me, purring loudly. "Hey," I said. "You can see me?"

The cat meowed, its short tail lazily waving above its back.

Excitement made me try to move my feet again.

If I was really there, not in the vision, I could help them fight off the monster.

Nope. Still glued to the street.

Son of a bunion!

A roar filled the silence of the vision, and I whipped my head toward the sound. Nicht was down and Hawk was on his back, his sword clattering to the street as the monster dove at him. As I fought to move, I heard the horrible sound of teeth crunching down on bone.

I screamed, ripping my feet, finally from the ground, and then felt myself falling through a deep, velvety black tunnel. The scream died in my throat and I forgot to breathe as I plunged through nothingness, as fearful of it never ending as I was afraid of what would happen when it did.

I never found out. The tunnel disappeared, and my flailing arms smacked against something warm and solid.

"Umpf!" someone grunted. "Goddess, Glynn! Stop thrashing around."

My eyes snapped open. I was looking up into Art's confused and welt-covered face.

I was back.

I struggled out of the chair, finding it difficult not because of magic but because the stupid thing was covered in flesh-thwucking foam. "Hawk's in trouble. We need to go!"

To my shock, as we ran toward home, Art reached inside his boring cotton shirt and pulled out a blade. The thing was about eighteen inches long and gleamed in the soft light of the moon high above.

I'd never seen my brother use a weapon before. I filed that away to ask him about later. I wasn't sure how I felt about my pole-up-the-posterior brother as a knife-wielding defender, but for the moment, I was glad of it.

I opened my senses to the residual magic in the air around us and felt Art's meager energy, automatically sifting it out of the mix as I embraced a variety of energies that included some of Della's fairy magic, a mix of other powers bleeding from the surrounding homes, and, as we came within a block of Victoria, a welcome rush of my home energy, waiting for me to accept it.

I yanked the power to me, letting it bleed from my fingers in a thick stream and form into a sword, long and deadly, its blade honed by focused intent.

The blade glowed silver as I lifted it, my hand wrapped securely around a hilt that had been created to fit my specific handprint.

I realized as we closed the distance that a small form stood in the street, facing the monster. I sucked in a shocked gasp at the sight of Sissy holding two miniature thunderclouds of magic in her hands, legs set apart and gaze locked with determination on her foe.

The lizard thing had reared up, standing on its back legs with the steadiness of a creature that was used to standing that way. Though its thick legs were bent and its back slightly bowed, it towered several feet above the small witch, making her look tiny in comparison to its height and bulk.

I dared a quick glance toward the spot where I'd seen Hawk go down and he was still there, an unmoving shape in the trampled grass

Nicht was starting to move, his enormous paws twitching helplessly against the ground.

Tears stung my eyes. I blinked them away as rage scoured through me, burning emotion back until I had the luxury of safety to expel it.

"I'll circle around behind it," Art said quietly.

I inclined my chin, my gaze locked on Sis. As soon as she hit the monster with the energy bubbling at her fingertips, I wanted to strike it with my blade. The thing was huge, and apparently powerful since it had taken down both Hawk and his hellhound. Our only shot at besting it was if we combined power.

"Sis," I said softly, my nearly silent voice gliding toward her on a gentle push of power.

She gave me a terse nod without looking away

from the thing looming over her. "On three," she responded just as softly.

"One," I said, lifting the blade over my head.

"Two," Sis said.

"Three!" I screamed, sending power into my voice that threaded through the space between me and the lizard thing.

"Die!" Sis screamed, her voice throbbing with magical energy. She hurled the energy storms she'd held in her palms at the lizard.

I leaped into the air, the hilt of my magic blade clutched above my head in both hands, and hit the beast just after Sis's magic thrust duel blades of pure defensive energy through its thick hide.

My blade sliced downward, spearing it through one dense shoulder, and I threw my weight sideways as it split the flesh, redirecting the tip toward the thing's heart.

The lizard screamed, acid spewing from its long, heavy snout, and pain sizzled along my leg where the nasty spittle landed.

It turned and punched the claws of its other leg into me, sending me flying across the yard. I hit the ground ten feet away and skidded until I bumped up against something big and soft that smelled like wet dog.

Sis threw another pair of magical firestorms at the thing as it turned with a roar to meet Art and his flying blade.

To my shock, my nerdy brother actually seemed to be doing some damage to the thing, blood and spittle flying around its flailing limbs and snapping jaws.

Deadly black claws sliced the air close, so close to Art, but he was too fast for it to touch. His big, lithe body leaped from side to side, seemingly dancing on the very air as he struck and spun away and then struck again, weakening the thing even as he kept it busy so Sis could continue to pelt it with boiling clouds of witchy magic.

I pushed away from Nicht, taking a moment to check his big body for damage. Claw-tracks scored his sleek black fur in a few places, a few of the wounds deep but no longer bleeding. I watched several of the shallower tracks close up before my eyes and realized he was healing himself as quickly as he could. His sides were heaving from the effort and, though his brightly glowing eyes were open, they were glassy with the effort of healing.

I crawled away from him and checked Hawk.

It wasn't good.

He was paler than pale against the dark ground—his color nearly the silvery-white of the moon high above us. Hawk was barely breathing and, it didn't take me long to find out why. His chest was caved in, a large chunk of flesh missing near his heart. Oh so very near. The monster had clearly been going for the life-sustaining organ and had probably only been distracted in its purpose by Sissy arriving on the scene.

She'd likely saved the big hunter's life. But it ultimately wouldn't matter, because he was a breath away from dying anyway. I leaned down and put my face in front of his, feeling only the smallest touch of warm breath against my face. "Hold on, Hawk. You hear me? You need to fight."

My mind roiled, as I churned frantically for a way to help. I needed healing energy and lots of it. I could take it from Nicht, but that might get in the way of the hound's attempts to heal himself.

Victoria's bones had absorbed all kinds of energy over the years, some of it the healing variety, but I knew instinctively that there wasn't nearly enough to fix the damage to Hawk's body.

"Glynn!" Sissy called out. "A little help here?"

I crouched beside Hawk, indecision locking me in place. If I didn't help Hawk quickly, he would die. I knew it with a certainty borne of experience and magical intuition. But If I didn't help my bestie and my brother, we could all die.

I really had no choice. Tears burned my eyes as I shoved upright and yanked magic from the air again, reforming my blade.

A soft, gray mist in the dark caught my gaze and my head snapped around. A wispy form glided toward me through the night.

The blade came up and I wanted to curse. Didn't we have enough on our plates already?

But the spirit pelting toward me from the darkened ranch house across the street was more friend than foe.

I hoped.

Della was nearly translucent, but I shoved worry for her aside. Her form was always wispy away from the fairy-infused fortress of her home.

My thoughts stuttered and took another direction. *Fairy dirt.* It had shown great healing powers when Della had been near death from the soul swallower. Would it work on someone other than Della?

I met her in the street, my gaze filled with hope. "Hawk's nearly dead. Is there anything…?"

She held out a hand, her touch on my arm cool and moist like mist. "Go, deal with the creature. I'll see if I can help him."

I clasped the icy hand. "Thank you!"

A scream spurred me into the fight. Sissy was down. The thing was standing over her, its horrible jaws gaping wide and acidic spit sizzling droplets against her skin.

She was fighting to build more magic in her palms, but full-on panic wasn't conducive to creating energy. Unfortunately, I knew that from personal experience.

Art was kneeling in the street, his face gray and his bloody blade still clutched in one hand. His chest was heaving, and deep bloody tracks scored one shoulder.

He was done. Too tired and hurt to help my friend.

I pushed worry for my brother from my mind and grabbed for the energy to make another strike. With a thought, I was flying through the air again, and the monster's terrible maw was opening wide, its feral amber gaze gleaming in anticipation.

17

I hit the monster hard, knocking the air from my lungs as I stabbed downward with the blade. The silvery energy speared through the flesh, but it was only a distraction. I knew it wouldn't be a killing blow.

My real goal had been to get hands on the thing. And with that in mind, I let go of the silvery hilt and wrapped my arms around the monster's neck, riding its back as it reared up on an enraged roar.

Spittle flew through the air, sizzling against every surface it touched. The monster careened sideways, causing Art to leap out of the way or be stomped.

Sissy climbed quickly to her feet and screamed my name. I had no idea what she was trying to tell me, and it didn't matter anyway.

I was kind of busy at the moment.

The thing roared with rage, its claws scraping

across both of my forearms as it swung around, trying to dislodge me from its throat.

Agony ripped through me. The wounds burning like fire. It was all I could do to hold on as my blood bubbled up from the slashes across my arms.

I forced myself to concentrate, despite the agony of being repeatedly bashed into the tree the thing was currently using to try to rub me off its back.

I closed my eyes, only vaguely aware of the monster juddering as something exploded near its feet. We wheeled sideways and my eyes flew open before I could stop myself. The monster slammed me into the tree hard enough to stun. Thankfully, the giant lizard took most of the damage. I wrapped my legs around its chest as I grabbed hold of my siphoning energy, fueled by pure desperation, and began to draw energy from the monster's core.

Sour, black acid filled me, burning my cells and drawing a horrifying array of screams from my throat as I siphoning the thing's energy and tried to make it my own. The energy burned a pathway through me, boiling my blood and melting my insides as I tried to force it to acclimate.

Sensing its weakening power, the creature turned manic, spinning and roaring and tearing at my thighs and arms.

Somehow I held on. I think I'd entered a kind of muscular rigor mortis, and I started to worry I wouldn't be able to let go even when I was done.

Slowly, the magic ceased to burn. I was half afraid it had simply burned away all my nerve endings, and my insides had become a melted pool of lava. But with the cessation of pain came a wash of phenomenal power. I felt as if I was swelling, my body becoming heavier and larger by the moment. My teeth began to ache, dual pools of amber light glowing against the dark wherever I looked.

A new kind of panic swirled through me. Was I *becoming* the monster? I hadn't wanted to do anything but siphon its magic and use it against the thing.

I'd never been transformed from siphoning magic before.

The monster gave a long, eardrum-shattering shriek and spun one last time, falling to its knees in the middle of the street. That was about the time the energy turned to fire in my veins again.

Sharp pain pierced my gums and blood ran from my mouth, my face boiling and rolling in a metamorphosis I didn't know how to stop.

My thoughts unfocused and then sharpened on memories I'd never owned. Blood-drenched pictures formed in my mind of me chasing and crunching things I never wanted to crunch with my teeth. I struggled to remember what I'd been trying to do. The disturbing pictograph continued to play across my mind.

I shook my head, trying to dispel it. Spital flew from my open mouth.

The creature below me crashed to the ground, its big head slamming into the asphalt and embedding itself there like a dinosaur fossil.

My mind finally formed words among the pictures. *Kill. The. Creature.*

Oh yeah. That was it. I focused on a quick, mental checklist:

Siphon energy from the monster so I could kill it.

Kill the monster.

Don't die.

I reached for the silvery sword sticking out of the reptile thing's body and wrenched it free, my long black claws clacking together against the magical hilt. Wait...what? I didn't have long black claws...

My self-image was still mixing with the monster's. Not good.

I swung the blade, my mind showing me a picture of a large, scaled arm striking in a powerful arc, and the blade sliced almost effortlessly through the thick neck, cleaving the ugly head from the struggling creature beneath me.

The creature stilled, its blood pooling like lava beneath its headless body.

Energy flooded me and I surged to my feet, roaring into the night.

The fire burst through my insides, making me

stagger away and fall to my knees. I retched pure acid into the street, feeling as if I were horking up my very organs.

Without warning, I collapsed to the ground. Voices droned around me. A soft light blazed from the dark and something soothing slipped over me. It was cool and smelled like peat and earthworms. I think I tried to push it away. But a soft gray mist gripped my flailing arms and cooled my enflamed brow.

And as the fire finally started to die, I let the nasty smelling stuff soothe me into sleep.

The whole passing out and waking up in Victoria thing was getting really old. Like before, I didn't want to open my eyes. I just lay there a moment and let the soothing drone of familiar voices roll over me

Unlike before, the crisply dancing flames in the fireplace were really not soothing.

Burning fire. Been there, hated that.

But the familiar small hand clasping mine would always be a comfort. I squeezed Boyle's little hand and he snuggled tighter against me with a sigh. I could tell by listening to his soft, rhythmic breathing that he was asleep.

I must have been lying on that stinky couch for a while.

"Glynn?"

I tried to ignore Sissy's voice, but she knew me too well. "I know you're awake. Here. You need to drink this."

I wrenched my eyes open. She flinched, which told me everything I needed to know about the state of my eyes. "That bad, huh?"

She set the cup of tea on the sofa table and gave me an assist as I sat up enough to drink. She stuffed pillows behind my back and then stuck the mug in front of my face. Steam rose from the surface of the strange-smelling tea.

I eyed it like it was snakes.

"You'll have to forgive me if I don't want to put anything hot inside my body right now."

"Drink it, Glynn. It will help get rid of..." She waved her hand in front of my face, and I frowned.

"Get rid of what? Do I have a pimple?" I let my eyes go wide in horror, and she rolled hers.

"Stop being a jerk. Drink your medicine."

I took the mug and sniffed it carefully, retching. "Ugh! That smells like butt."

She put hands on hips. "Okay, now I'm wondering whose butt you've been sniffing." She grimaced. "I won't be able to get *that* thought out of my mind for a while. Stop being a baby and drink up."

I took a quick sip and retched again. But the glower on my friend's face had me choking the rest down fast, hoping it would be over my tongue and down my throat before my taste buds realized I was trying to poison them.

"There," she said, taking the mug from me. "That wasn't so bad, was it?"

I wiped my mouth with the back of my hand. "Still retching here," I told her on the backend of a particularly violent heave. I didn't dare do anything besides gag though because the look on her face promised dire things if I did.

"If you throw it up, you'll just have to drink another mug full."

And there was that.

I closed my eyes and laid back onto the pillows, feeling better. The stuff had gone in hot but it had coated my innards in a cooling wash that seemed to numb a lot of the residual burning sensation. I sighed. My muscles softened. The sounds of people moving around the house eased away...

The floor next to the couch creaked. My eyes shot open and my hand flew up, fingers curved as if I'd claw the man standing beside the couch with them.

I would have too, except for two things. One, I didn't have claws. And, two, he'd grabbed my wrist in an iron grip and my hand couldn't get to him.

Art lifted a brow. "Cool your jets, Glynnie. I just

wanted to see how you were feeling. That nasty stuff Sissy made should have kicked in by now."

I laughed, jerking my arm from his grip. "In two minutes? What was it, instameds?"

He gave me a look filled with pity. "Glynn, you've been asleep for three hours."

I started to shake my head, then I glanced toward the spot where Boyle had been. He was gone. And I heard his cute little voice in the kitchen, telling somebody all about his favorite bugs.

I collapsed back to the pillows. "No wonder my mouth is so dry."

"I'll get you some water."

I shook my head. "No. I'm getting up. I'll get it."

He frowned and I added, "But thanks. I just need to move around a little."

He offered me his hand and I took it. Then I remembered Hawk and squeezed it hard. "Hawk and Nicht?"

"They're going to be okay," he told me. "Your neighbor pulled dirt out of the ground and dumped it on them. She did it to you too, by the way." He frowned. "I'm not sure why, but it seemed to help." He frowned. "What is she, anyway?"

I stiffened at the question. He noticed and looked hurt. Lifting his hands, he shook his head. "Never mind. I was just curious."

"Sorry, Art. It's not my place to reveal that. Della's a very private person."

He nodded. "No, I get it." He forced a smile, but it didn't reach his eyes.

I felt bad. But that didn't change the fact that I was telling the truth. Everyone in Render was in hiding. We all had our reasons for not going public about our magic. And we were only safe as long as nobody started telling tales.

Sis came into the room, my favorite little gargoyle skipping alongside her. She had a tray in her hands, which was sending a delicious array of aromas into the air. I eyed it hungrily as she placed it on the table in front of me. "Oh, my goddess! Is that homemade bread?"

She grinned, wiping her hands on the towel she'd jammed into the waistband of her jeans like an apron.

"And jellies!" Boyle said happily, holding out a tiny jar filled with something that was glossy and red. My eyebrows lifted. "Is that strawberry rhubarb?"

He nodded so enthusiastically, he almost dropped the jar.

Sis dove on it, rescuing the little jar from his fingers. "I'll take that, little man. Do you want to tell Glynnie what we made for dessert?"

He bounced on his toes, his eyes as big as saucers. "Glynnie, Glynnie, Glynnie, me and Sissy made chawcate cake!"

"Chocolate cake?" I clapped my hands, doing the happy carb dance on my butt.

Boyle giggled with pure joy, doing his own happy dance. He swung his tiny arms in the air and hopped from foot to foot, tipping his head energetically back and forth.

We all laughed at his antics. That only made him dance harder.

Sissy handed me a bowl of soup and I sniffed. "Mm, vegetable beef?"

She nodded. "Sorry it's not fancier. But you had fresh veggies in the fridge, and it's been sounding good."

"No, it's perfect. Thanks so much for doing this."

She frowned, handing my brother his own bowl. "I didn't do anything."

I lifted a brow. "No, you only took on a monster in the street. And probably saved Hawk's life."

She flipped a dismissive hand in the air. "You would have done the same." I watched her slather a thick slice of bread with jelly and hand it to Boyle. "Now, sit down next to Glynn with that," she told him. "Don't get jelly all over the place."

The little gargoyle took a bite, did an abbreviated form of the happy carb dance, and plopped next to me.

I watched him eat, the simple contentment on his face filling me with pleasure.

"He ate his soup in the kitchen," Sissy told me. "I

didn't think it was a good idea to give him soup in here."

"The jelly's dangerous enough," Art said. "I saw what he did with it at breakfast."

"You're not wrong," Sissy said.

"So, tell me what happened?" I asked my friend.

She rubbed her hands on the towel again, her gaze filled with concern. "I was washing the baking dishes and looked out the window. I saw that... thing...standing in the middle of the street and Hawk and Nicht circling it." She shook her head. "I have no idea where it came from. One minute the street was empty and then it was...just...there."

Sis twined her fingers together, seemingly lost in thought. I took note of the dark shadows under her eyes and a new tightness in their corners. Sissy had a headache. Probably a bad one, judging by the amount of energy she'd used out there.

"Where did Hawk come from?" Art asked.

"I don't know. That was strange too. He simply appeared when the lizard thing did. I guess it was just a coincidence. He must have either been out there when it showed up, or..."

I knew what she was thinking. Hawk always seemed to be around when trouble happened. It was like he could smell it or something.

Or he knew it was coming.

"You don't suppose he's some kind of Seer, do you?" Sis asked.

It was like she'd read my mind. "I don't know," I told her. "But I'm going to find out." I would go see Hawk. I'd give him the rest of the night to recover from the battle. But then I was going over to the place where he was living, and I was going to confront him. Whether he was friend or foe, we needed to know what we were dealing with.

"Did you find, Mitch?" Sis asked. She spoke softly and skimmed a quick glance at Boyle, who'd run into the kitchen to retrieve his favorite monster truck toy from the table.

"No." I frowned, remembering the vision I'd had. I couldn't explain it. And until I could, I was reluctant to talk about it. "There's no sign of him in the house. I couldn't feel any residual magic with his signature in the place. Except for in the chair, of course. That's saturated with it."

Sissy chewed a bite of bread, her expression grim. "It's not like Mitch to just pick up and leave. And if he had, he would have taken that chair with him. It was the only thing he cared about."

I nodded my agreement. "I'm not giving up. If I need to, we'll bring in one of the Body's hounds to find him."

Art, who'd been eating in silence for the last few moments, glanced up at my suggestion. His eyes met mine. "I can arrange that if you'd like."

"Thanks. But not yet. It has to be a last resort because if the Body finds out about Mitch, they'll pull him into Magical Indy. Mitch really doesn't want that."

Not to mention, I wasn't entirely sure the Body hadn't taken him in the first place.

"He might rather die than be forced into service," Sissy said on a frown.

I thought about that. She wasn't wrong. The Seer definitely might prefer to die rather than have someone forcibly take his freedom from him. In that respect, he wasn't unlike the rest of us in Render. It was one of the things that had bound us together.

"I know someone," Art offered, hesitation in his voice.

"Someone?" I asked, taking a bite of soup. It was beyond delicious. I gave Sissy a thumbs up, and she smiled with pleasure.

"She's a...bounty hunter seems like too harsh a word." But I noticed he didn't offer a better one. He leaned forward in his chair, warming to the idea. "She'll sign a blood-oath confidentiality agreement."

I was familiar with the blood-oath agreements. If the signer broke the agreement, he or she died a swift death. If you wanted an iron-clad agreement, there were none better.

I thought about it for a moment and then nodded. "I'll put that in as Plan B. After I talk to Hawk, if I think we need this bounty hunter of yours, we'll contact her. Okay?"

Art nodded, pleasure infusing his handsome

features. I couldn't help wondering if the pleasure came from being helpful, or because he looked forward to using the hunter.

If it was the latter, I suddenly wanted to meet the woman who could put that spark of pleasure in my brother's eyes.

18

There was a soft scratching on the front door as I was checking the locks and wards. I placed a palm on the door and tugged on the house's magic to read the life force of whatever was scratching there. I saw nothing at first, but then I adjusted the sight downward and stopped. There was a tiny, four-legged creature standing on the porch. Curious, I opened the door and looked down at the small black cat. It looked up at me and meowed indignantly. As if it had been standing out there forever and I'd been slow to meet its needs.

Wasn't that just like a cat?

"What's up, little boy?" I asked. I had no idea how I knew the cat was a male. It wasn't like I'd looked.

"Meow!" To my unending shock, the little thing pranced past me and into the house.

"Okay," I said, watching it bound up the steps all the way to the third floor, it proceeded to disappear into Boyle's room. I stood there a moment, unsure if I should make it leave.

Magic swirled from the door I still held into my hand, soothing and calm. The dense wood pulled from my grip and softly closed, locks clicking into place.

Victoria had spoken. The cat stayed.

I yawned and set the protections on the door, the multi-layered wards falling into place with a simple Latin phrase that was the key—*Nemo potest intrare*. None may enter.

Then yawning again, so hard my jaw cracked, I started for the stairs.

I jerked to a stop as the shadows shifted at the top of the stairs. I reached for magic and created a sizzling ball of energy in each palm, my heart pounding.

The shift sorted itself into my brother. I watched in fascination as he descended, looking like he was in a trance, and headed for the basement door.

I let the energy sift away. "Art?"

He didn't appear to have heard me. His movements were stiff, showing nothing of his usual lithe grace. He stopped in front of the basement door and stared blankly at it for a moment. I mentally kicked myself for not boarding it up. I needed to stop procrastinating on that.

Art stood there for so long, I thought he might not try to open it. He was clearly sleepwalking. But I was reluctant to do anything because waking a person who was in a sleep trance was risky enough. But waking a magic user who was sleep-walking was especially dangerous. If I scared him, he might attack.

I didn't think my brother had all that much magic. At least he hadn't cultivated much of it for use if he did. But anything he had could be deadly if applied in the right way to the right place.

A single jolt of magic to the heart was just as deadly as a bullet.

Art's hand came up and stopped, fingers curled over the knob but not touching it. I stepped forward, not sure what I was going to do, but realizing I needed to do something.

Without warning, his hand snapped in my direction. Energy flared from it, and my legs buckled. I fell, hitting the floor hard enough to send agony spearing up my spine. Shock kept me silent as Art's fingers grasped the knob and turned.

The door opened. The warding I'd placed on it simply sifting away, and a moment later, Art was on the stairs, closing the door quietly behind him.

"Goddess's galoshes!" I mumbled, trying to shove to my feet. "What just happened?"

Had Art used the same method I'd used at Mitch's to bypass my wards?

My legs felt like rubber, and the flesh was numb. Fear sliced through me. What had he done to my legs? Panic made my chest heave and my breathing speed. I couldn't stand. I feared I wouldn't be able to walk if I did.

I made a small panicked sound that seemed loud in the silence of the house. The pitiful cry jolted me, causing me to shove panic aside. I had a responsibility to protect the portal. It was more than a job. It was a calling. An obligation. A portal was pure, barely controlled power, which, in the wrong hands, could create untold devastation.

Normally, I wouldn't think Art was a danger. But he clearly wasn't himself.

With a jolt, I realized my brother was under some kind of influence. Worse, whoever was pulling his strings didn't seem to be on the side of protecting the portal.

And I'd brought him into Victoria.

I'd endangered us all.

The thought brought shame spearing through me. Followed by anger so thick I felt it crawling into my face as heat.

I'd screwed up. It would be up to me to fix it.

When I thought of little Boyle sleeping peacefully up in his room, helpless against whatever my brother might unleash, the anger flared brighter.

I tried again to stand and collapsed. Using my arms, I dragged myself over to the couch and used it to pull myself upright. My legs might as well have been rubber for all that I could use them. They collapsed out from under me and I fell, my back slamming into the table in front of the couch.

Pain ricocheted through my middle, robbing me of breath. I needed help. Shoving the rug back, I placed my hands on the smooth wood floor. "Help me," I implored the magic-saturated house. "I need your strength."

The wood beneath my palms warmed and pulsed. The floor seemed to roll slightly as tiny static sparks sizzled on the air. As I watched, the silvery sparks of electricity converged above the couch, spitting and dancing with manic energy. The sparks slammed together, forming a single, snapping ball of energy that throbbed like a beating heart.

The wood cooled beneath my palms and the energy ball just hung there. The house wasn't responding. I wondered with a despondent feeling if Art's magic had somehow blocked the house from giving me energy.

Disappointment was like a sour taste in my mouth. "Victoria?"

I lifted my hands and, as if the movement had unlocked a hidden restraint, the ball of sizzling energy shot in my direction, crashing against my chest.

I convulsed beneath it, my body juddering against the floor. My head slammed into the hardwood over and over and over again as the convulsions wracked me. I tasted blood on my tongue and realized I'd bitten it. Pain painted my hand, the knuckles smacking the table hard enough to bruise.

My heels struck the floor repeatedly. Only the heavy socks I wore against the natural coolness of the old home protected them from the assault.

Flame speared my chest. Burning agony came together in a focused area around my heart and slid outward in ribbons of fiery pain. The energy bit, but it didn't destroy. Finally, it began to ease, leaving behind a cool residue that soothed and strengthened.

Along with a feeling of amazing power.

Before the last dregs of pain had fallen away, I was on my feet, running toward the basement door. My skin still sizzled with residual energy, sparks flaring from my skin as I reached for the knob.

Victoria had given me too much magic, I thought. What I was carrying was overload.

But then I opened the door and saw the telltale flare of energy licking against the rock wall at the base of the steps. And I wondered if it would even be enough.

I flew down the stairs, my feet barely touching them. I was cognizant of a reluctance to use magic against my brother. Yes, he'd used it against me, but I was pretty sure he hadn't known he was doing it.

Or at least that was what I was telling myself to

keep from losing it. Art was the only family I had left.

If he'd gone bad...

I stepped down into the powdery dirt of the floor. My eyes flew to the place across the room where Art stood, his face in profile and his hands outstretched as the rocky wall in front of him rolled and changed.

Heat pulsed against me, drawing sweat from my body in copious amounts.

Beneath Art's hand, the hole in the wall had stretched into a circle about the size of a grapefruit. The inside of the circle was the color of flame, the surface shifting like fire and the wall around it pulsing as it stretched.

Art gave no indication that he knew I was there. That was good. It would buy me some time.

To do what, I didn't know.

I crept along the wall toward the siphoning table, my gaze locked on Art as the portal opened far too quickly in answer to his call.

How was he doing that?

I sent my siphoning energy toward my brother, sliding it around him like a cloak to read the magic he was emitting.

I'd never seen that kind of energy before. It was pale orange and formed of a series of octagonal shapes joined together in random patterns — like a knitted blanket made up of thousands of adjoining three-dimensional holes.

His magic throbbed against mine, growing more frantic as the first blush of my power gave a test tug on the knitted energy.

I tugged harder, pulling the energy away from Art with unusual difficulty. It came slowly and in thick, sticky ribbons.

Like pulling taffy.

There was no way I was going to be able to sift the power from him in layers as I usually did. The magic coating my brother would have to be torn away in one large, resistant piece.

It would take a lot of energy to siphon—more than I had.

The portal had grown to the size of a hula-hoop and heat pulsed through the basement, the walls shimmering beneath it like heat radiating off an Arizona highway in August.

I watched in horror as the first drop of melted rock slid down its surface.

Art was opening the portal!

I couldn't let it happen.

I grabbed the siphoning pot and sent my magic into it. There was no time to prep the pot like I usually did. My energy would have to do the job of nullifying the siphoned magic. Moving toward the widening portal, I focused the pot on the roiling fire within the opening in the stone.

Art's hand reached closer to the fiery gateway, his

already reddened skin starting to bubble as the burns dug into the deep tissue beneath his skin.

He didn't even wince beneath the damage. Though, I knew the pain had to be exquisite.

Something was desperately wrong.

I moved closer with the siphoning pot, and it slammed back against my stomach. My arms shook as energy hit the pot and swirled against it, resistant to the imperative of the siphoning spell.

It whirled like a hurricane on the boiling ocean, circling the edge of the pot and slowly being pulled inside. The pot heated enough to make my clothing smoke. The heat of the portal ate at my skin, pulling copious amounts of sweat from my pores. The moisture evaporated almost immediately, turning to steam in the superheated air.

I moved another step closer, my arms shaking from the effort of holding the pot in position. I'd never felt so much pushback from the portal. It was as if whatever Art was doing was agitating it somehow. Expanding its energy.

I took another step, my entire body shaking under the strain of standing against the energy. It swirled around me, pulsed against me, and pummeled my senses into mush.

It was like standing beneath a waterfall of boiling water.

Art spun around, too fast for my battered senses to comprehend. His hand came up and adrenaline cleared my mind. He was going to hit me with another arrow of the debilitating energy he'd thrown at me upstairs.

There was no time to consider my options. I dropped to my knees in the dust, flooding my hand with Victoria's borrowed power. I lifted the energy-drenched hand and grabbed the energy as he threw it at me.

It hit my palm and flung it backward, wrenching my shoulder as the impact overextended my arm.

I dropped the pot and fell onto my back. But energy rolled against my palm. Pale violet energy that was quickly drying to taffy against my skin.

I didn't wait for it to harden. I curled my fingers around it and, as Art prepared to throw another energy wave at me, I flung it back at him instead.

It hit him in the center of his chest, exploding outward in a thousand, tiny purple stars that chipped against every surface they touched.

Art's eyes rolled back into his head. His knees buckled. And he slumped slowly to the ground in a boneless heap.

Behind him, the portal stopped growing. The fire within seemed to dull and lose energy. And the opening in the rock began to shrink away until it disappeared.

I shoved slowly to my feet, though all I wanted to do was just sit and rest. I felt like someone had beaten me with a bat, and I was tired.

So tired.

Stumbling over to Art, I dropped to my knees beside him. Panic sluiced through me. He wasn't moving. And, at first, I couldn't see his chest rising and falling.

Goddess! Had I killed him?

But then he stirred, groaning as he opened his eyes. He looked up at me in surprise, blinking rapidly. "What are you doing here?"

I laughed with relief. "What am *I* doing here?"

He shoved up to one elbow, rubbing his eyes. "Yeah. Why are you in my room? I had such a nightmare. And my head is killing..." He stopped midsentence, his eyes widening as he realized where he was. Art frowned. "Glynn, why am I in the basement?"

I expelled air and shoved to my feet again. "That's a long, confusing story. How about if we go upstairs and I'll make us some tea?"

19

Art hadn't come down yet when Boyle and I headed out to see Hawk at dusk. I wasn't surprised. He'd looked like I'd felt that morning when we'd huddled around the table in my kitchen, filthy from rolling around in the dirt of the basement and exhausted from expending so much energy.

"I didn't know you had the portal protector's power," I'd told him.

"I don't," he'd insisted. "You know I don't, Glynn. If I had, do you really think I'd have left?"

His response hadn't eased my concern one little bit. I'd seen a lot of evidence to the contrary.

In the end, I hadn't gotten into the details of the night before with Art. I wanted to think about what I'd seen. I wanted to consider my options.

We'd both gone to bed confused and, in my case, concerned. But I'd called Sis as soon as Art stumbled back to bed. The door to the basement was getting a special ward on it as soon as Sissy could get to Victoria. And I was leaving it on until Art went back to Indy. The ward would be built with magical energy that he couldn't manipulate on his own.

Witch magic.

The black cat trotted out of the house and headed into the yard with a soft "meow!".

"Bye, kitty," Boyle said, waving.

I locked the front door and set the ward with a wave of my hand. I waited until I saw the telltale golden glow spring up along the door and walls before I took Boyle's hand and started toward the old firehouse across the street.

The baby dawdled beside me, stretching my arm to its full length so he could kick at rocks and pick ugly weeds to present to me like flowers.

I smiled and thanked him but otherwise stayed silent. My mind was full of thoughts about the episode in the basement. My brother was scaring me. Not only was he messing with the epically deadly energy of the portal, but he didn't seem to know he was doing it. Which made the situation so much more dire. If someone was riding his mind... affecting his actions...Art had become an extremely dangerous tool in that person's hands.

A dense row of enormous, overgrown trees nearly hid the front of the firehouse building. The red brick of the old building was still solid, though its face had aged with a black patina that spread to the concrete sills and coated the windows in a dingy film. It was magic residue, a remnant of the battle fought between Magical Indy and the Render magic users of the past. Several years past, a corrupt few magic users had gotten it into their heads that they should rule the land. Through coercion and promises of power, those few had managed to convince many other magic users to join them.

They'd come together to try to control those who had no magic.

Thus began the Disruption, as it was later named by those who'd been on the receiving end of that power grab.

The Disruption had engaged a marshaling of forces into the city. Where it was believed the close proximity would create an impenetrable axis of power that people without magic wouldn't be able or willing to breach.

Unfortunately, that particular blade had cut both ways. In typical human fashion, those who were driving the runaway train called Magic had decided that all magic users must comply with their edict to relocate to the city.

Anyone who didn't favor being told how to live their lives became just as much the enemy as those who, by nature of their lack of or limited abilities in magic, were automatically considered hostile.

The battle spread across the country, infecting

most of the major cities in most of the states. Many of the non-magic ran into the countryside around the cities, preferring to struggle and scrape for a meager existence of their own making, than to become fodder for the magic or turned into virtual slaves by magic users.

Those of us who'd wanted to remain in Render had either gone deep underground until the focus left our unprepossessing little town and we'd all been forgotten, or had fled deeper into the country-side to make a new kind of home amid the abandoned homes and buildings.

Those months had been particularly trying for me, and I tried not to think about them. I'd had Victoria to protect. And the portal. So I'd had to stay close enough to do my job, while staying out of the eye of the roving bands of Magic Indy soldiers.

Sissy had put a spell on Victoria that made her look like a fallen-down corpse of a building. Empty and uninhabitable. And I'd warded myself in the basement, leaving only rarely, when my stores of food and water had been depleted.

After a while, the soldiers lost interest in Render. And those of us who'd stayed behind had slowly come out of our mouseholes and reestablished our lives. But the event had scarred us. Deeply. We were a private bunch. Suspicious and borderline unfriendly.

But we were living under our own directives.

Surviving under our own rules. And for most of us, that was enough.

The Sheriff's station and the firehouse had been the first casualties of that war. The idea had been to remove those who were the most militant, the most physically able to fight back, and those who projected the ability and willingness to lead.

Many first responders died in those ugly days. Others had fled. Still others had gone to Magical Indy under the promise of wealth and comfort.

But no one had remained behind in the building that would be considered modest by most city's standards. No one had lived within its walls.

Until Hawk and his impressive pooch had slipped silently into town.

Hawk could have been one of the country-fled as we called them. He might have been one of those who run to Magical Indy but had decided it wasn't the place where he wanted to spend his days. Either way, I thought he owed us an explanation.

And I was determined to get one. Even if it meant planting my buttocks on his doorstep and refusing to leave until he did.

"Look, Glynnie! Fire tucks!" Boyle hopped up and down and pressed his little face against the glass in the big doors of the truck bay. "Red tucks!" He bounced so hard I was afraid he was going to put his face through the glass.

"Yeah, they're pretty, huh? You need to stop jumping, sweet boy."

A big shape appeared on the other side of the glass and Boyle squealed, jumping away in surprise as Nicht pressed a big, wet nose against the glass.

Boyle squealed again and pressed his nose against the glass in the same spot. The big dog barked, the sound startling in the silence of the night. Boyle answered in kind. "Bark, bark, puppy," he squealed, clapping his hands.

The smaller door next to the truck bays opened, and I found myself staring into Hawk's inscrutable gaze. With a supreme effort, I managed not to scour a gaze over his tall, muscular form, which was currently covered in a tidy white tee-shirt and a pair of loose, soft-looking jeans that were slung low on his hips. His feet were bare, showing me wide toes with tidy, well-groomed nails.

"Are you all right?" he asked me. His deep voice sounded a bit rougher than usual, probably a residual effect of nearly being eaten by that lizard thing the night before. "We're good. How about you?"

He shrugged, shoving his hands into his pockets. "Okay."

He looks good, my traitorous mind said. *Really good.*

We stared at each other for a few beats. I started to think he wasn't going to let us inside. Then, luckily, it was taken out of his hands when Boyle dove past him, through the door, and squealed as Nicht went snout down, butt up, in a classic playful pose. The two of them took off running around the big bays, and Boyle was soon climbing all over the fire engine parked there.

I lifted my brows at Hawk.

His lips curved in a wry grin. "Would you like to come in?"

"It appears one of us already has," I told him, matching his grin with one of my own.

He stepped back and I slid past him, my shoulder brushing against the heat of his chest. He'd left me just enough room to sneak past and not an inch more.

I didn't think it was a mistake when his hand came out to skim over my back. The touch pulsed heat straight through me and momentarily clouded my brain. To cover my discomfort, I nodded toward the dog sitting in the front passenger seat of the firetruck and my rambunctious baby, who was making siren noises and turning the huge steering wheel back and forth. "It looks like the firemen have come back to Render."

Hawk's gaze slid over the baby and warmed. He barked something to Nicht in a guttural language I didn't recognize. The big hound responded with a noise that sounded like a gruffly spoken word rather than a bark.

Hawk turned to me, indicating a sliding glass door into another part of the building. "Coffee?" he asked.

"I'd love some. Thanks."

I followed him into a large room that was sparsely furnished with an old couch and two old reclining chairs. The furniture all faced a television that looked like it had been around for a few decades. It hung on the wall between two sliding glass doors and filled most of the sixty or so inches of paneled wall space.

I inclined my head toward the television set. "Does that still work?"

"It does. I watch it every night."

"That must cost you a pretty penny in electricity." Since most of the population of Render had been drawn back to the city, power companies no longer fully supported the area. There was a skeleton crew that would still travel out to the country to fix existing equipment when service was interrupted, but they took forever to come and charged the customer triple what they used to charge for the service.

Hawk filled a saucepan with water and dropped a cone of coffee into it. I recognized the coffee pods used by people who either lived outside the grid or traveled through it. I mostly made tea because it was easier to find and didn't cost as much as coffee, but Sissy used the pods so I knew they made decent coffee. Her highly-placed parents sent her regular care packages, which usually included coffee pods.

Hawk turned the heat up under the saucepan and shifted to look at me, crossing muscular arms over his wide chest. "Everything okay?"

"Yeah. Why do you ask?"

He held my gaze for a moment. "I felt a surge of magic from your house last night."

Oh, oh.

I smoothed as much emotion as I could from my expression. "Oh?" I'd leave it at that because I didn't want to directly lie. A change of subject was in order. "How are you? That lizard thing really did a number on you."

Hawk stared at me long enough to let me know he'd recognized my tactic and then nodded. "I'm fine. Your neighbor's fairy magic is strong."

I noticed the way he'd referred to Della as *my* neighbor, despite the fact that she was his neighbor too. That seemed meaningful. As if he didn't consider himself a resident in Render.

Like he didn't intend to stay. And if he didn't, why not? Before I even realized I was going to ask, the real question I wanted him to answer popped out of my mouth. "Why are you here, Hawk?"

He turned to the coffee and lifted the pan, swirling the contents in a practiced move before pouring it into two large mugs. He carried them over and set one down in front of me, taking a seat across the table.

He didn't say anything for long enough that I thought he wasn't going to answer my question.

Finally, he said. "I'm trying to help."

"Help who?" I asked, sipping carefully so as not to scald my mouth.

He just shook his head.

So far, my information gathering wasn't going well. I decided to try a different tack. "Since you arrived, we've had several monster attacks. Do you know why?"

He blinked at me over his mug, looking genuinely surprised. "You think I'm responsible for those attacks?"

I just stared at him.

He lowered his coffee. "I was nearly killed last night."

"But you weren't. You've managed to come out of all of the attacks mostly intact."

"So have you," he said, his brows lowering with anger.

I realized making him mad wasn't going to get me what I wanted. So I changed course again. "Mitch is missing."

If Hawk was feigning surprise, he was really good at it. He leaned across the table, his expression filled with sudden tension. "When was he last seen?"

I shrugged. "I'm not sure. He keeps to himself. We only ever see him if we go to his place."

"You were there a couple of days ago?" The way he asked told me he knew the answer already.

"Yes. Sissy stopped over there yesterday and didn't find him. So Art and I went to his place last night..."

"Art? You took your brother?"

The question throbbed with hostility and caught me by surprise. "Yes. Is there a reason I shouldn't have?"

Hawk shifted in his chair, an irritated jerk of broad shoulders. "He works for the Magical Body. Do you really think it's a good idea to take him to the Seer?"

I was surprised that Hawk knew what Mitch was, but I tried not to show it. "Art is questioning his work at the Body. And I needed backup. Sissy had to stay and protect Boyle..."

"Why didn't you come to me?"

I laughed. "No offense, but I barely know you. And you won't tell me who you really are or even *what* you are. You just pop into town and insert your-self into my life." I shook my head. "Judging by your outrage that I would take my brother to see Mitch, you know how hard we try to protect each other here in Render. Yet you expect us to have full confi-dence in you. Since you won't tell us anything, we have no reason to trust you, Hawk. And every reason to fear your being here."

He inclined his head. "Point taken. But I've tried to prove that I'm trustworthy. I've tried to keep you all safe."

"We don't need you to save us. We've been taking perfectly good care of ourselves for three years. But, if you want us to rely on your help and integrity, you need to earn that reliance."

He sipped his coffee and stared at the table for a long moment. Finally, he caught my gaze. I noticed that he had really nice eyes. They were slightly tilted, making him look a little exotic, and they were mostly green with splinters of caramel brown running through them. "Okay, you're right. You deserve to know what I am. First, I'm an ex-cop from Magical Indy. I left because I couldn't stomach the way the Body was treating non and low magic people."

"What do you mean?" I asked, feeling the first nigglings of discomfort threading through my chest.

He gave me an incredulous look. "Surely, you're aware of the purgings?"

"Purgings?" Okay, that sounded bad.

"The Body has become arrogant and dictatorial. People's rights are being ripped away from them, especially those with weak or no magic. They're being watched and controlled and punished for non-compliance. And when any of them show a spark of defiance, the Body has them killed."

I was appalled. "But you say you're a cop. Can't you do anything about it?"

"That's the point, isn't it?" he asked me. His tone throbbed with anger. For a moment, I thought that anger was directed at me.

But it wasn't.

He leaned across the table, his face dark with rage. "Who do you think they asked to do the killing?"

Stars burst before my eyes. I swallowed bile and fought sudden dizziness. Then I realized what he was telling me. What he was *really* saying. "So you ran away? You're in hiding in Render, aren't you? You saw a tragedy and rather than help to stop it, you ran." I surged to my feet, disgusted. "I can't believe you just left those people to die."

"Sit. Down," he growled.

I shook my head and turned away. "Don't come near Boyle ever again."

He was out of his chair and on me before I managed to make it two steps. His hand wrapped around my wrist like a steel band and he yanked me around, slamming me up against the rock wall of his body.

"Let me go!" To my horror, tears burned my eyes. I had no idea whether I was crying for the loss of something I never really had, or for the nameless, faceless strangers Hawk had killed or abandoned.

"Listen to me, Glynn. This is why I didn't want to tell you…"

"I'll just bet. Why would you want to admit you were a coward?"

"I'm not a coward!" he growled out. Pressing his face closer to mine, he spoke through gritted teeth, his jaw rigid. "I didn't abandon them. I brought two dozen of them out of the city with me when I came. I kept them here until they could catch a ride to their next destination."

I blinked, surprise ripping words from me. I shook my head. "There's no way you could have kept that many people here without my knowing."

His smile was smug. "Are you aware there's an underground shelter in back of this building?"

My mouth snapped shut. I hadn't been aware. Rather than admit it, I said, "I would have seen you arrive."

He shrugged. "You sleep during the day. And we're very good at moving through an area without so much as kicking up a dust bloom. I chose this building for a reason. It's on the edge of town and there's a very nice woods behind it that gave us good cover until we got close to the shelter. It wasn't nearly as hard as you seem to think."

He must have sensed he finally had my attention because he released my wrist. "I'm not hiding in

Render. I'm looking for people who are strong enough to stand up to the Body."

I frowned. "You expect me to believe there's nobody in Indy who can stand up to them?"

"There are a few, he conceded. But the strongest are part of the Body. I need rebels. I need people who are good at hiding what they can do. In other words, I need people just like you and Sis and Mitch and Della."

Realization brought my eyes wide. "You came to recruit us?"

"No. Well, maybe. But only once I'd proven to myself that you were suited to the job."

I dropped my butt onto the nearest piece of furniture, feeling slightly dazed by his revelation. Then I remembered what had brought me there. I looked at him. "How are the attacks we've been experiencing tied to Indy?"

He blinked in surprise.

I realized he hadn't made the connection. "They have to be," I argued. "What I said before...about the attacks starting after you arrived here. That was true. If you think about it, you have to admit it to yourself."

"I don't know. Besides, I'd been here for three weeks before you realized I was here. Secrecy was key to getting those people safely away. You don't know when I came, so you can't tie the attacks to me."

I wouldn't be so sure about that, I thought. "I know you've been watching us for over two weeks."

He hid his surprise well. Inclining his head, Hawk laughed softly. "I guess I'd better brush up on my reconnaissance skills."

"Why were you watching us?" I asked, not because it mattered anymore. But because I'd been wondering for a while and just wanted to know.

"Habit, I guess. I've had to be very careful. I make it a practice to know who's around me and what they're capable of. We're working on moving the next bunch of refugees and I didn't want to bring them into an unsafe situation."

I didn't believe him. I wasn't sure why. He didn't give anything away by look or movement. But something told me that had been a lie.

We sat in silence for a few moments as I tried to absorb his story. I was willing to admit he could have done what he'd said. It was plausible. But there were still a couple of things that weren't plausible. One was his excuse for watching me. The other...

"Tell me what you are, Hawk."

His brow furrowed. "I did..."

I shook my head. "No. You didn't. You gave me your profession. But you have magic. And even Mitch couldn't tell me what you are. Only that he wasn't sure if you were good or evil." If Hawk's story was true, Mitch's confusion finally made sense. "*What* are you, Hawk?"

He seemed to be considering my question. I figured he was trying to decide whether to lie or not. Finally, he lifted his gaze and locked it on mine.

And proceeded to rock my world with three little words.

"I'm a daemon."

20

I stared at him, a huge lump in my throat. "You're a demon?"

His expression tightened slightly. "Not a demon. A daemon. Long *A* sound."

"Aside from pronouncing it differently, what's the difference?" I asked, my muscles tightening for flight. I glanced quickly at the door dividing the house from the big garage.

Could I get to Boyle before Hawk reached me?

"Daemons are protective spirits," he said, a knowing look on his handsome face. I could tell by the way his jaw had tightened, he was annoyed. He was probably used to the reaction I was having. "This is why I didn't want to tell you. I think I've more than proven that I don't mean you and Boyle harm, Glynn."

He was right. He'd certainly helped us a few

times. But that made me wonder if he was just trying to get into our good graces before doing whatever dastardly thing he was going to do. I shifted sideways on my chair, ready to plant my feet and make a run for it.

Hawk sighed. "You don't have to run." He crossed his arms over his chest. "I'm not going to try to stop you. Go ahead if you have to."

I stood up.

"But just know this. Something bad is coming, and you're going to need my help to stop it."

An uncomfortable feeling razored through me at the words that everybody around me kept repeating like a mantra. I narrowed my eyes on him. "What's coming?"

"I don't know…"

I shook my head. "If you know something's coming, you must know what it is."

"I promise you, I don't."

"Then how do you know there's trouble heading this way?"

"When you teased me about sniffing magic at Della's the other night…"

I let my eyes narrow further.

"That was truer than you know. Before I left MI…"

When I frowned, he clarified. "Magical Indy."

I nodded.

"I was part of a special tactical group there. We

were responsible for finding non-registered magic users and bringing them before the Body to be tested."

I slid back into my chair, interested despite myself. "For what purpose?"

His expression tightened. "To be judged and given designations."

"Designations?"

"Yes. The Body controls everything in MI, Glynn. Those who live there have no choice in what they do, who they associate with, how they live their lives. It's a good system if you're at the top." He shrugged. "But if you're not lucky enough to have the right kind of magic in the right amounts..."

"You become a slave," I finished, horror making it hard to breathe. I'd known on some level that I needed to avoid the Body and Indy. Until that moment I hadn't known why. "That's horrifying," I told him.

"Yeah. It is."

"So you decided to do something about it," I guessed.

"I did. Whenever I located someone whose magical energy was low or a target for an undesirable designation, I held them back until I could interrogate them to determine if they were candidates for rescue."

I frowned. "Wasn't that dangerous? Any one of

those people might try to buy their own freedom by giving away yours."

He nodded. "That is always a concern."

"You did all this by yourself?"

"No. There is...was a small group."

"Was?"

Pain flashed across his face. "Some of us were discovered. A couple of us were killed and the rest scattered with as many refugees as we could take with us. My cover hasn't been blown completely yet. I was already out of Indy when everything hit."

"You're going to try to stay with the Body?" I wasn't sure how I felt about that. I'd called him a coward for leaving, but after what he'd told me, staying seemed nearly as bad.

Hawk's gaze sharpened. "All I did was buy myself some time. It won't last long. But the longer we have a contact inside the city the better."

I thought about his story for a moment, trying to wrap my head around it. Guilt clutched my gut with dagger-like claws. All that evil happening a little over an hour away, within the walls of Magical Indy, and I'd been happy to hide in Render. Safe from all of it.

I'd never spared a single thought for what was happening there. On some level, I suspected I didn't want to know. Because then I'd have to do something about it.

Shame heated my cheeks. "I'm sorry. I didn't realize..."

He shrugged. "Don't feel guilty for surviving the best way you know how. You have a life here. I'm not sure I would have risked losing it either if I'd been in the same situation."

It was kind of him to say. But did nothing to ease my guilt.

Suddenly, Sissy's parents' denial of her magic and their seeming indifference that allowed her to stay in Render took on another flavor altogether. The realization hit me like a fist on the nose. *They'd been protecting her.*

Had she known? Somehow I doubted my best friend could stay silent about the kind of thing Hawk was describing. No doubt her parents had protected her from it, keeping her in the dark.

What about Art?

Stars burst in front of my eyes. If I hadn't been sitting, I might have passed out. "Son of a bunion," I murmured.

"What's wrong?" Hawk asked.

My gaze lifted to his. "My brother. He works for the Body."

Hawk frowned. "I know."

"But..." I stared into space for a moment, swallowing hard. Then I leaned forward and clasped Hawk's wrist in a frantic grip. "He's been trying to open the portal."

Hawk's neutral mask slid away. "Are you sure?"

"I've seen him with my own eyes. Twice. The last time he nearly managed it." I let go of Hawk, twining my fingers together nervously. "I didn't even realize he had the power to do it. I believed that was why he left after Grams died." Leaving me to pick up the pieces and protect the portal and Render.

Hawk's gaze was intense. "Glynn, are you aware what that means? If Artur shouldn't have a power that he currently displays..."

"He got it from someone else," I finished, all the pieces sliding together at last. "It's worse than you think, I told Hawk.

"I'm not sure that's possible," he growled out.

My eyes found his. "Art's not functioning under his own steam. In fact, he might not even know what he's doing."

"What do you mean?" Hawk asked.

I described the way Art had moved, the glassy gaze, the fact that he didn't seem to remember what he'd done.

Hawk shook his head. "You can't believe him, Glynn. He could be trying to make you think you were dealing with something harmless like sleep-walking."

"I thought of that. But I know my brother, Hawk. He's not consciously trying to open the portal. I'd stake my life on that."

"You very well might be," the daemon growled,

pushing out of his seat to pace the room. "You might be staking everybody's life on it."

Boyle! I thought, my chest tightening enough to cut off my breath. "I'll talk to Artur."

Hawk shook his head. "You're too close to this. I'll talk to him."

"No!" I stood up, glaring at him. "You'll kill him." I hadn't even realized I'd been considering that possibility until the words leaped from my mouth to slice the space between us.

Hawk slammed his big hands onto the table, his expression hard. "Do you realize what will happen if the wrong person gets hold of that portal?"

"Of course I do!"

"Yet, you'll allow it to fall into potentially evil hands?"

"My brother's not evil!" I yelled.

"You just told me you don't think he's doing this himself. You can't have it both ways, Glynn!"

I opened my mouth to argue.

"Glynnie?"

The tiny, unsure voice made me clamp my lips closed on the vitriol I wanted to spew in Hawk's direction. I turned to find Boyle standing just inside the door, one hand resting on Nicht's broad back as if for comfort.

I forced a smile. "Hey, sweet boy."

"Why is you and Hawk tho mad, Glynnie?" The soft lisp told me he was scared and it broke my heart.

My gaze caught Hawk's, filled with warning. "We're not mad, honey. We're just talking about something important." I lowered my voice, filling it with steel. "I will talk to my brother. The portal is my responsibility. I will do what needs to be done, and you will stay out of it. Are we clear?"

A vein jumped in his jaw as he compressed it so hard it was a wonder he didn't break a tooth. His eyes were hard. "See that you handle it, Glynn. Because, if you don't, I can promise you that I will."

I held his gaze long enough to let him know I wasn't backing down. And then whipped around and strode toward the door, scooping Boyle into my arms as I slammed a hand against the door and shoved it open.

I didn't slow my footsteps until I was back on Victoria's lawn.

And then I pulled Boyle against me and wrapped him in a comforting hug. He vibrated against me. I felt like the worst kind of parent for having scared him. "It will be okay, sweet boy."

"You thure, Glynnie? Hawk wath really mad."

I kissed his tiny nose. "I'm sure, honey. I'm going to make this right. I promise." But even as I opened Victoria's front door and stepped into safety, I couldn't push the worry away that I had lied to Boyle. That I couldn't make it right.

Not without doing something terrible to my only living relative.

Hawk watched her disappear into Victoria. Anger raged with fear in his mind, prickling against his skin like a physical presence. She was in terrible danger. He knew it with the certainty of long experience. The Body was coming. He had little doubt of that. He'd recognized the foul stench of the Magistrate's magic in the lizard creature that had attacked them. He'd smelled it all the way from inside the station. He'd run out the door just in time to see it step from a weak, wobbly gateway, pulsing on the edge of Glynn's property.

So close to her home.

Too close.

If the Magistrate was involved, everyone in Render was in danger. Hawk watched Glynn's front door close and started to pace. He had to do something. If her brother was working for the Magistrate, a near certainty in Hawk's mind, he would bring the Body to Glynn's doorstep and hand them the portal.

Stubborn woman! Why wouldn't she listen to reason?

In an act of pure desperation, Hawk yanked the phone from his pocket and began punching buttons. A moment later, a smooth voice answered. "Yeah?"

Hawk's gaze slipped one last time to Glynn's house, and then he turned and headed into the station. "We have a problem."

My stomach twisted with dread and I was finding it impossible to sit still. I'd asked Sissy to take Boyle to her house while I spoke to Art. She'd been full of questions, especially after seeing the expression on my face. But I'd put her off, promising her I'd tell her what was going on as soon as I could.

Artur hadn't been home when Boyle and I returned from Hawk's. He hadn't left a note and wasn't answering his phone.

I couldn't imagine where he'd gone, but a tiny part of me hoped he'd gone back to Indy. If he'd left, I wouldn't have to do what I was about to do.

Of course, I couldn't be that lucky.

Twenty minutes later, Art opened the door and came inside. He jerked to a surprised stop when he saw me waiting for him. "Glynn? Is something wrong?"

My face must have given me away. "You tell me, Art." Okay, that hadn't been how I'd planned to start. My voice was confrontational, and I watched my brother bristle at the sound of it.

"What are you talking about?"

"Where were you just now?"

He frowned. "Just out for a run. Why?" He glanced around. "Where's Boyle? Is he okay?"

His question caught me off guard and made my

heart hurt. His first thought was for the baby. I was such a jerk for thinking the worst of him. I sighed. "He's fine. Can you come sit down?"

When he hesitated, I added, "Please?"

He complied, his worried gaze finding mine. "You're scaring me, sis. What's wrong?"

I sat too and stared down at my hand for a minute, trying to find the words to ask what I needed to ask.

"Glynn?"

I took a deep breath and plunged in. "I know you've been trying to open the portal, Art. I need to know why?" I'd tried to soften the accusation with a softer tone. But I didn't get the hostile reaction I'd expected.

Art frowned, looking confused. "I'm not trying to open the portal. Why would I do that? You and I both know I don't have that kind of power."

"Yes, I thought I knew that. But I saw you myself. Last night you managed to get the portal nearly all the way open."

He paled. "That's not possible!"

I watched him carefully. Art seemed truly shocked.

"I can assure you it happened. You seemed..." I dug deep for the right word and finally said, "I spoke to you and you didn't hear me."

"You mean like I was sleep-walking?"

"Maybe." I narrowed my gaze. "Are you telling me you really didn't know?"

He hesitated a fraction of a second and my stomach twisted with dread. "Art?"

"I didn't know. I promise, Glynn. But…"

"But?" I nudged when he didn't go on.

He looked down at his hands. I noticed that the skin was still angry-looking where he'd been burned by the portal. I'd given him first aid but hadn't asked Sissy to heal it. Guilt tightened my chest. "I'll admit that I wondered where I'd gotten these burns." He lifted a haunted gaze to me. "Glynn, what if I'd opened it? What if you hadn't caught me?"

"That would have been bad, Art. Very bad," I told him. I didn't bother to hide my concern. He needed to be fully aware of the reason for my next words.

I was afraid that he'd never forgive me for them otherwise.

"That's why…" I hesitated, the words tasting like excrement on my tongue. I shook my head. "Art, I'm afraid you need to leave Victoria."

21

Art and I stared at each other for a long moment. I tried to read a reaction in his expression, decipher it from his steady gaze. But he'd all but grown up in the political Magical Body. He'd learned to mask his emotions well.

My pulse pounded with fear. I didn't want to fight with my brother. I didn't want to have to come out and tell him to his face that I didn't trust him. But, I began to realize he was going to force me to do it.

The floor beneath my feet rolled a warning. The door trembled.

My gaze shot toward the door. "Somebody's here."

Art's face didn't change.

I realized he hadn't read Victoria's warnings. He might be a political creature, but he'd never paid attention to his heritage. I'd learned the language of the house as a small child, sitting on Grams' knee.

"It's someone Victoria doesn't trust." I glanced toward the ceiling before remembering Boyle was with Sissy. Good. He was safe.

As I started toward the door, Art grabbed my wrist. His eyes were bright with a silent plea.

I shook my head. "We need to deal with this. Then we'll talk."

He relaxed noticeably. In that moment I realized he'd been stiff with unhappiness.

The floor rolled again, slightly harder the second time. The boards rippled from the threshold of the front door toward the back of the house, as if trying to pull me away from whatever waited on the porch. My pulse spiked and my heart beat hard against my ribs. Whoever it was, Victoria really didn't want me to answer the door.

I took a moment to check the nullification warding on Victoria, finding it fully engaged, and then opened the front door.

A man stood on the porch. He was tall, with graying black hair and piercing blue eyes. The visitor was dressed unrelievedly in black, wearing a black shirt under a black coat with fashionably long tails and wide lapels. His slacks were also black. They were a narrow cut, fitting him tightly enough that they looked like they would restrict movement. But I knew better. I might be a country mouse by choice, but I was aware of what the magical elites in Indy wore. If only from Sissy's laughing descriptions. His clothing looked fussy and restrictive, but the black cloth had been spelled to shift as needed. To support any movement or shape the magic-user chose.

My visitor's cold gaze scraped over me, brimming with disdain. The man's smile was little more than a curling of his upper lip. "Miss Glynn, I presume?"

I blinked as something cold and invasive tested me, looking for signs of the magic I had locked down and hidden from his probing energy.

I gritted my teeth against reacting to the invasion. Any reaction on my part would be the end of my autonomy and my time in Render. "Can I help you?"

"He's looking for me," my brother said, his tone dull.

I turned to find Artur standing just behind me. His gaze was on the coldly severe face of the man on my porch. "Magistrate."

I blinked, stepping to the side but not away. I didn't want the man to think I was inviting him inside.

"Artur, how are you, son?"

My gaze slid to Art, finding him stiff and unhappy. That was curious. Unless I missed my guess, the man on my porch was Magistrate Cole Martin, Artur's boss at the Body.

"What are you doing here, sir?" Art responded.

Martin made a face that seemed to express disappointment, hurt and surprise all at once. No small feat. "I was worried about you. I came to see how you're doing." He skimmed the yard and the street a glance, the curl in his thin lips deepening. "You're out here in the wild and all alone." He laughed, the sound like the chuff of a feral hound. "I hadn't heard from you."

"I'm hardly alone in the wild, sir," Art said, frowning. "As you can see, I'm with my sister and..." He stopped abruptly, and I realized he'd been about to mention Boyle. I wasn't sure how the Body was handling magical species who weren't humanoid, but I could guess. And my guess was that Boyle would be treated no better than a rabid dog. "And her neighbors," Art finished smoothly. If I hadn't been paying attention, I might have missed the slight hesitation.

But I had been.

And so had Martin. His icy gaze tightened. "I see. Well, now that I'm here..." He lifted hands that were without callouses, with nails that were perfectly manicured. His message was clear.

My stomach twisted as I realized I had to let him inside. If I didn't, he'd know that I felt his magical hostility. I couldn't afford that.

Besides, like Art, I was curious as to why the man had come.

I stepped back. Forcing a smile, I said, "Goddess, where are my manners. Please, come inside. Can I get you something to drink? Coffee? Tea?"

"Just a glass of water, please," he said as he slid a disapproving look around my tatty but comfortable living room.

I forced myself to ignore his judgmental glances, swinging an arm toward the couch. My gaze fell on the knitted throw still laying across the furniture and I reached for it, using the pretense of folding it to take it into the kitchen with me. Like everything in Victoria, the blanket held a residual stain of Grams' prodigious magic. It had provided me hours of comfort in the years since Grams had died. But I couldn't risk the Magistrate sensing the magic.

"You look well," Martin said to Art.

"I'm feeling much better, sir. Thank you for checking up on me." Artur's tone was colorless and without inflection. I was sure that even someone as self-involved and superior as the magistrate would hear the coolness behind the words.

"Not at all. I had business in this area anyway. I just thought I'd stop in and check up on you."

"Oh?" Art said, sounding genuinely interested. "What business?"

I thought of Mitch, and my stomach twisted. Had the magistrate found him? Was that why he'd disappeared? Had they come back to search for others like the Seer?

The thought turned my spine to ice.

I filled a glass with water and carried it back into the living room just in time to see Martin wave a dismissive hand. "None of your concern. Just busywork." Martin glanced up, his smile cold. "Thank you, dear."

"You're welcome." I skimmed a glance toward Art, finding his expression closed off, his gaze carefully neutral. "I'll just leave you to visit."

Martin swallowed a sip of water and shook his head. "Not at all, dear. Please, sit and visit with me for a bit. I'll admit to curiosity about Artur's sister. I've heard so much about you."

"Oh?" I said, worry tightening my chest. "What have you heard?" I forced my legs to carry me to a chair near the fire and sat. It was as far from our visitor as I could get without leaving the room.

Martin made the dismissive gesture again. It was apparently his, *you're too simple to understand*, signal. "Just a proud brother's fond ramblings, I assure you." He fixed a speculative gaze on me.

My palms started to sweat.

I wasn't sure what to say. I'd barely spoken to Art for two years. When we'd parted last, it hadn't been under the best terms. He'd tried to get me to abandon the portal and come to Indy with him. That had been the last thing I'd wanted. But Art was looking at me with a plea in his brown eyes. I didn't know what he wanted me to say. I decided on the simple truth.

"It's been a while since I've seen him. I was glad he could come for a visit."

The Magistrate inclined his head. "I'm sure." He plucked at something on his slacks. "It's a shame you must be separated, given that he's the only family you have."

I tensed. That was a dangerous subject. I had no idea what Art had told him about our situation, so I said nothing.

Martin seemed to take my silence as a sign to stick his nose deeper into my business. "I understand you're sensitive about not sharing your brother's prodigious magic..."

I blinked, keeping my gaze on the magistrate by sheer force of will. I wanted to glare at Art for spreading lies about me. But then, I realized he'd done me a favor. If the Body believed I was magically useless, they'd probably leave me alone.

"I don't know if you're aware, Glynn, but there are many things a nonproficient can do in Indy. You could create a very nice life for yourself there."

"Nonproficient?" I tasted the word, swallowing the insult framed within it.

"Yes, you know, the non-magic. It's nothing to be ashamed of, dear. We all have our strengths. Magic isn't the only important thing."

"No?" My smile was strained. "What other

important things are there?" I asked with forced pleasantness. Hawk's terrible story about how "non-proficient" people were treated in the magical city danced through my mind.

Hawk! If the Magistrate became aware that his magic sniffer was across the street, what would happen to him?

"...shops and restaurants..." Martin was saying. "Magical Indianapolis is just like any other city, dear. Everyone needs to eat and shop, no matter how magically inclined they are."

I finally turned to Art. He sat mutely, staring at me. I couldn't read the emotion in his expression.

I nodded, smiling as I stood. "I'll certainly keep that in mind," I told Martin, my gaze locked on Art's.

"Please do, dear," the man said in a cool but pleasant tone. "I'm sure Artur would appreciate having you there with him."

I made my escape upstairs as quickly as I could, my mind spinning. Why had the man really shown up at Victoria? Why had he been badgering me to move to Indy? If he truly had no idea of my magic or my role in Render, why would he lobby for me to return with my brother?

And what was Art's culpability in the visit?

With a start, I realized Artur had not looked the least bit surprised when Martin appeared at my door. Had the magistrate's arrival been planned? And, if so, why?

Then I thought of Art's seemingly unaware visits to the portal. My pulse sped and a deep cold moved into my bones. Was Martin the reason Art had tried to open the portal?

It would make sense. I detected powerful magic within the Magistrate. Which, of course, made sense. He was one of only thirteen ruling members at the Body. Only the most powerful sat on the Regnant Bench, the ruling elites of the city.

So, what would one of the city's elites want with me?

Then it hit me. It wasn't me they wanted.

They were after the portal and its almost infinite power.

And I suddenly found it hard to breathe.

22

I hovered in the shadows at the top of the stairs, trying to hear what Art and the Magistrate were discussing. The conversation seemed fairly mundane, focused on people and things I didn't know. None of it seemed imperative. But there was an undercurrent in their voices that told me there was more to the conversation than it appeared.

The front door flew open and Hawk strode in, his face dark with rage. Hawk's gaze was locked on the Magistrate, and he looked ready to bite nails. "What are you doing here?"

Martin tensed briefly, his cool gaze heating with sudden pique. Then the anger melted away and he gave Hawk a smile. "Well, look what the universe dragged in." He clasped his hands around his crossed knees, sparks all but flashing from the stormy ocean of his blue gaze. "I could ask you the same question, dog." He laughed when Hawk tensed, fists clenching at his sides. "Although I shouldn't be surprised, I guess, that you'd come sniffing around here. Miss Glynn is a very pretty young woman."

Ice formed on my spine at his words, and Hawk's expression turned hard.

"You have no business in this place," Hawk growled out.

Martin stared at his hands as if they'd touched something filthy. "I'll give you a pass this time, Hunter. But do not presume to speak to me like that again."

Hawk's chest heaved with what looked very much like rage. "I wasn't told you'd be arriving....sir." He ground the last word out through his teeth as if it cost him something to say.

"Funny, Hunter, the last time I checked, I wasn't obligated to keep you apprised of my daily activities."

"Of course not. But if you want me to do my job..."

Icy fingers of dread danced along my nerve endings. *His job? What exactly did that mean?*

"Your job doesn't revolve around my comings and goings." Martin's gaze hardened. "But, since we're on the subject, I believe a report was due to me last week on your findings. I'll expect that in my hands within twenty-four hours. Now leave."

"No."

Martin stiffened. "Excuse me?"

"No...sir. I require a moment of your time." Hawk bent such a tiny amount the bow was really more of a twitch. "If you please."

Martin sighed. He pushed to his feet. "Very well. I believe my business here is finished." He slid an oily smile over Art, whose skin tone had turned slightly green since Hawk had arrived. "Artur, I'll expect you in Indy in the morning."

Art's eyes went wide. "Sir?"

Martin laughed. "You need to finish what you're doing here tonight and report in at ten sharp." He held Art's stare for a long moment, something dark throbbing through the stormy gaze, and then turned toward Hawk. "Walk me out, Hunter."

I watched Martin leave with mixed emotions. Relief warred with worry and fear.

Hawk's gaze rose unerringly to where I stood in the shadows, and I barely bit back a gasp of surprise. The gaze lingered for a moment and then slid away as he followed the older man outside. There'd been a message in that stare, but I couldn't read it. My mind was too busy dealing with the disappointment of learning that he'd been in Render on the Body's business all along.

Everything he'd told me had been a lie.

All of it.

And I'd believed him, despite my better instincts.

I was such a sap.

The door closed, and Art jumped to his feet, hands twining nervously as he paced.

I hurried down the stairs. "What's going on, Art?" I asked.

He shook his head. "I wish I knew." His head came up as if he could hear my disbelief. "I promise, I don't. I didn't come here with any plans except to rest and think."

"And yet, you've spent a good part of the time down in the basement, trying to open the portal," I said, my voice filled with the suspicion I couldn't help feeling.

Was there nobody I could trust?

Art stopped pacing. His face paled as if he'd had a sudden thought. "Glynn, I swear on Grams' grave I didn't come to Render to cause trouble. I don't know why Martin showed up here. He usually doesn't pay any attention to me. I'm just an assistant...one of five. I've made it a practice to keep a low profile at the Body for just this very reason. I didn't want Martin sniffing around the family business."

I watched him carefully and couldn't help feeling like he was telling me the truth. "You didn't know he was going to come?" I asked my brother.

"I swear I didn't."

"Why do you think he did?"

Art turned away, his shoulders going stiff.

"Art?"

He shook his head. "There's only one reason I can think of." He turned back to me, his face tight with pain. "He knows about the portal. Someone had to have told him."

Yeah, someone, I thought. Someone like a hunter sent from Magical Indy. Someone who'd done his best to insert himself into the goings-on in Render, pretending to be a friend.

My legs gave out and I dropped into the nearest chair.

Someone who knew every secret I'd been trying to guard my whole life.

It had to be Hawk.

"Oh goddess," I whispered, dropping my head into my hands. "We're all in danger."

"You're right," Art said, lowering into a crouch in front of me. "Martin is dangerous. He's evil to the core. But nobody in the Body will believe it. He's hurting people, Glynn. Killing them. But he's able to skate from all of it because he has the connections to keep his activities secret. He's a snake with enough charm to lure people into his evil." Art collapsed onto the carpet as if his legs had given out on him. "And I brought him here."

"Yes," I told him, anger making my voice hard. "You did. But I've made some mistakes too. Big ones." My voice trailed away as I considered how dire our situation was. I scrubbed my hands over my face, jerking them away and fixing Art with an angry look. "But it's too late to worry about any of that." I grabbed his hand. "Could the Magistrate be somehow manipulating you to open the portal?"

He turned white. "What? No!"

"Think about it," I told him. "You claim you don't remember going into the basement. And, after seeing your face...your mannerisms...I believe you. But, unless you're walking in your sleep..."

He emphatically shook his head. "If I was a sleepwalker, I'd have known by now."

"Maybe not," I started to say.

But Art's face hardened. "Yes. I would, Glynn. I spent the first year at the Body in a dormitory with ten other low-level assistants. They were my friends. And something like sleep-walking will get you killed at the Body. It could be used against you and would be a potential tool for someone else to utilize. The Body is a place that respects power and abhors weakness. If they thought I had a weakness that could be leveraged against them..." He shook his head again. "No. The other guys would have told me if I was a sleepwalker. We protected each other."

"If someone craved influence they didn't have, it might seem to them like selling *your* secret would be lucrative."

But he shook his head again. "I just don't believe one of my friends would betray me like that."

"Why?"

"Because we had each other's backs through all the evil crap the Body tried against us."

I thought about that for a minute, not fully convinced. Someone in that position might be really motivated to do whatever was necessary to get out of it.

Art must have seen the doubt in my expression because he went on. "And because they had secrets too. It would have been really risky for any of them to open that can of worms."

"Okay. Then we have to consider that someone is manipulating you."

"Like Hawk?" He frowned.

My own feelings about the hunter might have been influencing me, but I didn't think Art looked like he believed it.

"Maybe. Have you ever met Hawk before coming home?"

"Not that I remember."

"Who would benefit from getting hold of the portal?" I asked, knowing the answer already. I needed Art to verify it for me.

"Who wouldn't? It's a passage into another dimension, Glynn, with the potential for untold power."

What we'd been told from a very early age, was that there were creatures in the dimension at the other end of the portal that contained strange powers not found on Earth. Some of those creatures were dangerous, but others were benign. Anyone looking to gain power from other magic users would quickly recognize the opportunities presented there.

My family had once come from that other dimension. Outvald, they called it. *Other world.* We knew the damage the Body or someone who was equally unscrupulous could do there. It was our job to keep that from happening.

"Yes, but only for someone who knows how to handle it," I said, my chest tightening with fear.

Artur laughed, but there was no humor in the sound. "The powerful elites in MI all think they can do anything. The only thing more potent than their magic is their egos. Any of them would believe they could handle the portal. It would never occur to them that they couldn't."

I sighed. "That doesn't narrow it down much."

"I know."

"What is the Magistrate's magic?"

Art frowned. "As the title implies, he runs the prisons. Indy has one for magical humans and one for non-magical humans. But that's just his job. His power is in finding weaknesses and exploiting them. He reads the energy signatures in reactions, identifying what they mean. For example, if he suggested to Hawk that he might be interested in you, romantically, Martin would read Hawk's energy and realize he'd guessed correctly." Art's eyes narrowed slightly, his gaze a question. "He'd use that against Hawk,

Glynn. Which would put you in Martin's crosshairs."

Goddess's Galoshes! Trying to cultivate a carefree expression, I shook my head. "Hawk isn't interested in me." The very thought made my stomach twist into a painful coil. And sent heat flooding through me.

"It was just an example, Glynn."

So he said. But his face told me he'd believed it.

A quick change of subject was in order. "And Hawk?"

"What about him?"

"What does he *do*, exactly?"

Art's gaze slid to the door. "Hunters sniff out magic and bring in anyone who hasn't been registered by the Body. The Body used to just manage those of us who lived inside the city, but recently they've been sending the dogs..." he flushed. "That's what they call the hunters."

And I'd seen how much Hawk loved that nickname. "Because they smell magic?"

He nodded. "They've been sending them out to scour the countryside looking for unregistered victims."

"Why?" I asked. "Why drag more people into the city?"

"Power. They know there's magic out here that they don't control. Their egos won't allow them to let that situation stand. Besides, the cities have been competing lately. Magical Chicago has been claiming more power than MI, and the Body can't stand it."

I let myself consider that for a moment. The thought that powerful magical humans might try to wrest my independence away from me just because they could, filled me with fear and rage. I shook my head. "Hawk lied to me. He said he'd brought people out of Indy so they could disappear into the countryside."

Art went very still, lines forming between his brows.

I looked at him. "What?"

His gaze slid to the door again, and something flared in it. Something that looked like excitement. "No. It couldn't be."

"Art? What couldn't be?"

He looked at me. "I've heard rumors. But nobody believed them."

"What rumors. Come on, Art, tell me. Hawk might be back any minute."

Art stood up and hurried over to the window, peering through the glass and watching with a narrowed gaze. "The lowest level of magic users in the city are treated worse than dogs," he said, his muscles taut. "Many of them are imprisoned. Those are the lucky ones."

I could have sworn I saw my brother shudder. "Why?"

He finally turned back. "Because they won't submit to having their magic scraped from them. Even the lowest level of user has *some* magic. It isn't much when taken individually, but culled from a hundred, five hundred, a thousand…"

I felt all the blood leave my face. "They're scraping people's magic from them?" Outrage pulsed through me.

"Yes. If they can't make themselves useful to the Body in some other way."

"Goddess," I murmured, horrified.

I thought of Mitch and my stomach twisted. "Will they scrape Mitch?"

The horror throbbing in my voice pulled Art away from the window. He crouched in front of me. "No, Glynnie. I doubt it. He's too valuable. The Body values Seers. There aren't many of them."

I relaxed, but only slightly. "Mitch won't give in to them. He won't help them against his will."

"Then they'll imprison him," Art said.

Something in his face told me that wouldn't be a good outcome. I scrubbed a hand over my face and stood up to pace the room. "We have to get him back."

Art shook his head. "No, Glynn. We have to keep them from getting the portal. That's the real danger here. If we don't stop the Magistrate and the Body from getting the portal, there's no telling how much damage they can do."

He was right. I knew it. Our first priority was the portal.

But I made a silent promise to myself that, as soon as the portal was secure, I was going after my friend.

23

The floor shivered beneath my feet. Panic turned my breath to knives in my chest. Without thinking, I pulled magic from the air and formed it into twin blades that fit my hands like they'd been made for me.

Power shivered along the twelve-inch blades like silvery light and snapped the air at the tips.

Art circled his hand and energy roiled around his fingertips, unfocused but just as deadly for its ability to wash the air with pain and death.

The door opened and Hawk stood silhouetted by the moonlight behind him. His eyes glowed briefly and then dulled. He held up both hands, palms outward. "I'm a friend," he told us.

"I'm not so sure about that," I answered. Power throbbed in my voice, turning it husky as it sliced the air between us.

Hawk shoved his hands into his pockets. "Glynn, I didn't lie to you. What I told you was true."

Art's energy dissipated, and he stared at Hawk as if he was seeing him for the first time. "Are you him?"

Hawk's face tightened. He stepped inside and the night thickened behind him, horking an enormous black dog into Victoria's living room. "Don't believe everything you hear," Hawk said.

I looked from one man to the other. "Is he who? What's he talking about, Hawk?"

"An urban legend. Nothing more."

"You're saying he doesn't exist?" Art asked, looking almost angry.

"No." Hawk bit off the word in a tone that brooked no further discussion. "We need to talk about where we go from here."

"Go?" I asked. "I can't go anywhere. I'm not leaving the portal unprotected."

"Can you move it?" Hawk asked.

I felt my eyes go wide. "Have you lost your mind?"

To my surprise, he chuckled, the sound almost a growl in his throat. "A long time ago, yes. But that has nothing to do with this."

Nicht trotted over and shoved his enormous head into my belly, nearly knocking me off my feet. I scratched his big ears and he tilted into the caress, one of his big feet whacking the air near his belly.

Goofy dog.

"How about closing it down?" Hawk asked.

I frowned, the enormous black head still pressing into my stomach. Years ago, I remembered reading something about that in my Grams' journals, but I couldn't remember much about it. "It's been theorized about. But I don't believe it's ever been done," I told him. Because I did remember that.

"But, it's possible?" His expression was hopeful. If I didn't know better, I'd think he really did want to help us.

"I don't know. I'd need to research it." I fixed him with a hard stare. "But that will take time. If Martin acts quickly, we might not have that much time."

Hawk scraped a hand over his chin, the crackle of his stubble filling the silence. "I'll get us some help in case the Body attacks. But we need to convince your neighbors to leave."

Art and I shared a look. His eyes were as big as mine felt. "They'll never leave," I told Hawk.

"These people," Art added, "—have been here all their lives. They've gotten really good at hiding...at giving up everything but the bare necessities, to stay below the Body's radar so they don't have to leave their homes."

"You need to help me convince them," Hawk said, his gaze locked on mine. "Or they'll be killed."

I finally gave in to the twin pressures of shock

and Nicht's big, hard head, and dropped onto the couch. What he was asking for was impossible. But watching all of them die...all my neighbors... friends...people I'd known all my life.

I suddenly found it hard to pull air into my lungs.

There was movement across the room and Hawk was suddenly crouching down in front of me. "We need to make them understand, Glynnie."

I blinked at the sound of my nickname on his lips. I stared into his handsome face for a long moment, a mixture of emotions roiling through me. The battle between the divergent feelings made me dizzy. For a long moment, I couldn't speak. Then he reached out and placed a hand on my knee.

It was firm and hot and comforting.

And I didn't want that comfort. Not from him.

I placed my hand over his, hesitating only the briefest of moments as his eyes widened, and then shoved the hand away. Nicht lowered himself to his belly with a long sigh.

"You lied to me. Again!"

Hawk didn't look away. He didn't deny. He didn't try to persuade. He only looked into my eyes and showed me the pain in the wide hazel gaze. "Glynn, I want to help."

I could see the sincerity in his eyes. In the tightness of his shoulders. In the proud lift of the square jaw. "Did you really bring people out of Indy? Release them?"

"I did."

"Then why did the Magistrate...?"

"Like I told you, I haven't burned that bridge yet. I'm trying to keep my job for as long as I can. Once they know what I've been doing..."

"You won't be able to save any more people," Art said softly.

Hawk's gaze shot to my brother and settled. "We need to know whose side you're on in this." he told Art.

My brother didn't hesitate. "Glynn's." But his gaze fell, and a new tautness found his shoulders.

Hawk stood, moving to stand slightly in front of me. "But?"

Artur slid me a look. "But, I might be compromised."

Hawk's hands curled into fists. "Compromised how?"

"He's talking about the portal," I said when Art merely glowered back at Hawk. "He has no memory of trying to open it."

Hawk swore softly at the confirmation. "Who's been in your head?"

"I don't know. But I'm going to find out."

"How are you going to do that," I asked.

Art glanced my way. "Sissy can do a scan, can't she?"

Hope flared. "She can."

"The witch?" Hawk asked, his brows lowering. "Does she have enough juice to pull that off?"

Art and I shared a look and, for the first time in what felt like days, shared a real laugh.

———

W e'd pushed all the furniture against the walls and rolled the ancient oriental rug away from the center of the floor. Art, of course, took the opportunity to tweak me about my housekeeping when we uncovered what looked like a few years of debris beneath the rug.

"It's not my fault," I told him after slugging his arm. "Boyle shoves dirt under there so I won't make him clean it up."

"Uh, huh," Art said with a smile.

I slugged him again.

He was sitting cross-legged in the center of the room, surrounded by a chalk circle Sis had drawn on the hardwood floor.

Sis worked around him, placing candles in strategic spots and arranging an array of crystals between the candles.

Boyle rode the hellhound through the house, one arm waving above his head like he was a bronco rider. "What is that on my baby's head?" I asked my friend.

Sis glanced up and grinned. "It's a cowboy hat. He's a cowboy."

I arched a brow in her direction. "It has pictures of fish all over it." I was pretty sure the hat had been Sissy's fishing hat when she was ten years old. The wide brim drooped over Boyle's tiny face, the shock of orange hair between his ears sticking out the front like a bright, silky arrowhead.

Sis shrugged, her lips twitching. "It was the only one I had with a wide brim. He likes it."

I didn't tell her my brother had brought him a cowboy hat. She thought she was making the baby happy and tweaking me at the same time. Why should I spoil her fun?

Hawk was bent over the kitchen table, talking strategy with someone on the phone. I assumed he thought it would be useful should we end up in a confrontation with the Body. I had no idea what he was planning. There was no strategy which would allow us to win that battle.

We simply didn't have enough firepower.

Sis caught me staring at Hawk. I must have been scowling.

"Judging by the glower on your face, I'm guessing you haven't found any magic bullets in Grams' journal?"

Sighing, I ran a hand over the yellowed pages,

my fingers mapping Grams' large, curlicued handwriting and feeling the occasional indentation where she'd pressed too hard with the pen. "It's not that I haven't found any bullets," I told my best friend. "It's that I could be looking at a whole six shooter full of the things and not know it."

Sis raised her brows. "A bit rusty in your Latin?" All trace of Sissy's amusement fled her pretty face, replaced by a decidedly "I told you so" glint. I'd always hated Latin when we were growing up. Sis had excelled in it. She'd nagged me incessantly during our years at Render High, explaining over and over again how important Latin was. It was the language of both magic and science. Which made it more important than anything.

"It's not the Latin. I can read Latin," I told her, narrowing my gaze in defiance. "But Grams used a shorthand type of Latin that completely eludes my deciphering abilities."

Sissy shook her head and returned to her task.

Hawk disconnected and strode into the living room. He looked at me. "Have you found anything?"

I felt my glower deepen. "This will take some time," I told him.

He held my gaze for a moment, and I thought he was going to call my bluff. Then he nodded. "I'm going out to meet someone. I'll be back in a couple of hours."

"Who are you going to meet?" I asked.

He shook his head, sliding his phone into his pocket. I envied him that phone. I hadn't had one since we'd gone into hiding over three years ago. Like electricity, phone service was too easy a trail to follow. "I don't have permission to tell you that. Hopefully, when I get back, I'll be able to fill you all in."

I didn't respond. He wanted us to trust him, but he seemed unwilling to trust us.

"Glynn?"

I resisted looking up. "Yeah?"

The floor creaked and I felt him moving close. My head jerked up when he crouched in front of me. "What?"

He fixed his intense hazel gaze on me. I felt oddly unwilling to look away. "It's not my information to give. This person has a lot to lose by joining our fight. It's not that I want to keep secrets."

I looked for any sign of evasion in his expression and found none. Though, to do what he did, he'd have to be really good at lying. I shrugged.

He stayed there for a moment longer and then brushed my bare ankle with a feather-soft touch— just the tip of one finger. The contact happened so quickly I might have imagined it. And then he stood.

I watched him leave and glanced at Sis. "How much longer until you're ready to perform the spell?"

"Twenty minutes. Maybe more. This is complex."

I made a sudden decision. "I'll be back."

Sis didn't ask me where I was going, but I could feel her gaze burning a spot between my shoulder blades as I left. I climbed the steps to the third floor of the big house. Boyle's bedroom door was open, his room cluttered with toys and strewn with discarded clothes. With everything that had been going on, I hadn't had time to tidy it up for a couple of days.

It was amazing the amount of mess one small gargoyle could make in just two days.

I sighed, grabbing a muddy pair of shoes near the window and dropping them into the laundry basket. I hung up a few shirts and folded some shorts, settling them into a drawer in Boyle's long dresser.

I knew I was putting off the inevitable. I also knew why. Some things were just uncomfortable. I wouldn't do what I was about to do if I had any other way. But my world was tilting on the edge of a dangerous precipice. And I was going to need some help to save it.

Finally, when I'd delayed as long as I dared, I settled cross-legged onto Boyle's bed, closing my eyes. I rested my hands on my knees, palms up to give the energy an open space within which to move. With a final, deep sigh, I pulled the energy I needed forward.

The first thing I noticed was her scent. It had

always been distinctive, a combination of vanilla, lavender, and clean sweat.

Grams had worked hard all her life. She'd worked with her hands, bending her back into every task. She'd never sought out the ease of machines to do her work. As far back as I could remember, she'd washed her clothes by hand and had done every job in Victoria without the advantage of electricity or mechanized tools. Where Grams had grown up, electricity hadn't been a thing. And she'd clung to those early experiences until the day she died.

Grams eased into view. The familiar sight of her, rocking back and forth in her favorite wooden rocker, nearly made me smile. The light played over her slender form, indistinct and wavering. The diffuse illumination stole a dozen years from her face and softened the droop in her narrow shoulders as she worked at something in her lap.

"Hello, Grams," I said, the hands resting on my knees burning slightly as the calling magic oozed through my palms.

She turned as if surprised, her wiry gray hair falling into her eyes with the sudden movement. She shoved it away, favoring me with a wide, sweet smile. "Child. What a nice surprise."

In my mind, I unfolded myself from the bed and walked over to her, bending to kiss her soft, crepey cheek.

Her touch slipped over my face, rough with

callouses and dry from spending too much time in soapy water. Beyond her usual scent, her skin held the familiar aroma of portal magic.

I always wondered if mine held the same scent. I suspected it did.

"You're looking well," I said.

She barked out her familiar laugh. "Liar. But things are not nearly as difficult here as they were. I'm getting the rest I need." Her gnarled hand cupped my chin with fond tenderness. "How is your brother?"

I didn't stop the impulsive roll of my eyes because it had always made her laugh. Most adults found sibling bickering tiring. Grams had always been amused by ours. "She used to say it was a sign that we were forging our own ways. And that, in the end, we'd be all the better for it.

But her sharp features folded into a frown. "What's wrong, Glynnie?"

The fond nickname in her voice nearly brought me to tears. She'd always called me that, never using my full name, Glynneth. I hated that name. And with her usual intuition, Grams had known.

I wrapped my fingers around her warm, calloused hand. "We have trouble, Grams. I need your help."

"Of course, dear. What can I do?"

"Tell me about the portal. How does Victoria protect it?"

24

I descended the stairs to the living room a half-hour later, my mind spinning. I found Art still in a cross-legged position in the center of the circle, eyes closed.

He was levitating a foot above the floor.

A painful pressure clogged my ears and made my skin feel tighter than normal. The candle flames flickered in an unnatural rhythm, their light a dancing golden glow against the walls. Between the candles, the crystals glowed steadily, their illumination throwing fractured light that bathed Art in geometric patterns of silver, purple, and green.

Sis stood at the apex of a triangle she'd drawn around the circle, its curved lines bisecting each of the three "walls" of the triangle at their exact center.

My friend's eyes glowed with an eerie yellow

light. Matching yellow energy sifted through the air above her raised palms.

As I stepped down onto Victoria's living room floor, the glow left Sissy's eyes. The candle flames rose a dozen inches above their waxy columns, and the clogging pressure popped.

Art's body slowly dropped to the floor and his eyes opened. He looked dazed, his eyes blank. He stared straight ahead, but I got the impression he wasn't seeing what was in front of him.

Sissy walked over to me as the light slowly died from the crystals. She looked tired. She dropped heavily to a step and rubbed her temples in small, tight circles. "He's definitely under the influence of someone."

The weight of worry in my gut grew heavier. "Can you tell who?"

"No. I wish I could." She frowned. "But it's someone powerful. And the foreign energy has been building for a while, slowly accumulating at his core."

"Like how long? Are we talking weeks? Months?"

"Years," Sis told me, looking worried. "At least three years."

Art had lived at the Body headquarters since becoming an intern at eighteen. "It's someone at the Body," I told my friend.

She nodded. "Most likely. Or, at least, someone in Indy."

I contemplated her words for a moment, considering the possibilities. "A friend?" I asked, thinking about what Art had told me about the other ten assistants he trusted with his secrets.

Sissy thought about it for a beat. Finally, she shook her head. "Hopefully not. To do this to someone is..." She frowned. "This is the worst kind of invasion, Glynn."

I thought about that. "It would be someone he spends enough time around to create a deep, slow layering of the intrusive energy."

She nodded.

"Can you sever the connection," I asked, my voice hopeful.

Sissy's expression was sad, touched with pity. "No. I'm sorry. If I knew who'd placed it...maybe."

I shook my head. "I don't understand. Art has very little magic."

Sissy's eyes went wide. "You're wrong, Glynn. Your brother is brimming with magic."

"That's impossible. He's never shown any signs of it," I objected.

"That might be," she told me. "But he's very powerful."

My gaze slid to my brother, who sat unnaturally still, his gaze blank. "Why would he hide it from us?"

Sissy shrugged. "He might not know how to access it. Or he might not have *wanted* to access it." Her gaze held mine, filled with unspoken meaning.

Memories slid through my mind. Artur resisting Grams's instruction, disappearing to play with his friends, messing up his portal homework so badly it didn't seem possible. His almost gleeful declaration that, since I was so obviously better suited to protecting the portal, he was going to go to Indy and find something else to do.

I'd supported him then—even been happy that he was taking his lack of magic so well. If I'd known...

Anger burned hot in my breast. He'd left me to bear the full weight of our family's legacy because he hadn't wanted to be tied down. He'd wanted to go sow his wild oats. Enjoy life. And he'd thrown me to the wolves to gain his freedom from responsibility.

Sissy's eyes widened. "Simmer down, Glynnie," she warned.

I looked at her. She nodded toward my hands. I followed the direction of her stare and flinched. Angry energy swirled between my fists, biting the air in a deadly arc.

I forced my magic to recede. "I want him out of Victoria."

Sissy looked sad. "I'm so sorry."

I didn't respond. I was too mad.

Victoria's walls shivered in warning. I quickly yanked the magic back to my fists and turned to face the front door.

It opened and Hawk stood silhouetted against the darkness beyond. His gaze slid over the energy spitting at my fists and one eyebrow lifted in question. "Can we come in?"

I blinked. "We?"

He stepped aside to reveal a woman standing on the porch behind him. She stepped into the light, her deep-set eyes sparking with unnatural energy as the golden illumination of the lamp hit them. She was almost as tall as Hawk, broad-shouldered and narrow hipped, with smooth, tanned skin and dark eyes the color of an evergreen forest. Her long blonde hair was pulled back from her face and twined into a thick braid that fell over one shoulder, resting on the full curve of one breast. She wore a black tee under a black leather jacket that dipped in at her narrow waist and flared slightly over her hips. Her long legs were encased in tight black leather, and short leather boots covered her narrow feet.

The hilt of a sword showed over one shoulder, and two large guns of some kind rested in holsters at her hips. She looked like a warrior princess.

"Glynn, this is Alina."

The woman inclined her chin and then skimmed her fiery gaze over Sissy, quickly dismissing her. The dark green gaze widened slightly when she saw Art, the first sign of emotion she'd shown since she arrived.

"You know my brother?" I asked, my voice slightly hostile.

She jerked her gaze away from Art and narrowed it on me. "We've met."

Her voice was deep and smooth—beyond sexy. Alina was perfection from head to toe.

I hated her on sight.

"Alina and I work together," Hawk said, tension on the word "work" as if there was hidden meaning there. Was he telling me she was part of the network sneaking low-magic humans out of Indy? If so, they wouldn't want to speak of it in front of Art.

I slid my brother a look and found him still staring blankly into space.

Hawk nodded as if he'd taken a message from my worried glance. "Is he in stasis?" Hawk asked Sissy.

She nodded. "Until I release him."

The two sniffers walked into the room and the door swung quietly shut behind them.

"What did you find?" Hawk asked my friend.

Sissy filled him in on what she'd told me.

Hawk stared at Art for a long moment, his expression tight. Finally, he said, "He's a liability. He needs to go."

I knew he was right. I'd had the exact same thought myself. But it didn't stop me from getting my back up about it. "That's not your decision to make," I told him angrily.

He opened his mouth and then snapped it shut, apparently deciding to let that particular disagreement simmer between us for a while. Instead, he said, "Alina has news from MI."

Sissy and I looked at the intimidating hunter.

Alina gave us a smile that turned my bowels to water. "As suspected, we've learned that the Body is behind the recent attacks here in Render. They've been cultivating a stable of magical boogies for years, intending to create magical weapons."

Sissy and I just stared at her, our eyes wide. Finally, I asked, "Where are they getting them from? Those things aren't from this dimension." I thought of the lizard thing that had stepped out of my vision onto the streets of Render.

She shook her head. "The Magistrate has been able to open limited-use portals to other dimensions. He's gotten many of them through those portals. Some, like the wraith, were created by feeding terrifying amounts of magic into unwilling victims to see what would happen." Her lips compressed into a thin line, her expression grim. "Much of the energy he's harvesting goes to his experiments."

"Harvesting?" Sissy asked. I hadn't thought she could get any paler. But then Sis had always been an over-achiever.

"I'll explain later," I murmured, not wanting to sideline the conversation right at that moment. To

Hawk and Alina, I said, "If the Magistrate already knows how to gain access to other dimensions, maybe he doesn't really want Victoria's portal."

"I wish that were true," Alina said in her rich, smooth voice. "But his gateways are unpredictable and take a tremendous amount of energy to create. They last for only a few minutes. He craves the ability to come and go into other dimensions at will."

"This all just reinforces my point," Hawk told me. "If Martin gets hold of your portal, think of how much damage he can do."

I frowned, crossing my arms over my chest. "Art is not going to be sacrificed to the Magistrate's lust for power," I insisted.

"Be reasonable, Glynn," Hawk said. "Your brother is under the control of someone. We don't know who it is. And you've caught him trying to open the portal twice already. If he stays, our enemy will have someone inside who can undermine everything we try to do. And we'll be fighting this battle on two fronts."

His argument was perfectly reasonable. I even agreed with him. But the space between agreement and action was too large for me to travel at the moment. "He stays. At least until we know what's going on. We might be over-reacting. We might not even be under attack."

Hawk and Alina stared at me, and I couldn't help

thinking they were judging my intelligence for keeping my brother close. I didn't blame them. I didn't really think it was smart either. But he was family. The only family I had left. And his situation wasn't his fault.

Not entirely.

"I can take him to my house," Sissy offered. "I'll ward the house so he can't leave."

I frowned. If whoever was riding Art decided Sissy was in his way, he might use my brother to hurt her. "I don't want to put you at risk."

"I can take care of myself," Sissy argued, visibly annoyed at my lack of confidence.

"I know you can, Sis. But they've already taken Mitch," I told her. "He was the most careful of all of us."

"Your brother can't find out what Alina and I have been up to," Hawk said. "He'll jeopardize our entire operation."

"If the Body comes after the portal, your operation is lost anyway."

"Not entirely," Alina said. "We have other... outlets for our work."

She was telling me they used other small towns outside the city to move their people through. Of course they did. It only made sense. If they always moved into one area, the Body would become suspicious.

I thought about my options, not liking any of them.

"The decision doesn't belong solely to you," Hawk finally said. His tone was soft, but the resolve behind them was rock solid. I knew he was right.

Still.

"I can monitor the witch's house," Alina offered. "Keep an eye on things there. If she needs me, I can be there within seconds."

I didn't like it but saw no way around it. Hawk was right. Too many people had a stake in what was about to happen. I didn't have the right to jeopardize it all to protect my brother. I nodded. "Okay. But he's not going to like it," I said.

"I can keep him in partial stasis until we get him settled at my place," Sissy said. "Once the wards are in place, I'll release him and explain the situation."

I stared at Art for a long moment. He'd never forgive me. And I didn't blame him. "Okay. But I'd like Hawk to be there when you tell him. Just in case."

"No," Hawk said.

"No?" I asked, incredulous.

"Alina can handle that. He knows her. I'm going to be doing something more important."

I knew my eyes flashed with anger, but I didn't bother to restrain it. "What could be more important than protecting my best friend?"

"Saving the people of Render," he told me. "You

and I are going to get them together and convince them to leave."

———

W e decided to hold the meeting at Della's house because it was warded the best of any of the homes around us except for Victoria. Since I was the one coming to them with an impossible request, I thought it would be best to hold the meeting on relatively neutral ground.

Della didn't seem surprised to find us at her door. Which surprised *me*. Then again, things clearly were changing rapidly in Render. It wasn't exactly a leap to find out we had a problem that needed discussing.

Inside her home, Della looked solid again, her white hair thick and shiny and her silver eyes clear. The blue ring around her irises was so dense it nearly covered the silver.

But despite her apparent health, the usually smooth space between her eyes was creased with dual lines of worry. "They're coming," she told me. The hand that rose to push a wisp of errant hair off a pink cheek shook slightly. "They'll invade Render and take everyone."

Della didn't like being touched. I'd always thought it had something to do with the fact that she was a spirit form. But something inside me tightened at the fear in her eyes. And I reached out to clasp her cool hand. She looked surprised for a beat and then squeezed my hand back. "We're not going to let that happen," I told her.

She held my gaze for a long moment. It was probably just my imagination, but I thought I sensed her magic probing my mind, looking for the answers I was only pretending to have. After a moment, she nodded. "What can I do to help?"

"Call everyone? Ask them to meet us here tonight? We have a plan." Okay, it wasn't a plan so much as an escape strategy. But it would have to do.

She nodded. "Yes. When?"

"Eight o'clock?" Hawk asked.

Two hours. I hoped that would be enough time.

Della nodded and we left.

I turned to Hawk as we headed across the pitted lawn to Victoria. "I have something I need to do."

"I'll come with you," he said.

"No. I need to do this alone."

"Are you sure?"

I held back a shiver of fear through sheer force of will. "Yes."

He inclined his head. "I have to speak with my crew. Make sure you're at Della's by eight. They'll be more likely to listen to you than me."

I nodded and stood there as he melted into the

darkness. Some instinct screamed at me to call him back. To ask him for help.

But I couldn't do it. Grams had said I needed to do it alone.

With a sigh, I headed into the house.

25

I crouched in the shadow of an enormous bush at the edge of the property. I'd been watching the shed for twenty minutes. Nothing had moved inside or around the place. Still, I couldn't shake the feeling that something was there. Something I couldn't see.

All around me, crickets sang a familiar song that leeched some of the tension from my muscles. It was just another night in Render. Crickets were singing. The night was calm.

Then the crickets' song ceased, and a soft panting sound broke the sudden silence behind me.

I hadn't intended to bring Nicht along on my questionable adventure. But I'd had to bring Boyle because I had no one to keep him safe at the house. Everyone was doing other jobs where it would be too dangerous to include him.

And I couldn't leave him alone at Victoria. The

house could engage powerful wards to protect herself from attack, but she couldn't anticipate the guardian spirit of a baby gargoyle that would inspire Boyle to climb up to the roof and try to protect her.

No. The baby was safer with me.

Apparently, he and his pony-sized dog were an unbreakable pair.

I turned to the dog and shushed him softly.

He slammed his mouth shut with an audible snap, the large, white teeth disappearing into the unrelenting blackness of his face. In fact, if it wasn't for his glowing red eyes, the entire dog would have disappeared.

I frowned at him. "Can't you do anything about the headlights?"

He whined softly.

I sighed, reaching back to scratch his big nose. Unfortunately, he took that as permission to start panting again.

"Okay," I whispered, "I've put this off as long as I can."

Nicht stood carefully so as not to jostle the sleeping baby draped over his back. Boyle mumbled softly in his sleep and resettled himself into the dog's thick fur, his skinny legs and arms draped loosely over the sides.

"I'm going to hire you as a sleep nanny," I told the hound.

He made a soft, "woof!" sound, and we started toward the shed.

Motioning for Nicht to stand near the door, I walked around Mitch's tiny home a couple of times to evaluate the area, stopping at the small window of the kitchen and peering through with each rotation. I listened carefully each time, hearing nothing inside.

No light.

No movement.

No sound.

Finally, I opened the door. It creaked slightly and I jumped a foot into the air, emitting the high-pitched squeal of a sissy girl before I could stop myself.

Mentally flagellating myself, I stepped into the shed.

Nothing had changed since the last time I was there. The air might have been a bit mustier. But the kitchen was the same, and Mitch's Seer chair still stood empty in the center of the main room.

I settled the small, wooden box I'd carried in onto the floor and opened it. Nicht stood near the door, his nose pointed outside, keeping watch.

I pulled out the bag of portal ashes, the grave dirt I'd dug from behind the house, and the small medallion I'd also found buried there. Grams had told me that the answers to the portal had to be found in the place where it led.

Outvald.

The information had brought an icy shiver climbing down my back. I didn't want to go to Outvald. There was nothing but horror for me there. But Grams didn't share my fear.

"It's where we're from, child," she'd told me. "It's where our legacy magic began."

I'd shaken my head, pacing the room as pure terror ripped through me. I'd fought the portal enough times to know. What tried to escape was evil. Pure and simple. It was death.

"You must trust your heritage, child," Grams had said, her voice hardening in the face of my resistance.

"I can't," I'd told her. "Don't you see? The portal sheds evil like hair from a balding man. It reeks of it. If I go into that portal..." I'd shuddered, the motion so violent it nearly took me off my feet. "I won't survive it."

"You must go to Outvald, child," Grams told me in a voice that rattled the windows. "You must find the portal entrance and place the medallion there. It is the only way. You came to me for answers. Now you must do as I say."

She was right. I'd known it. But that didn't take the stink of fear away. It didn't make it any easier to breathe. I'd nodded. "Tell me what I need to do."

And so, she had.

She'd told me that I must go to her grave and dig

in the space six inches in front of the cross we'd marked it with. She told me to dig six inches into the soil with my fingers and extract soil from that spot. And that I must use my power to draw the energy from the medallion, pulling it from the place six feet down, where her bones lay.

The mystical power of Thrice Six. Not an evil symbol as many humans believed. But a magical one.

I'd done as she'd said, trying not to think of the fact that the medallion had been lying across her cold fingers when we'd buried her. It had touched her cold skin, its power infusing her with the magic that allowed me to speak to her even after death.

By taking the medallion, I'd silenced her. And I felt the severing of that tie like a knife to my heart.

I'd walked away from that interview intending to do as she'd said. But I couldn't just open the portal and wander through it into Outvald. I had to know what I'd be walking into.

So I'd come up with the plan.

The plan sucked giant water balloons. But it was better than going in blind.

I would use Mitch's Seer energy to peek at Outvald. I'd use the tools that tied me to the other dimension and try to focus my visit, so I didn't just emerge psychically in some random spot. I needed to see the other end of the portal.

I needed to know what was waiting for me there.

I didn't really know how to prepare for what I had to do. I only knew I needed to shed some light on the task.

I glanced at Nicht, seeing the small form draped bonelessly atop him. I walked over and lifted Boyle from the hound's back. "In case you need to move," I told Nicht.

The hound made a soft, chuffing sound, his gaze never leaving the night beyond the door.

I lay Boyle atop Mitch's soft bed and brushed my fingertips across his tiny cheek, tears burning my eyes. How was I going to keep him safe if I had to go into the portal? How would I protect him from the Body? The thought of those human-shaped monsters in Indy getting hold of the tiny gargoyle made me see stars.

I couldn't let it happen.

But I couldn't take him through the portal with me. It was much too dangerous.

I scrubbed at the tears and bent toward Boyle, kissing his soft cheek. "I'll be right back, sweet boy."

I forced myself to move to the chair, to pick up the three items I'd carried with me, and to settle into the overstuffed sucking behemoth of a recliner.

I slipped the chain of the medallion around my neck and sat back. I'd barely tucked my fingertips into the ash and the dirt before I felt the magic pull me in.

I'd expected to land somewhere in Outvald, looking at the end of a portal. Instead, I was plunged into the heart of raging, ravaging flame. Heat sucked all the oxygen out of the air, pressed against me like an actual physical presence, and made me want to turn and run.

But there was nowhere to go.

I was inside a vision. A vision that felt oh so very real. But which was still a vision.

Though the fire was hot, it didn't seem to burn my skin.

Hmm.

I could either just stand there, immobilized by terror, or forge onward to see what I'd come to see. Since that wasn't a tough decision, I started moving.

The fire wrapped around me, forming a tunnel that blazed with unnatural light and moved like a living thing. Sweat poured off me, drenching my clothes and making my thick brown hair cling to my face and neck. I shoved it away, scrubbing at the unrelenting moisture with the sleeve of my tee, and moved more quickly.

I wanted nothing so much as to reach the end of the fiery tunnel. Surely when the fire ended, the portal would end too.

But it seemed to go on forever. My steps slowed, my legs feeling as if lead weights had been strapped to them. My back screamed at me, and I realized I'd been walking half hunched over because the portal seemed to shrink as I walked. Pain made me straighten slightly, testing the result. To my surprise, the fire above my head rose to accommodate it.

Interesting.

I plodded onward and realized the sides were closing in on me, smoke filling up the available space.

I coughed until I felt as if my lungs would explode from the stress.

I prayed for clear air.

The smoke shifted away.

Hmm.

Did I have control over the portal? I'd expected fire and found myself in fire. I'd assumed smoke and smoke appeared. But those elements appeared to be malleable.

Was that possible?

I tested the theory by wishing for cold.

The flame disappeared on a blustery breeze, and ice formed beneath my feet. The walls of the portal that had been defined by flame were obscured by white as snow sifted downward in dense sheets.

I closed my eyes and let the cool air slide over me, refreshing and sweet. The coolness quickly dried the copious amounts of sweat coating my skin.

It was glorious.

But, within moments, I started to shiver, chilled

to the bone. The light dusting of snow beneath my shoes was soon up to my knees, and I was struggling to move forward.

I thought of Spring and a fresh, flowery scent wafted over me. My sneakers sank into thick green grass and butterflies danced on the air around my head.

I laughed in delight. "Now that's much better," I murmured to myself.

On I trudged.

And on.

And on.

And...

Okay, it was getting ridiculous. "How long is this thing?" I yelled in frustration.

I had no idea how long I'd been in the vision, but it felt as if I'd wasted the better part of the day. I started to stress out over what might be going on back in Render. And Boyle! What if the baby woke up and I wasn't there?

I needed to finish what I'd started and get back.

Suddenly the walls around me were gone. I found myself standing in the darkness, silence throbbing around me.

I spun in a circle and saw...nothing. No portal, no lights, no people.

Light filtered down on me, and I looked up. A dense bank of clouds released a full, silvery moon, allowing its light to paint the area around me. The gray bulk of bushes sat nearby. They were familiar despite the fact that the enormous flowers had closed into tight, tulip-shaped buds with the night. Their scent permeated the air, sweet and full.

Silvery light bathed a distant line of trees, massive trunks spearing into the sky, straight and unbending. Their arrowhead-shaped tops pierced the clouds.

I knew that place. I'd been there before.

Remembering the horrible lizard creature we'd battled on the street in front of Victoria, panic slipped through me. My gaze jerked toward the trees, and I spun around to view the entire area again, looking for the monster.

I didn't see its massive form moving through the night, or smell its horrid, fishy scent. I relaxed slightly. But the memory made me realize I needed to get out of there.

I looked down at the medallion hanging around my neck and tugged it off. Bending down, I clawed through the grass, scraping the dirt until I'd made a narrow hole about six inches deep.

I dropped the medallion into the indentation I'd created and covered it again with the black soil, patting it down. Standing, I looked around for something to mark the spot. I found a small stick laying half under the bush and grabbed it.

It didn't come free at first. I realized it was still attached. Bending the stick back and forth at the spot where it was still joined to the bush, I finally wrenched it loose.

I jabbed it into the soil where I'd buried the medallion.

I brushed dirt off my hands. "Now, I just need to find the portal entrance," I mumbled softly.

The ground shook.

I went very still. Waiting. Listening.

Something snorted, loud and close.

I panicked, throwing my hands up and dragging on the available magic. The energy slammed into me, hitting me like a fist in my core. I stumbled backward as magic bit my skin, a thousand tiny stings of power.

The darkness shifted and something lumbered out of it, a nightmare of legs and claws and...eyes. With a thought, I imagined dual blades forming from the magic dancing at my fingertips. The blades shot into existence, eighteen inches long and shimmering with silvery power. A gleam of energy danced along each edge, promising pain.

The creature stared at me for a moment and then opened its enormous jaws, showing me several rows of conical teeth. My gaze was riveted on its terrible face, the deadly-looking teeth and the chaotic blinking of its many eyes. I got caught on that blinking, mesmerized by the hypnotic flicker of the black orbs.

The thing was almost on me before I realized it

had moved.

Claws slashed past my face, an inch away, and I only had time to slice blindly at the thing and dive away.

Despite its size and the confusing number of its limbs, the monster moved fast.

Really fast.

By the time I'd rolled to my feet, it was on me again, and I barely got the knives up between us before its claws flashed past. A burning ache found the skin of my belly, and I knew it had scored a hit.

I swung one blade high and one low, slicing through its wide, scaly chest and across its face. The huge, spider-like creature howled in pain and outrage and rose onto four of its back legs, its front legs flailing the air in front of my face.

I moved fast, dancing close enough to perform crisscrossing slices to its exposed belly. The monster hit the ground, its enormous maw snapping toward the blades and missing my skin by a fraction of an inch...close enough for me to feel the heat of its breath.

It struggled to its feet as a soft glow eased into view just behind it.

The portal!

I tried to duck around the spider and was cut off by the slash of a razor-sharp claw. Blood welled through my jeans before I even felt the pain.

I swung the blade, slicing off the claw.

The monster responded with another strike, opening a fresh gash in the calf of my opposite leg.

I slashed again, severing another claw.

But the monster had too many legs. As quickly as I cut them off, another one joined the fight.

I dodged left and jumped right as it struck again, hoping to confuse it enough to allow me to get to the portal. But a hairy, muscular limb swept my legs out from under me and I fell, landing against the monster's horrid blue body. The body was hard and shaped like a tick.

I gagged at the thought.

To my horror, the massive jaws were opening again. I was too close. I wouldn't be able to get away in time.

I couldn't let it score another hit. I was already losing too much blood. And that mouth would rip me apart in seconds.

I stabbed out in desperation, the blade carving easily through the thing's oblong head, and it screamed again. The sound was horrible, filled with pain and manic rage.

I rolled off as the monster thrashed against the agony, flailing from one side to the other.

Climbing quickly to my feet, I dove into the portal and hit my knees in the thick grass there.

I took off running, not looking back. All I could do was pray the portal would close quickly enough to keep the spider-like thing from following.

26

I came out of the vision with a gasp, jerking upright in the chair. For a moment, the foresight clung to me, seeming so real I could still smell the putrid stench of the monster's blood, and feel the wiry hairs of its tick-like body against my skin.

I shuddered violently from the memory.

My hand clasped the locket around my neck. It was hot to the touch, residual energy still churning inside it.

Good. I hadn't been sure if the vision had used the physical locket or a magical replica to do its work.

Sucking air as if I'd run a marathon, I shoved myself out of the chair, desperate to put some distance between me and the vision. I looked around the shed, my gaze flying toward the spot where I'd left Boyle.

Still there. I nearly collapsed with relief. His little chest rose and fell in sleep, and my own breathing soothed under the sight.

Nicht wasn't standing where I'd left him. That brought my pulse spiking back up. The only reason he would leave his spot was if there had been a threat.

Even as I had the thought, I felt an alien undercurrent on the air—unknown magic.

Someone was outside in the dark.

I hurried over and grabbed Boyle off the bed. He murmured something that was too soft to hear and burrowed into me with a soft sigh.

The warm weight of him against me was both reassuring and terrifying. I had to protect him at all costs.

But the silence beyond the shed door told me that whoever was out there was confident we would come to them. Whoever it was had cloaked themselves in shadow, waiting.

Nicht would find them, I told myself. He had to.

My heart still pounding as if I'd run a race, I looked desperately around, wishing Mitch had given himself a back door. But I knew why he hadn't. Because, short of digging a tunnel, a back way out would do us no good. The building was too small. One person could easily keep watch on the entire thing from a single vantage point.

Son of a bunion!

The shadows around the door morphed and a long form eased through, silent as death.

I grabbed for latent magic before I realized who it was.

I sagged in relief. "Nicht," I whispered. "Where have you been?"

The dog whined softly and spun, moving quickly to the door and peering out into a night that felt moist and was dark as pitch.

I became aware of the soft ping, ping, ping of raindrops hitting the roof. Good, Nicht could see perfectly in the dark. He'd guide us out of there. "Lead the way," I told him as I walked up and rested a hand on his tall, furry back.

He moved through the crack in the door and I eased through behind him, rushing to lay my hand on his soft fur again as he picked up speed.

We were nearly to Della's house when the night exploded around us.

Jagged golden light flared past me, so close I could smell the ends of my hair burning. Boyle jerked awake with a cry, his howl almost drowned out by Nicht's enraged snarls and the shouts of the people boiling out of the night in our direction.

I didn't hesitate, grabbing magic from the air and

firing it at our attackers like bullets. I had no time to form blades. The raw energy bolts would have to do.

Boyle stopped crying as I dove behind a tree to give us some protection. "Up!" I told him. "Get high and stay there." I threw his agile little form toward the trunk of the tree and flung energy toward two people who suddenly appeared behind me.

They went down, but one of them jumped back up almost immediately.

I ripped more energy from the air with one hand and threw it with the other. The night was thick with magic, bulging with it. And my pickings were varied and full.

I yanked it to me with a rabid kind of energy, frantic yet determined that the soldiers the Body was pelting us with would not win.

The man in front of me yanked a sword from the sheath on his back and slashed at me in a single, fluid movement. He danced away from my narrow energy bolts, so I fanned them into a shield and then yanked more power from the woman lying on the ground. Her body jerked as I ripped energy from it, arching off the ground at the force of my attack.

With a manic kind of focus, I twisted the energy into a coil that was as thick as my wrist and as long as my arm.

The man with the blade dodged sideways and lunged, the blade nicking me over my ribs.

Pain sent fire through me, a biting reminder that I couldn't afford to lose.

I thickened my shield, wrapping it around me on three sides. I had the tree at my back and my energy padding me from the front and sides.

I had bought myself some time.

But not a lot. Because two more people had just melted from the dark.

There was a distant snarl and my already pounding heart sped. *Nicht!*

Two more people appeared before me.

"Give it up, Ms. Forester," a deep, male voice said. "The Magistrate requires your presence."

I was out of time. I needed to change my strategy from shielding and single weapon offense to something faster and more globally effective.

I knew just the thing.

My hands found the small box I'd shoved into my pocket. I worked the lid off with one finger. "So sorry. But my dance card's full for tonight," I told them. "In fact, I'm pretty sure it's full for the distant future, as far as the eye can see."

Three more people joined the crowd in front of me. All of them had magic dancing around them or weapons in their hands.

My stomach twisted.

I licked a finger and stabbed it into a baggie, dropped that baggie and jammed my finger into the second bag. "Please give the Magistrate my regrets."

I yanked power into my hand. As wild energy flared brightly over the dirt and ash covered finger, I took a deep breath, dropped my shield, and stabbed the finger against Gram's locket.

Energy boiled toward me from the night. I closed my eyes, praying my magic would be in time and felt the night turn white and explode around me.

Power punched me, shoving me back against the rough bark of the tree. The air was so thick with it that breathing was like trying to suck molasses through my airways. I coughed, choking on the residual fog, and dropped to my knees.

Then I remembered Nicht and forced myself to stand. I tried to see through the smoky air but couldn't.

Nothing moved through the fog. Nobody came for me, so I guessed my little death bomb had worked. I stumbled around the tree and found a nightmare waiting.

Boyle had climbed down from the tree. Apparently, in concern for Nicht. The big dog was badly wounded, his sides heaving and smoke rising from several spots in his fur. He was on his feet between Boyle and a crowd of what looked like a dozen Body soldiers, each dressed in the form-fitting black suits that I knew were like magical chainmail, impervious to fire, magic, bullets and blades. They wore long cloaks with blood-red lining, and those who had light-colored hair covered them in close-fitting caps that looked as if they were made from the same stuff as their suits.

They all but melted into the night. Only their paler faces showed through the darkness.

Every soldier had a weapon in one hand and magic roiling around their clenched fists.

Boyle turned to me when I stepped around the tree, his round eyes filled with fear. "Glynnie?"

I moved slowly toward him. "It will be okay, sweet boy."

"Call off your hound," a tall woman with straight black hair that reached past her broad shoulders demanded.

"What do you want?"

The woman, who stood at the apex of a wide vee formation, smiled unkindly. "You and the gargoyle need to come with us, Ms. Forester."

"Why?" I asked, fighting to stay calm. Approaching with slow, hesitant steps, I stumbled slightly, trying to give the impression of weakness. The ploy worked because none of the soldiers tried to stop me.

"The Magistrate will explain everything," the woman said, "Now call off the hound. You can't win this battle. You're badly outnumbered."

I reached Boyle and took his hand. "I'm not calling him off until you tell me what you want."

The woman frowned, pursing perfectly shaped lips. "It's a shame to kill such a fine specimen of a hellhound." Even as she said the words, the energy roiling around her fist grew.

I tensed, my mind churning. I glanced toward Della's home, only about twenty feet away.

I wondered...

"Ms. Forester?"

I swayed, stumbling sideways. "I'm not feeling very well..." I let myself fall to my knees and tugged Boyle down with me. "Just give me a minute."

Placing my palm on the ground, I shoved sensing energy into it, reaching for the magic-saturated earth beneath Della's home. It had responded to me before. Maybe I could call to it again.

The woman sighed. "Your theatrics aren't helping, Ms. Forester."

A ribbon of sleeping energy stirred at my touch, reaching for me, but it was just a thread. It wouldn't be enough. I needed more magic density. I kept reaching for it, my vision blurring as I extended myself into the distant, foreign magic.

"Ms. Forester?"

The Earth tugged against my hand, insistent and eager. I shoved seeking energy through it, looking for a specific power signature. My questing senses slipped through the cool energy of normal Earth magic and emerged into a heated pool of intense power.

Bingo!

I glanced up at the woman, nodding. "I know. I'll

call him off." I looked at Nicht. He'd been standing perfectly still the entire time, his wary gaze never leaving the soldiers in front of him. The barest growl throbbed at the base of his throat, only discernible by the faint vibration in his big body. "Nicht?"

The big hound whined softly. I fixed him with a stare, wishing I could send a mental message to him. "It's okay, boy. Come here."

The soldiers stirred slightly, but not a single one dropped their focus or their weapons. It was a testament to how much fear a giant hellhound could cause in even the most powerful people.

"Come on, boy," I urged softly.

He gave a final, spittle-filled snarl and backed toward me. "Good boy," I said softly enough that only he could hear. "Don't turn your back on them."

I didn't need Mitch's magic chair to see a vision of what they would do to the dog if he turned away. I reached out and placed my hand on his tense, muscular thigh. Nicht jolted to a stop, still staring at the soldiers. His eyes glowed a fierce red in the dark.

I sent a ribbon of energy into him. His thigh twitched slightly under my hand, but to his credit, he gave no other outward sign that he'd noticed.

Boyle grabbed the dog's other leg and leaned his head against Nicht's hip.

I looked at him, widening my eyes. Boyle's sweet blue gaze flared with clear blue light. I flinched in surprise.

He'd never done that before.

I sent the fae energy I'd culled from the land beneath Della's home into Nicht in a steadily growing stream. Beneath my hand, the dog seemed to gain flesh and grow taller. Boyle watched me with an intense gaze, his little body wrapped tightly around Nicht as if to protect him.

Boyle's eyes flared again, brighter. I realized with a start that Boyle was sucking in some of the energy I was giving to Nicht.

"No," I told him, trying to keep my voice soft.

He favored me with a sweet smile.

"Ms. Forester, step away from the hound."

I heard chains jangling and knew what they intended. They would chain Nicht, magically muzzle him, and then he'd be helpless against whatever they wanted to do to him.

That so wasn't going to happen. With a final push, I sent everything I had into the big hound and screamed, "Go!"

Nicht launched off the ground and flew at them in a whirl of teeth, claws, and flying spit.

Horrific screaming tore the night as Nicht ripped into the soldiers, tearing them apart and flinging the parts across the yard before they even had time to react.

I helped where I could, using my own depleted magic to slow the soldiers on the outside of the vee so they couldn't overwhelm the hound.

A tiny woman flew toward me, flinging herself to the ground and flipping to land on her feet with energy coiling around her small fist.

I shifted forward and her eyes went round with surprise as my knife sliced into her throat just above the black suit. She sagged to the ground and I turned to face the next one.

Nobody came. Everyone was focused on the big hound. I cleaned my blade off on the grass and slipped it back into its sheath.

I watched just long enough to be sure Nicht would be all right. Then I looked down at Boyle. "We need to go..." I blinked.

Boyle was gone.

Panic sheered a path through my insides, drenching me with adrenaline. "Boyle!" I screamed, my gaze scouring the area for him.

I didn't see him. And I didn't see anyone who could have taken him. There were several soldiers moving in to take the place of their shredded peers against Nicht, but none of them were even thinking about Boyle.

Then I caught a glare of pale blue shining brightly from an enormous tree behind the Body soldiers.

I looked up...and up....and up...and... *Goddess's galoshes!* "No!" I screamed.

But the baby 'goyle wasn't paying a lick of attention to me.

A horrendous cracking noise rose above the snarling and screaming on the ground. And I watched in fascinated horror as my sweet baby boy ripped an enormous limb from the tree and dropped it on the heads of the soldiers still standing at the back of the formation.

27

V ictoria was under siege.

Magic flared bright and hot against the night — coming from everywhere at once. I crouched beneath a giant evergreen tree sitting on the boundary between Della's land and mine and watched for a moment, trying to form a plan.

Answering magic flared from Victoria, the streams every bit as harsh to the senses, but the numbers of them much fewer.

Whoever was trying to fight off the Body was badly under gunned.

Panting behind me, Nicht's glowing gaze was dimmed by pain, and I knew he needed care. We needed to get inside Victoria so I could tend to him. I reached out and placed my palm on his wide chest. "Hang in there, boy. I'll get you some help as soon as I figure out how to get inside."

Nicht swung around on a snarl.

Sitting on the ground in front of me so I could keep an arm around him, Boyle jumped to his feet, his eyes glowing in the dark.

I wanted to cry.

Now what?

I stood and turned to face...Della?

Her form was nearly translucent, her tiny feet hovering above the ground. She beckoned to us and turned, floating quickly toward her house.

I grabbed Boyle's hand and followed. Something about Della's form bothered me. She was much too wispy, considering she'd been inside her home for days. She usually only looked that wispy when she'd been away from the supportive magics built into her house for a while.

Or when she was badly injured. Like she'd been the night Hawk and I had come to help with the soul swallower.

My pulse picked up and I hurried to catch up with her. "Have you been attacked again?"

She turned to me, the bricks on the wall of her ranch home showing through her form. She raised a silvery finger to her lips, silencing me.

We slipped through the open back door and I turned to set the bolts, feeling the protective wards snapping into place.

Della floated through the kitchen, heading for a

back room. She didn't gain additional solidity from being inside the house.

Ice climbed my spine. Della wasn't well. Something had happened to her.

I tried to talk to her again but she shook her head, pointing through a door at the end of the hall.

Warning bells rang in my head. Was it a trap?

I peered at Della, narrowing my gaze. "What do you want?"

She pointed again, never speaking, never growing more solid. Behind me, Nicht started to growl softly.

Della went very still, her head coming up, and she motioned frantically toward the door.

At the front of the house, a horrendous crashing sound spurred me into action. I didn't know where the fairy spirit was leading us. But any option of escape behind us had just been blown away.

I jerked Boyle into my arms and started running, Nicht on my heels.

We plunged through the door at the end of the hall and it closed silently behind us, a ward snapping into place. It was a powerful ward, fae magic, and it bit at my skin when I moved too close. I moved deeper into the room and saw Della, framed in another open doorway. It looked like a closet.

With a final nod, she turned and disappeared into...nothing.

Heavy boots slammed down the hall. Beyond the

closed and warded door, wood splintered and glass shattered.

Voices boomed through the empty house and I recognized the arrogant, insistent voice of the Magistrate. "Find them!"

I hesitated only the length of another heartbeat and then looked at Nicht. "We have no choice." I placed Boyle on his back and lifted the baby's chin with a finger. "Hold on tight," I whispered to him. I needed my hands clear...just in case.

He nodded, his round blue eyes as big as saucers.

And then I ran toward the closet. Something crashed into the warded door and someone yelped in pain, then swore. Energy flared, its silver light sifting through the narrow space at the bottom of the door.

We were out of time.

As I plunged into the closet, Nicht trotted quickly in behind me.

***

I jerked to a stop inside a black vortex. There was constant movement, but I couldn't see what was moving. I got the sense that the walls were rotating around me, like an enormous drill with me at its core.

Nicht shouldered past and kept going as if he knew where he was. The sight of him disappearing into the blackness with Boyle giggling and riding him like a horse jolted me out of my inaction.

I ran after them. My footfalls were nearly silent, the ground squishy under my feet. I was cognizant of a soft swish of fabric rubbing against fabric as I ran. The sound seemed to revolve around me like the walls, but I realized after a moment that I was hearing the movement of my own clothing.

The portal, or whatever it was, displaced sound in a strange way.

I became aware of a soft light ahead and sped up, thinking it was the end. But it wasn't the end. I plunged out of the blackness into an enormous cavern. The walls of the cave were steep, jagged with rock formations, and an odd charcoal gray color.

Scanning the huge space, I spotted Nicht standing in the center, his head down.

A pale hand rested on his midnight fur.

Della!

I cut the distance between us in seconds, dropping to my knees to clasp her cold hand. She looked fully corporeal, her features pale but solid and smooth. There was no color in her cheeks. Her skin was a solid, alabaster white.

If her eyes hadn't been open and glossy with life, I would have thought she was dead.

She lay on a pallet covered in pale moss, the center of an enormous wheel carved into the rock.

Each spoke of the wheel was glowing, the energy a pale, silvery-white like Della's spirit form.

"Della, what's going on?"

She smiled. "I never wanted you to see. I didn't want anybody to know. I'm...vulnerable here." Her voice was broken, rusty, as if she hadn't used it in a while.

I frowned. "Is this your true form?"

"Yes. I can't explain now. There is no time."

Della's smooth brow puckered but she went on. "There is no time. You must go to Victoria and close the portal. We cannot let the Body gain access. They are nearly inside, Glynn. They are beating back the home's defenses and its defenders."

She stopped to take a deep breath.

"No," I said, squeezing her cold hand. "I want to help you."

She shook her head. "There is no help. But don't fear for me. The Body won't find me. My home is abandoned. And once they are gone, I'll return and keep watch on Render."

"But why?" I asked, not even sure exactly what I was asking.

To my surprise, she laughed. "The answer to that would take hours. Suffice it to say that I know why I am here, and I have made my peace with it. Now go! Protect that adorable baby and your friends who are standing against the Body with little hope of winning."

She tugged her hand from mine and I stood. I looked around. "But I don't know how..."

"Stay safe, Glynn. Be strong." Della lifted an arm and threw magic over Nicht, Boyle, and me. It drifted downward in silver flakes that felt like snow against my skin. And when the snow fell away, we were standing in Victoria's living room.

To my surprise, Hawk and Art were at the windows, they'd barricaded them with bits of broken furniture and one of Victoria's heavy doors, and were firing some kind of energy weapon through small holes they'd left in the blockade. Hawk's head whipped around when we appeared and alarm turned quickly to relief. "Thank the goddess. We thought something had happened to you."

Art's gaze swung to mine and held. I saw no anger there for what I'd done to him. I gave him a tentative smile and he returned it.

Sissy was leaning over the couch, her softly glowing hands gliding above someone who wasn't moving. I hurried over and looked down, finding the bloody and torn form of her next-door neighbor, Micah Blunt, sprawled across the couch.

The living room floor held several other blanketed figures in various states of injury. And, in one case, death.

My heart fell at the sight. I recognized a few more of our neighbors, but there were at least three I didn't know. I assumed they were Hawk's people.

Yanking my attention back to the man on the couch, I pulled on Victoria's magic and created healing magic, adding the energy to Sissy's as she tried to repair torn flesh and broken bones. She pointed to his legs. "See what you can do with those."

I laid my palms over Micah's ankles, sliding them slowly up the legs as bones cracked and shifted beneath his skin, returning to the proper spots and sealing the breaks.

Micah's handsome face was ashen against the deep red of his hair, and his full lips were pressed into a taut line, no doubt from pain.

"Why is my brother here?" I asked my friend.

She didn't look at me, her attention focused on her work. "If I'd left him at home they would have killed him," she told me, her voice throbbing with anger. "I gave him a tattoo that is temporarily blocking his energy. I figured that would lock whoever was influencing him out for a while."

I frowned at the idea of a magical lockdown but nodded. "Thanks, Sis."

"Don't thank me. If we survive this, we'll have to deal with it more permanently." She turned to me, her gray gaze filled with fear. "I have no idea how to do that, Glynn."

I frowned. She was telling me I might lose my brother. The thought dug deep, slicing into my heart like an energy-infused blade.

I shook it off. One problem at a time. I had confidence in my friend. She'd find a way to help Art. I clung to that thought because I had to.

We worked in silence for a few minutes, as the world outside crashed and flared and generally imploded.

"What did this to him?" I asked Sissy, jerking my chin toward Micah.

She shook her head. "The Body has all sorts of horrible things out there," she said, rage throbbing in her voice. "They've been going house to house. They got Edna..." Her voice broke on the name, and tears glimmered in her eyes. "They...killed her because she had no magic," Sissy breathed out. Her chest heaved with emotion, and I leaned against her for a moment in shared mourning. Edna Backus had been a non-magic resident of Render. She'd been married to a mage who'd abandoned her a decade earlier to go to Magical Indy. The last I'd heard, Festu Backus was calling himself Fox and had somehow managed to scrape decades off his age. The man was a selfish cad. And if I found out that he was behind Edna's death...

My pulse pounded in my temples and I suddenly found it hard to breathe.

Hawk appeared behind me. "Do you know how to close the portal?"

I looked at Sissy and she nodded, sniffling. "I've got this. Go. Do what you need to do."

I grabbed Hawk's arm and pulled him away. "I have it all set up. But I need to go through the portal to close it, and once I close it, I'll be..." I forced myself to say the words. "I won't be able to come back."

Hawk's gaze held mine. "You can't do that, Glynn."

"I have to," I told him. "We have no choice." I thought of Della and fought a wave of renewed sadness.

"Then I'm going with you," he said.

I started to shake my head but he grabbed my arms and yanked me close, his gaze intense. "You're not going to Outvald alone, Glynn."

Something sparked between us. Something bright and needy and warm. But I didn't have the emotional bandwidth to examine it. I pushed him away. "I don't have time to argue with you. Can you get the others away?"

Beyond Victoria, the night suddenly ignited with golden flares of energy. I ran to the nearest barricade peephole and peered out in time to see bodies across the street flying into the air, surrounded by an aura of pure golden energy.

More blasts of pure power flared into the night, bringing screams of pain and flinging more dark-clad bodies into the air.

Hawk ran to the door and placed a palm over the thick, wooden surface. The door rumbled in its frame, and the knob jittered as another flare of energy blasted the night to pieces.

He grasped the knob, opened the door about ten inches, and reached through to grab something on the other side.

He yanked a woman through the narrow crack, his hands grasping the back of her black leather jacket. She had an enormous black energy gun clutched in each hand, and she kept firing until the door closed in her face.

Alina.

Hawk slammed the door closed. Victoria sealed the ward back into place. He turned to Alina. "Did you get them out?"

She nodded, stumbling to a chair and collapsing.

I hurried over to her, yelling at Boyle. "Get her some water!" The little gargoyle took off, running full speed into the kitchen.

Alina was covered in blood, but I didn't think much of it was hers. She mostly looked exhausted, and she had some superficial cuts on her face and throat. I tugged more healing energy from Victoria, feeling her stores thinning, and ran my hands over Alina's cuts. They closed quickly.

Boyle handed the Hunter a large glass of water and she took it, gently tousling his orange hair. "Thank you, young man."

Boyle beamed up at her with stars in his eyes. He looked like he was meeting his favorite hero for the first time.

All right, I thought. *That's enough of that.* I shoved jealousy away, and tears burned in my eyes. If I went through with my plan, I would have to leave Boyle behind. I couldn't take him to Outvald. It was too dangerous without Victoria serving as a safe space.

The realization cleaved my chest in two, burrowing into my heart with ruthless savagery.

I was going to lose my sweet baby boy. I reached out and yanked him to me, enclosing him in a fierce hug that made him squirm. "Glynnie, let go!"

I held on another minute and then kissed his forehead. "Stay close to Sissy, okay?"

He nodded.

Sissy and I locked gazes, hers darkening with sudden understanding. She stood up and walked over to us. "Hey, Boyle, can you get Mr. Blunt some water too?"

When the baby bounced away to do as she asked, Sissy stared at me, crossing her arms over her chest. "You can't, Glynn."

I sniffed, scrubbing the heel of my hand over my

cheeks. "I have to, Sis. Promise me you'll keep him safe?"

Fresh tears glistened in her eyes and ran down her cheeks. "Of course I will. But you'll be back. Right?"

I never got a chance to answer because the front wall rumbled under a horrendous new attack. One of the barricades exploded inward, sending shards of wood through the room like deadly spears. An enormous, clawed hand shot through the opening and scraped the air.

Alina and Hawk flew to the breach with their weapons, firing thick, golden energy at the beast. It roared in pain, but the claw continued to scrape the air, flinging furniture and chunks of the wall around the room. One enormous eye filled the opening, surrounded by scaly black skin.

Alina flung a knife at the eye and the monster reared back, roaring its rage.

I gave Sissy a quick hug. "Get out of here, Sis. All of you. Now!"

Then I ran toward the basement door and threw it open. Plunging down the steps before I could change my mind.

28

I set a ward on the inside of the door and ran down the stairs. Tears nearly blinded me. The constant explosions and rumbling above my head kept me moving forward. Dirt sifted down from the rafters, the soft whine of latent magic singing through the basement, like the keening of a dying animal. I shoved emotions away, allowing the urgency of the moment to replace my painful thoughts.

Placing a hand on the rock wall hiding the portal, I felt Victoria throb like the beat of a frantic heart against my fingers. "I'm so sorry," I told her, sadness softening my knees. "I can't save you too."

The heartbeat beneath my fingers slowed, softened, and a warm draft slid over me. The breeze was filled with comfort and love, and I knew it was from Grams.

Grams was the heart of Victoria. She was the soul of the big old house, her magic keeping it alive and magical. And she had told me how to do what I needed to do. She had to have known what it would mean.

The loss of everything I loved.

I suddenly found it hard to breathe.

The door at the top of the stairs shuddered under a brutal assault. My fingers started moving of their own volition, forming the spell to open the portal on the air. Black dots and slashes formed on the surface of the wall in front of me, sliding into symbols that claimed their existence in ancient times in another dimension. The spell had been passed down to me through Grams, who'd learned it at the knee of her own grandmother, and back through time. I'd used the spell only once before, when Grams had been teaching me how to protect and manage the portal. She'd drilled it into me relentlessly then, as she'd explained that I would probably only use it in an emergency situation.

Her words had been prescient.

The door quaked under another assault. Dust sifted down onto my head. Whatever was pounding on the door was strong. And determined.

I prayed Sis had gotten everyone out in time. And that they'd made it to safety before the Body gained access to Victoria.

I was a little surprised I hadn't felt the breach

through Victoria's bones. That was worrying. What if the Body had already figured out how to rip the house's influence away from me?

The portal began to open beneath the spell, which glowed an eye-searing amber as the magic worked.

The door shuddered.

The floor beneath my feet trembled as something big hit the house.

I was out of time.

I completed the spell just as the door crashed back on its hinges. With one last look around the familiar space, I stepped through the portal and began crafting the spell to close it again. I worked fast, my fingers flying and my heart pounding against my tonsils.

Still, the portal was only half closed when a large figure jumped off the bottom step and barreled toward me.

My heart stuttered. My fingers stalled. And Hawk threw Boyle at me before diving through the quickly closing portal.

Sobbing in relief, I hugged the baby close. Hawk rolled to his feet. "We have about five minutes before the whole house comes down, and every one of your friends is killed inside."

As motivational speeches went, it was a good one. Brutal but succinct.

I didn't stop to ask what he meant. I already

knew. They were on the third floor, maybe on the roof. Victoria had barricaded them inside her emergency wards. It would take a massive strike to get through that ward.

The only reason the house was still standing was the portal. The Magistrate wouldn't deliberately bring the house down as long as the portal existed. Assuming his thugs knew the plan.

From the sounds of the assault, I somehow doubted they did.

Once I'd closed the portal down, maybe Hawk and I could find a way back to help them beat the Body back for good.

It was an impossible situation. I knew that even as I started running down a portal with a grassy floor and bright blue sky above.

I'd learned a little something about portal travel in my vision.

And I was about to shorten the learning curve a bit more.

Because I didn't have time to run endlessly through a long, long tunnel.

While we ran, I quizzed Hawk. "What's happening at Victoria?"

"They're safe for now. Sissy was creating a triple wall of wards that will take the Body some time to break through. Alina is on the roof, doing what she can to keep them at bay."

His eyes darkened, swung away.

"What?"

"They were trying to burn the house. We need to move fast."

Son of a bunion! I picked up speed, trying to grab the magic of the portal with my mind. I needed to demand that it shorten. Override its obvious tendency to prolong the passage.

But it wasn't working.

And panic at the idea of Victoria burning made it hard to think. Hard to imagine...

I slammed to a stop, jerking a short bark of surprise out of Boyle.

"Glynn?" Hawk asked, his handsome face dark with worry. "What is it?"

I shook my head, breathing too hard to speak. Instead, I shoved Boyle at him and dropped to my knees, burying my hands in the thick grass. I closed my eyes and reached for Grams. It was her consciousness that had brought me to Outvald before. Her magic infused into the medallion that allowed me to set the process for closing it.

I was dimly aware of Hawk shouting my name, of Boyle softly crying, but I forced my mind away from them. Into the power infusing the big house I'd left behind. *Grams?* I queried softly. *Help me.* Even to me, my voice sounded weak and terrified. I hated being weak. I knew Grams would hate it too. But I was beyond the point where any of that mattered. All that mattered at that moment was saving my friends.

And Victoria.

A soft haze swirled through my mind. It offered a calming energy, warm and soothing amid my roiling thoughts. I recognized the signature of the energy and reached for it, digging metaphysical fingers into the mist and letting it infuse everything inside me, bathing me in knowledge.

Grams's face appeared in the mist—the sharp, knowing gaze I remembered so well, the gentle curve of her smile.

You know what to do, child. Set aside the doubts and embrace your magic. No one controls the portal but you. No one speaks to its energy as you do. You have been chosen to protect it...to mold its power until it serves your unique purposes. You are its mistress. And you have the power you need to inform its actions.

The mist expanded, sliding through me and leaving behind an energy that sparked my own power, drawing it forward like a breeze that fans a flame. Power rose through me, warming and strengthening, and I fed it into the soil beneath my fingers.

It surged deep into the earth, feeding it with the power to accept my commands. I gasped in surprise as my fingers touched the bright spark of the medallion in the soil. Heat flared from its twin around my neck.

The power burned my skin, painful and bright. I shuddered violently as the medallion slipped beneath my skin. Its energy shot away from my core and melded seamlessly with the energy pulsing in the pendant I'd buried in my vision.

Power blew upward, blasting into me. My body arced away from it, my eyes snapping open. Heat and energy exploded into a tunnel of pure energy that stretched as far as the eye could see. Hawk gave a sharp cry as he was thrown backward, out of my line of sight.

The power burned into me, through me, searing the air and scorching its way through my lungs, eyes, hands, and heart.

It painted the world in a conflagration that boiled the very air around me, bathing it in light.

As quickly as it erupted, the power sliced off. I slammed forward from the loss of resistance, my face smashing into the deep, soft grass.

A high-pitched, wobbly whistling sound sheered past a few feet in front of me and then cut off with a decisive snap.

My gaze spun toward it, just in time to see the portal snap closed.

I lay there a moment, taking inventory of all my limbs and finding them all in working order. My chest still heaved from the expulsion of so much magic. There was a sooty taste on the back of my tongue and my skin felt as if I had been boiled alive. But I wasn't burned, just sore.

I was okay. I'd survived.

Boyle and Hawk!

I shoved upward in a full-on panic. My gaze scanned the area around me and I found them. Hawk stood with Boyle still cradled in his arms. The big man's gaze was focused somewhere behind me, filled with awe.

"Glynnie!" the baby screamed, shoving free of Hawk's grip and running to me. "Our house!"

I hugged him tightly, tears of relief and sadness filling my eyes. "I'm sorry, sweet boy. I couldn't save it."

He bounced in my arms, ripping free before I could stop him and running away.

"No! Boyle, stay close," I turned. "It's danger..." My words cut off, astonishment made me step back, away from the sight before me.

Victoria? How was that poss...

The front door opened and Sissy burst through it. "Glynn!" She was smiling, her gaze alight. "Look what you did."

Art came through next, followed by a slow-moving Micah Blunt and Alina, looking confused.

"What in the goddess's supreme power just happened?"

The voice came from Victoria's roof, and it was one I didn't recognize. We all looked up to find a Body soldier standing just outside my bedroom window, an energy weapon clutched in each hand. His gaze slowly scanned downward, focusing on Hawk. His eyes widened and his hands came up, taking deadly aim with his weapons.

"Glynn," Hawk said.

"Yes," I whispered back, rage making it hard to breathe.

"Cover Boyle's eyes," he said.

I didn't hesitate. A beat later, energy flared from two weapons, spearing the man on the roof and lifting him into the air. Then Hawk and Alina redirected the energy downward with a quick flick of their wrists, slamming the man to the ground in front of Victoria.

He hit hard enough to break every bone in his body, bounced once, and then lay perfectly still.

I narrowed my gaze on him, and something opened up on the air behind him. I didn't even have time to panic before the portal sucked the man inside and yanked him away, snapping cleanly closed a heartbeat later.

Alina nodded happily, blew on her gun, and jammed it back into its holster.

Well, I thought. *That just happened.*

"Where are we?" Art asked, looking around at the arrow-shaped trees and strange vegetation.

I winced. He wasn't going to like my answer. So I evaded his question like a champ. "I could really use some tea."

Sissy spun in a slow circle, taking in her new surroundings. Her eyes widened. "Beautiful!" She clapped her hands. "I love it!"

Alina seemed to take it all in stride. "I could use something to eat."

Art laughed, throwing an arm around her shoulders and leading her into the house. To my vast surprise, the two of them made comfortable small talk on the way. I hadn't thought the gorgeous Hunter capable of small talk. In my experience she barely spoke at all.

Micah tapped Sissy on the shoulder. "I don't suppose we could get you to bake some of your righteous brownies?" His eyes were alight as Sissy smiled back at him. "Maybe. If you talk real sweet to me."

He chuckled, the sound warm and intimate. "I can do that."

Goddesses galoshes! Why hadn't I known about that? I made a mental note to verbally flog my friend later for not telling me she had what gave every indication of being a blossoming relationship with her sexy neighbor.

Boyle bounced toward the house. A big, black shape burst through the open front door and bounded across the yard, black tongue lolling happily.

Nicht!

The big hound skidded to a stop in front of Boyle

and went into a playful half-crouch, butt up and tail manically wagging.

Boyle shrieked with happiness as Nicht's big tongue scoured his little face.

I sniffled and scrubbed at happy tears. I'd thought I'd lost all of it. My son, my friends, my... Hawk. I really wasn't sure how to classify him. But I was willing to put the time into finding out.

Somehow I hadn't lost any of them.

Eyes moist and heart pounding with happy excitement. I slid my gaze over the old house sitting in the center of a thick copse of vibrant green grass. Even the big old oak tree had come along on the trip. And as I peered carefully at the tree, I saw a pair of bright blue eyes and a small black form perched on one of the lower branches, tail snapping.

The small black cat.

Hawk came up beside me. We watched in silence as everybody else disappeared into Victoria. He slid an assessing glance around the area, frowning. "I'm guessing this is Outvald?"

I winced again. "Yeah."

"So, somehow, you managed to bring everybody, including the house and the tree along with us when you closed the portal?"

I nodded, unable to speak and not knowing what I'd say anyway.

He expelled a long breath. "Okay then. Well, I

guess that's that." I watched him walk away, admiring the view, and felt real happiness for the first time in days.

Yeah. That was that.

EPILOGUE

I sat on the porch in Grams's favorite rocking chair, the small black cat nestled happily in my lap. I rocked gently, listening to the silence surrounding the house and enjoying the enormous silver moon high above my head in a clear night sky.

We'd quickly realized the wards Victoria had engaged in Render were about ten times stronger in Outvald, encompassing the entire house and several acres of ground around it. Despite my initial fear of the monsters I'd seen around the portal and in my visions, none passed by close enough to be a concern. It was as if the house's protections worked better and spread farther in the new dimension. Which made a twisted kind of sense, since our family had originally come from Outvald, a couple of centuries earlier.

I made a mental note to spend some time in

Victoria's library reading the family histories I'd avoided like the plague to that point.

My mind was brimming with worries and uncertainty as I sat there rocking. I was exhausted, and specters of the past and future had always held sway with my mind when I was tired. I told myself that I'd shove them away for one night. We'd begin working through the logistics of our new home in the morning.

We'd need to figure out a food source, an energy source, and so many other things in the morning. There were the injured, though with Victoria's enhanced magic and Sissy's help, I expected we'd get them fixed up pretty quickly.

Then we'd have to figure out how to feed everybody, clothe them, and find them a place to live.

We didn't even know if there were other people nearby and, if there were, what they were like. Would they be friendly? Or warlike?

Then there were thoughts of what we'd left behind. Della sat high on the list of those thoughts. I worried about her. She was all alone in Render, vulnerable in her spot below the earth. I'd promised myself we'd find a way to help her.

I fully intended to keep that promise.

And Mitch. Sadness swamped me. I needed to somehow break him free from the Body's clutches.

Then there were the people in Magical Indy.

They were being preyed upon by the Body. We needed to stop that and save them.

I frowned, having no idea how to do any of it from Outvald.

Somehow, I needed to return us to the Earth dimension.

The thought filled me with fear and worry. Could I do it? And would Victoria come back with me if I did?

The house fit into the Outvald countryside as if it belonged there. It sank deep into the land like it had never left. I'd felt a new peace within Victoria's walls when I'd gone inside. And I worried she wouldn't want to return to what was basically a hostile world on Earth.

I sighed, stroking the cat's silky fur as I pushed my thoughts away, trying to find some calm.

"I've missed this beautiful place," Grams said.

My eyes shot open. My head jerked around. To my surprise, a very solid Grams sat in the other rocking chair. Her head was bent over a soft cloud of yellow and green yarn, her gnarled fingers guiding the needles through it with a dexterity gained from hours and hours of knitting. "Grams!"

Her head came up and she smiled at me. "Don't look so surprised, child. You've always known I was here."

I half-turned in my chair. "In spirit yes, but..." I

reached out and gently squeezed her arm. It felt cool to the touch but solid enough.

Grams chuckled softly. "Still in spirit, child. But Outvald is my home. My spirit is stronger here."

"Oh. Of course." Disappointment yanked some of the excitement from my voice when I responded.

The needles ceased their movement. Her smile turned gentle. "Don't look like that, child."

"Like what?" I asked, trying to appear happy.

"Like someone kicked your favorite puppy." She patted my arm. "You don't need me anymore. You're fully invested as a portal protector. You've finally embraced your destiny."

I frowned. "I embraced that years ago. When you died."

She shook her head. "You've just been playing around the edges. It's not your fault," she hurried to say when I frowned. "There hasn't been any need for you to accept the full force of your power until now." She grinned, her small teeth yellow in the moonlight. "I'm so proud of you, Glynnie."

I looked away, guilt and fear making my heart beat faster in my chest. "Don't be proud, I don't have a clue what I'm doing."

She returned to her knitting. "You will."

She seemed so sure that it made me want to yell at her. I couldn't possibly live up to all that confidence. "I have no idea where we go from here. There is no portal to protect anymore. And I dragged all my friends here, to Outvald. We don't know how to live here. And there are monsters roaming around." My fingers must have dug too deeply into the little cat's fur because he jumped off my lap and returned to his favorite perch in the tree. "Everybody's going to expect me to tell them what to do, and I..."

Grams clucked her tongue with displeasure. "Child, no one knows the right thing to do all the time. You're a smart girl. You'll figure it all out."

I thought about it for a minute and then sighed. "Yeah. I'll figure something out."

"You're not alone, child," Grams told me. "You have your friends." She reached a gnarled hand to clasp mine. "You have me."

Her words filled me with warmth and made me finally smile. "I do?"

"Of course," she said. "I won't leave you to cope all by yourself."

"You know about this place?" I flopped a hand to indicate Outvald.

"I do."

"I have so many questions."

"There will be time enough for that tomorrow, child. Get some rest tonight. Tomorrow will be a new day."

I rested my head against the back of the chair, closing my eyes as I nodded in agreement. I don't know the exact moment when Grams left me. I might have drifted off for a moment or sixty. But my dreams were calm, and my nerves were soothed.

I would tackle my new challenges tomorrow. In the meantime, everyone I loved was there, safe and sound. I fully relaxed for the first time since coming through the portal to Outvald, and let Victoria's welcoming magic wrap around me, lulling me back to sleep.

The End

ALSO BY SAM CHEEVER

If you enjoyed **Magis**, you might also enjoy these other fun mystery series by Sam. To find out more, visit the **BOOKS** page at www.samcheever.com:

Enchanting Inquiries Paranormal Mysteries
Reluctant Familiar Paranormal Mysteries
Yesterday's Paranormal Mysteries
Gainfully Employed Mysteries
Silver Hills Cozy Mysteries
Country Cousin Mysteries

ABOUT THE AUTHOR

USA Today and WSJ Bestselling Author Sam Cheever writes contemporary and paranormal mystery and suspense, creating stories that draw you in and keep you eagerly turning pages. Known for writing great characters, snappy dialogue, and unique and exhilarating stories, Sam is the award-winning author of 80+ books.

To learn more about Sam and her work, visit her at one of her online hotspots:
www.samcheever.com
samcheever@samcheever.com

---

*I'm Glynn Forester and I'm Magis. **More**. I enhance and strengthen magical energy. My power augments rather than creates. But sometimes More is not enough.*

My world is fractured between magic and non-magic. The magical elite rule. And they are ruthless and corrupt. They want what I protect. But protecting it has been my family's job for time before time. So I hide. I hide from those who would attempt to use my abilities for unscrupulous purposes. I hide to save innocents from their venom.

But something's changing. The world around me is pulsing with malevolent magic, I realize I no longer have the luxury of anonymity. It's hard to give up my old ways. But I may not have a choice. Others will need my help. And if I deny them I'll be no better than those who threaten my world.

Will my magic make a difference in this new reality? I can offer *Magis*. More. But will it be enough? And will there be anything left of me when it's done?